SYLVIA MERCEDES

THE VENATRIX CHRONICLES BOOK 3

This one is for Stephanie,
With many thanks for her insights, opinions,
and typo-crushing skills.

THE VENATRIX

Drauval Borou

Aalis River

Skada Mountains

Castra Brean

Wodechran

Sang River

Aelianor City

CHRONICLES

Aldreda Borough

The Great Barrier

Dulimurian
The Witchwood

Sang River

KINGDOM
OF
PERRINION

THE VENATRIX

Aalis River

Rivanduru

Caiduru

Hollen

Elsinoe

Dunloch Castle

Milisendis

Cabralet

WODECHRAN
BOROUGH

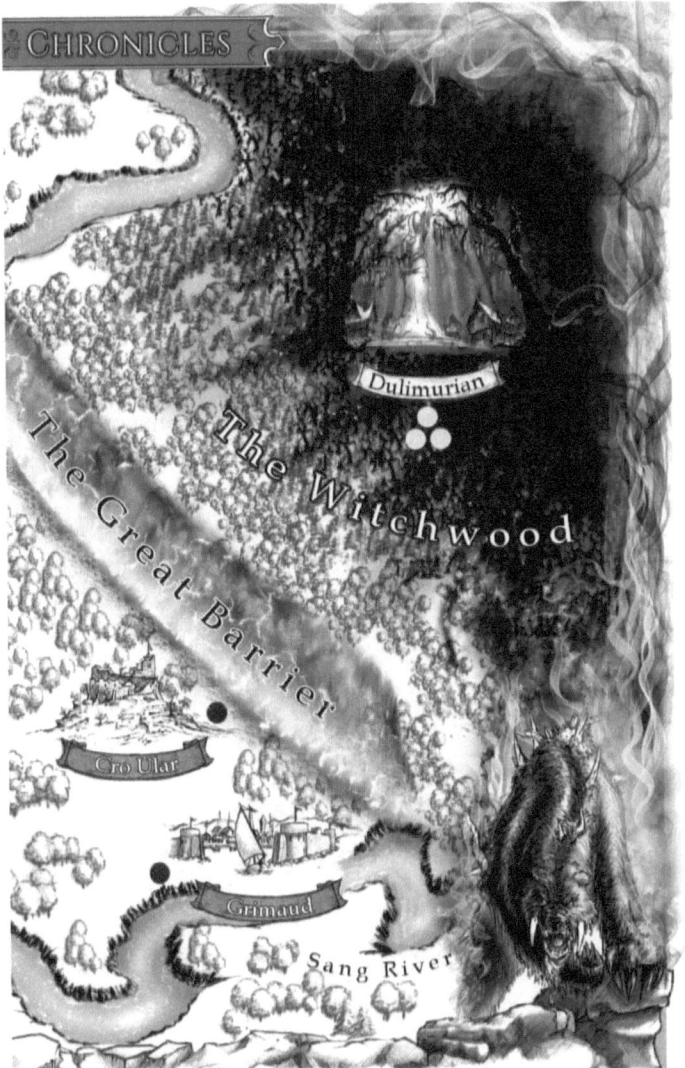

Dulimurian

The Witchwood

The Great Barrier

Cro Ular

Grimaud

Sang River

GLOSSARY OF SHADES

Shades: Disembodied spirit-beings who have escaped from their hellish dimension—the Haunts—and entered the mortal world. They cannot exist in a physical reality without mortal hosts, whom they possess and endow with unnatural powers. If left unchecked, they will gain ascendancy within a host-body and oust the original soul, taking full possession.

The following are the known varieties of shades as catalogued by the Order of Saint Evander:

ANATHEMAS
Abilities pertain to blood and curse-casting.

APPARITIONS
Abilities pertain to mind control and manipulation.

ARCANES
Mysterious entities with abilities not fully understood, but which seem to pertain to energies such as heat, motion, light, magnetism, and electricity.

ELEMENTALS
Abilities pertain to the natural elements of wind, fire, water, earth.

EVANESCERS
Abilities pertain to *evanescing*, or instantaneous distance-travel.

FERALS
Abilities pertain to heightened senses, augmented strength and agility.

LURES
Abilities pertain to enchanting voices and siren calls.

SEERS
Abilities pertain to visions, foretelling, and predictions. May also look into the past.

SHIFTERS
Abilities pertain to temporary transformation of host-bodies.

TRANSMUTERS
Abilities pertain to the transformation and manipulation of material substances.

PROLOGUE

SIVELINE TEMPLE, KINGDOM OF PERRINION

CERINE HASTENED ALONG THE CLOISTER, HER HEAD bent to avoid attracting the attention of any nun strolling at a more solemn, prayerful pace.

With one hand she gripped the edge of her sky-blue hood, pulling it low to shadow her face. It wasn't much of a disguise. Even beneath her overlarge novitiate robes, her petite figure was easily recognizable. Besides, she didn't walk like a novice. Her stride was too graceful, her posture too correct: telltale signs of her upbringing in one

11

of the noblest houses of the kingdom.

At times she paused to bow as a personage of exceptional holiness swept past. Otherwise, she made her way uninterrupted. A satchel bumped against her hip with each step, and she rested her hand on it to keep its overstuffed contents from falling out.

Only after stepping through the doorway into the scriptorium did she release the edge of her hood and lift her face. The ceiling arched overhead, shaped to catch and channel as much daylight as possible onto tall writing desks, at least twenty of which stood at intervals down the long chamber. Books, quills, trimmings, inks, parchments, pumice stones, binding instruments, and other tools of the scribe's trade cluttered the expansive top of every desk as well as the floor space beneath. Only three were currently occupied, however.

The two scribes nearest her didn't bother to lift their heads from their work as she passed by. Over their hunched shoulders she stole glimpses of illuminations in progress. One scribe was adding gold leaf to a magnificent embellished G, which took up the bulk of a single page. The other painted a border of lordivine blossoms around a carefully copied prayer. A pouch of vermillion sat at her elbow, and her fingertips were stained crimson.

It was painstaking, eye-straining work, but the Siveline Sisterhood pursued their labors tirelessly in the wake of the Witch Wars, striving to undo the destruction wrought by Dread Odile. For two hundred years the Witch Queen had captured temples and destroyed libraries, burning the sacred texts. Now, twenty years after her fall, members of the Order of Saint Sivella devoted their lives to copying and translating holy texts from many languages in the effort to replenish decimated libraries across the kingdom.

A third scribe sat before a desk at the far end of the scriptorium. The novice wove her way through the desks without calling out a greeting or announcing herself in any way. Nevertheless, that bowed back straightened and a voice cracked with age said, "Good morning, Sister Cerine."

"Good morning, Sister Ilda," the novice answered. She took a seat, not at one of the desks, but on a low stool beneath Sister Ilda's desk, among the books and papers and implements. She set her satchel off to one side, flipped open its flap, withdrew a stack of scribbled work, and arranged it in her lap. "I've been going over our readings of the last three days," she said, "and I believe I finally made a break-through. That phrase, that Occidian phrase, *dalath-mi'talrythe,* I found it again in—"

"And how is your noble father?"

Cerine stopped. When she tilted her head up, the sky-blue hood slipped off her scalp, recently shaved of its new growth according to the practice of the Sisterhood. She met a pair of too-knowing eyes set amid numerous delicate wrinkles, the sort of wrinkles caused by squinting long and hard for many years at many books. Ilda's face was otherwise unremarkable—never beautiful even in its youth. Soft features, a bit doughy. But those eyes were arresting.

"I, um . . ." Cerine briefly considered the merits of lying to Sister Ilda. But she'd known the old nun far too long to attempt it. "He's well," she answered instead, and looked down at her work.

"Sister Ducette came by with my morning crust and cup." Ilda leaned back in her chair, folding pudgy arms across her ample bosom. "She's never been one for keeping her peace, Sister Ducette. She told me another courier had come from Aldreda. Am I wrong, or has your father taken to writing to you with more regularity of late?"

Cerine pinched her lips between her teeth, biting down hard on the words trying to slip through. Haunts blast that Ducette! They shared a room in the novices' dormitory, and Cerine had long ago learned never to share anything of a personal nature with her roommate. But Ducette's eagle eyes had a way of spying out everything her cat's ears didn't overhear.

Cerine felt Ilda's gaze fixed intently on the top of her head. She heaved a sigh, fingertips brushing against the papers she'd spread before her. But she would get nowhere with her Occidian translations until this conversation was behind her.

"My father is . . . applying some pressure."

"Ah. It's the marriage question again, is it?"

Cerine nodded.

"The Night of Hallow's Well is coming up soon," Sister Ilda continued. "Was that not the night foretold as the wedding date of the Golden Prince?"

"The night, yes. But not the year."

"But your father wants it to be this year."

exactly as he'd wanted it to be last year. And the year before.

Cerine slumped on her stool. Her hand moved unconsciously to pull the blue hood back up over her head, hiding her face. Not that it did any good. Ilda knew her too well.

The old nun hummed to herself, one finger tapping her upper arm. Then she leaned forward on her seat and delicately selected a quill with one hand and a knife with the other. She set to work trimming, each cut of the knife precise.

"You ought to do it," she said at last.

Cerine looked up sharply. "I can't marry the prince!" Her voice echoed against the stone arches. The scribes at the other end of the scriptorium looked up from their work and hissed viciously, fingers to their lips. Cerine ducked her head in apology but continued, her words tight and tense in her throat. "I can't. Our work is . . . It's too important. The translation is nearly complete. The discoveries we've made in the last few months will change everything! I can't leave now, not when we're so close. We have to finish and—"

"And what then, girl?" Ilda set her quill aside but continued playing with the trimming knife, turning it in her fingers. "What good will a translation do anyone, hidden away here in Siveline?"

Cerine bowed her head. She didn't want to answer. Her hand rested on the page, her fingers tensing.

"Did you think we could sit on our knowledge forever?" Ilda persisted. "That we would never take it out into the wide world?"

"I . . ." Cerine swallowed. "I thought we would travel together to the Holy City of Liane and there present our findings to the High Priestess and the Council of Magali."

"And end up beheaded for heresy?" Ilda sniffed. "You're a good-hearted child, Cerine. You do not understand the corruption and danger of the Holy City. All of our work would be burned, right along with our headless bodies."

To hear their fate proposed in so calm a voice was chilling. Cerine shuddered and tucked her arms around her body.

Sister Ilda breathed out a long sigh. Then, setting her trimming knife aside, she leaned down and placed a hand on Cerine's bent head. "My child, you know how it is. A queen may whisper in the ear of her king. A queen may say things in the safety of the marriage bed that a holy sister dares not speak aloud in public places."

A hot flush crept up Cerine's cheeks. Unable to make herself look up, she stared hard at the pages of scrawled lines before her.

Ilda patted Cerine's head, then settled back on her tall stool. "Tell me, is the idea of marrying the Golden Prince truly so dreadful? By all accounts, he is a noble soul. And not unpleasant to look upon, or so the rumors say."

Cerine tucked her chin in closer, grateful for the protection of her hood.

But Ilda shook her head, *tsking* gently. "I may be old. I may have lived most of my life shut away in dry scriptoriums, but I'm not dead. I've seen the look in your eyes when those letters from Dunloch arrive. You expect me to believe you harbor no tender feeling for young Prince Gerard?"

"His heart belongs to Fayline." Cerine looked up and

met the old nun's eye. She schooled her face into a careful mask despite the color staining her pale cheeks. "He loves her. He always has. He always will."

Ilda nodded her understanding. "Your sister," she said, tilting her head to one side. "Your sister, who was shade-taken."

Her throat thickening, Cerine nodded.

"Tell me, Cerine," Ilda said, "what would happen to your sister if the Evanderians were to find her, were to catch her?"

Cerine didn't have to answer. They both knew. "They would kill her. To save her soul."

"Exactly." Ilda's hand reached out, catching Cerine's chin. Her face lost its sweet docility and became hard as stone. "And that is why you must make this marriage. That is why you must speak to the prince, tell him of our findings. So that people like your sister will no longer be murdered in the Goddess's name."

Her grip on Cerine's face tightened painfully. Then, abruptly, she let go and leaned back in her chair, her breath rasping in her old lungs. Her gnarled hand hovered over the book she was hard at work composing, each letter carefully shaped with no embellishments to distract from the meaning. As she gazed upon those words, her soul was so bright in her eyes, it might almost have burned up the pages.

"It's high time all of Gaulia knew the truth," Ilda said, "that Saint Evander of Roihm was a madman."

CHAPTER I

TWO MONTHS LATER

THUNK!

Ayleth landed hard on the straw-littered floor and momentarily believed her chest had been crushed. She could not move, could not think, could not make her flattened lungs draw air. The world spun around her in a maelstrom of light and darkness without meaning, and everything inside her focused on that one, single, desperate need to breathe.

A great gasp, and her lungs inflated. Her whole body

spasmed with relief. Short-lived relief. The gasp turned into a gagging choke as smoke poured down her throat. Her eyes stung even as her whirling vision steadied. She stared up into a horror of flames engulfing the rafters overhead, as smoke coiled through the air.

A crash shuddered the structure, and Ayleth flung her arms up to keep off the burning straw and bits of the roof raining down on her. At any moment the whole building would collapse.

Somehow, she managed to roll over, her boots scrabbling for foothold in the straw lighting up all around her. Through the smoke, she saw a monster-shaped hole in one side of the barn.

Her entire will fixed on reaching that hole.

"*Laranta!*" she screamed inside her head.

Out of the smoke, a massive black form manifested. Eyes bright with shadow-light, it loomed over Ayleth, lips drawn back from enormous fangs. A rumbling growl filled her mind: *Up, Mistress! Up! Up!*

"*Give me your strength!*" Ayleth cried internally even as she choked and gagged.

The dark being dissipated before her eyes, transforming into a formless stain blacker than the smoke clogging the air. That darkness funneled like a small tornado of pure power and magic into Ayleth's mouth, her nostrils, spreading through her and flooding her limbs. Galvanized with sudden strength, she pushed herself up and ran, ran, *ran*.

The horrible shriek and groan of breaking, plummeting rafters. The devouring roar of flames. She burst through the hole in the wall and out into open air, where brilliant red firelight illuminated the night. Her own shadow danced like a phantom before her as she hurtled away from the flaming ruins. She made it twenty paces before collapsing to her knees in the long grass.

Her body quivered with the need for air. For several heartbeats she could only breathe. Nothing in this world mattered more than sucking in breath after breath. Her hands felt her chest, not quite believing her ribcage hadn't been shattered.

Then she heard the screams.

Her teeth clenched in a sudden snarl. She snapped her head up, tossing back her long dark braid, and stared out into the night. Fire glare illuminated the little village of

Cabralet. Two, no three . . . now four other buildings caught ablaze, their thatch roofs disturbingly effective tinder.

Amid this destruction, a terrible figure threw back its head and belched a spurt of flame into the air. From the straining cords of its throat dangled a feathered dart.

The wrong dart. Tipped with the wrong poison.

Shade! Shade! The growling voice of the being inside Ayleth's head urged her with bloodthirsty eagerness. *Hunt! Hunt!*

Ayleth sprang to her feet, the fingers of her right hand curled, her thumb pressing against the trigger mechanism of the wristbow attached to her arm bracer. She'd been certain she'd sensed an Anathema shade in the body of that smelly old goat. The stench of curse magic had been all over it. Unseen, she'd crept into the barn, sighted the goat down her arm, and taken the shot.

No sooner did her dart strike home than those evil yellow eyes had opened wide . . . and the goat exploded with magic. Its body had warped before her eyes, breaking and re-knitting the skeleton with utterly malicious magic. It was like something out of a nightmare—jutting bone spines dripping blood down the ridge of its back, massive yellow teeth clacking from disjointed jaws. It had stood up on its hind feet, weirdly humanoid, and its front hooves split, broke, and transformed into sinister, twisted hands tipped with enormous claws.

Then it had started breathing fire.

"An Elemental. An Elemental, you idiot!" Ayleth cursed. Her hand went to the quivers strung across her chest. To her dismay, she discovered they had all broken when that warped goat's head butted her directly in the chest and knocked her off her feet. Her poisoned darts were gone, scattered beneath the rubble of the decimated barn she'd just escaped.

She would have to find some other way to take this monster down. Her hand moved to the knife at her belt. If the death must be violent, so be it.

With her shade's power pounding through her veins, Ayleth hurled herself into the flaming village. All around her, men, women, and children fled in terror, their screams slicing the air. Ayleth pushed the sights and sounds away, concentrating her every sense, mortal and shade, on that demonic creature. Its mouth dropped open, and a burst of flame roared from between those rasping teeth to set a leaning shed ablaze. Lost in its own chaotic rage, it didn't see her coming.

Ayleth leapt for the monster's back, plunging her blade straight for the base of its skull.

At the last possible instant, the monster turned its head, and one of those wicked horns knocked her sprawling to one side. Her knife flew from her hand.

The earth shook under pounding hooves as the monster turned to look down at her. Its yellow goat eyes gleamed with far too much sentience as the ascendant shade glared out at her. It opened its mouth, and Ayleth rolled, avoiding another burst of flame by inches.

She scrambled to her knees, unarmed yet undaunted. Laranta's strength was in her; she wasn't powerless. She leapt and landed only to find the monster charging her again, head down. Prepared this time, she spun lightly on her feet, her braid whipping through the air behind her. She felt the rush of the shade-taken's passing and sank into a crouch, ready to spring as soon as it rounded back to face her.

But it did not stop. Ayleth's eyes widened with pure horror. As the creature careened down the burning village street, its clawed fingers snatched up a wailing child. Before Ayleth found even the breath to shout, it leapt with the child into one of the burning cottages.

"No!" Ayleth screamed and flung herself in pursuit. Her boots pounded the hard-packed dirt of the street; her eyes fixed on that flame-filled doorway. For an instant— less than an instant—her mortal soul blenched in the face of those flames.

Then she sprang into the inferno, her arms up to protect her face. Smoke stung her eyes, her lungs, and flames blistered her flesh. *"Laranta, find the shade-taken!"* she cried inside her mind.

Eyes blazing with shadow-light, she peered through the smoke and the fire. No sign of the monster. But there! There! The child lay on the floor, his thin garments beginning to singe, to burn. A perfect distraction from the hunt.

Ayleth threw herself over the child and wrapped that small body in her arms, shielding him from the flames. To her relief, she heard weeping and coughing. The little one was still alive. Holding the child close under her cloak, she rose to a crouch.

Her vision filled with fire.

"*Laranta!*" she cried.

Her wolf shade roared in her head, but it wasn't the roar of the hunt. It was a sound of pure terror. Laranta was never afraid, no matter the danger. But faced with those flames on all sides, faced with that raging heat, she writhed inside Ayleth's head.

"*Laranta! We've got to get out of here!*" Ayleth choked, staggered. She felt her limbs weakening, felt the shade-power reducing inside her. The fire closed in, and . . .

Darkness.

Ayleth collapsed to her knees. Had she died? She must have died. The heat, the flames, they must have killed her. And this darkness, this must be death. The void of the Haunts, ready to claim her and her shade's souls. She could only hope the soul of the child in her arms would escape to find the Goddess's Light. She could only . . .

She blinked. And realized she couldn't be dead. If she were dead, she wouldn't be able to blink, would she? Her eyes stung with lingering smoke, but there was no more fire, no more heat.

"*Laranta?*" she said, and felt her panicked shade stir. Still clutching the child, Ayleth staggered out into the street, coughing smoke from her lungs.

The world was a pandemonium of screaming and terror. But there at the end of the street loomed a tall figure in a long cloak, his head covered by a red hood. His arms were outstretched toward one of the other burning cottages, and it seemed as though he somehow— impossibly—pulled the fire out of the thatch in a long stream, straight into his hands. His curved fingers turned and twisted as he appeared to crush its life between his palms.

Staring at him with her eyes full of shadow-light, Ayleth saw the brilliant pulse of magic coursing through his soul.

She collared a villager running past and pressed the wide-eyed child into the man's arms. "Take him," she growled, and the terrified man obeyed without question, carrying the little one out into the open countryside. As soon as Ayleth turned back to the tall figure working his strange magic, she glimpsed the goat-monster pounding toward him from the other end of the village. The shade inside the goat had sensed yet another shade presence, another threat to its existence in this world.

The monster took a wide, powerful stance some ten yards from where the tall man stood, opened its mouth, and belched another gout of flame. The man shifted one hand, palm out. The oncoming fire seemed to strike an invisible barrier and snuff into nothing.

The shade-taken goat, roaring, sent another burning stream, this one long, continuous, and so hot it must surely overwhelm the other magic-user. But the cloaked man defended himself with both hands now, catching the fire and collapsing it into itself.

Ayleth saw how the magic inside the man shuddered. His shade, however powerful, was not fully ascendant, unlike the Elemental in the goat. He would not be able to withstand such a concentrated magical assault much longer.

Using the goat's own fire blast for cover, Ayleth dashed up behind the man. Even as sweat streamed down his pale face, he acknowledged her arrival with a single expressionless glance.

"Hullo, Venator du Balafre," Ayleth said, her smoke-seared voice rather hoarse. "So glad you could join us." She reached over his shoulder, avoiding the fire he was crushing between his hands, and plucked a dart from one of the quivers he wore strung across his chest. A dart tipped with Elemental poison.

The shade-taken goat, spying Ayleth, attempted to direct its flame at her instead. But Terryn du Balafre stretched out one long arm and caught the long blast, giving her a chance to glide away. She assumed a firing position and moved to load her scorpiona with a dart—only to find that the string of her wristbow had burned away.

No matter. She would deliver this poison, come what may.

"*Laranta, to me!*" she roared. Tucking her chin to her chest, she set her sights on her goal and ran. Straight at the shade-taken, straight for those evil horns, straight for that open maw which even now filled with heat ready to burst straight into her face. The power of her shade drove her with incredible speed, and she covered the distance in the space of three heartbeats. At the last possible instant, she dodged to one side, avoiding the spouting flames. Then she lunged and planted the dart directly into the warped shade-taken's heart.

The monster caught Ayleth by the throat with its long-fingered hands before she could take even a single step back. She choked but latched hold of its wrists and braced herself before it could pull her from her feet. The brutish creature, although strong in body, could not match Laranta's power flowing through Ayleth. With a single tug, she yanked the clawed hands off her throat. Her knee came up, striking hard between those hairy goat legs. "Sorry!" she gasped even as the goat-creature doubled up, bleated, and sank to the ground.

At last the poison took effect, paralyzing its limbs, slowing its heart. More importantly, it took hold of the shade as well. The Elemental soul burning so viciously just moments before flickered, faded, and fell into a numb spirit-slumber.

"There." Ayleth rubbed her throat. Vague awareness of any number of hurts plucked at her mind: the burns, the stabbing pain in her chest from various cracked ribs, the bruises on her neck. For the moment she ignored them. The swell of triumph overcame all else. "He's ready for the Gentle Death," she said, turning to Terryn.

Her voice trailed off, and the blood drained from her face.

Venator Terryn stood in profile to her. Not one of the village huts still burned, but now his veins glowed beneath his skin with red light, illuminating the lines of pain scoring his face. She saw the rising power of shade inside him, mounting like the pressure of a volcano ready to burst. He had to suppress it. Now. And there was no time to weave spell songs.

As Ayleth watched, Terryn grabbed for the iron spike fixed to the bracer on his left forearm. Unlatching a hook, he let the spike spring back on its mechanism, driving it deep into the flesh of his arm. A single short cry burst from his lips, but he bit it back, his teeth grinding against the pain, against the iron poison he'd sent bursting through his own body.

As terrible as that pain was for him, it was a thousand times worse for the spirit possessing him.

Ayleth drew back a step but couldn't tear her gaze away. Her shadow sight saw it all: the sudden lashing and writhing of the shade he had called up from its suppressions just enough to access its powers. Now, iron poison from the spike drove the shade deep down inside him again, where he could bind it, control it.

Terryn released the spike. Blood ran down his arm into his hand. He ignored it. His hands trembling, he pulled a set of pipes from its sheath at his belt, the Vocos pipes, carved from bone. Putting the instrument to his lips, he called up the Song of Suppression. With true musician's skill, he wound layer upon layer of binding spell song around the soul of his shade.

Ayleth, listening to that song, staring at the blood still streaming down her fellow venator's arm, realized that the truly dangerous shade she'd faced here tonight might not have been the one in the goat.

CHAPTER 2

SHE WAITED UNTIL TERRYN FINISHED PLAYING THE Suppression and the last sonorous notes of the drone had faded away. Then, very quietly, Ayleth said, "The Gentle Death. Please."

Her fellow venator looked up at her as he lowered the Vocos from his lips. Strain tightened every line of his face. The circular scar on his right cheek stood out white and ugly against his dark complexion. At first, he stared at her blankly, too caught up in the aftereffects of the binding song and the pain still coursing through his bleeding arm to comprehend her. Ayleth waited, holding out her hand.

Terryn gave his head a short, sharp shake and slipped a dart fletched in black feathers from one of the quivers across his chest. He offered it to her, his bloodied hand trembling. Ayleth stepped forward and plucked the dart from his fingers, careful not to look too closely at him . . . which she knew he sensed, which she knew made it worse.

Returning to the goat, her back to the other venator, she studied the monster lying in paralyzed repose. If anything, it was more hideous in sleep than when it was awake and raging. The warping of its body was so extreme, so horrifying. Those spines, stained with its own blood, having ripped through the flesh of its back. Those hands that did not belong on a goat.

She'd seen warping like this before. The shade inside the goat was an Elemental, but the shade that had worked this warping magic on it was much more powerful. The goat could not help what it had become while in thrall to a curse, and Ayleth felt a momentary pity for it. But then her nostrils flared, breathing in the stench of burned thatch and wattle. After she took a quick glance around at the ruined cottages, no longer actively aflame yet blackened beyond repair . . . suddenly the monster didn't seem so pathetic after all.

She knelt and pricked the dart directly into a vein.

The Gentle Death took almost immediate effect. Watching with her shadow sight, Ayleth saw the exact moment when the mutated host body died and the spirit inside it slipped free. Only a single spirit: a dangerous, smoldering shade.

Ayleth slid her double-headed Detrudos from its sheath and began to play the Song of Expulsion. The drone rumbled out in a low, steady pulse, while the melody wrapped around the exposed shade-spirit even as it worked free of its mortal host. Had she dealt the goat a violent death, that escaping spirit, empowered by the violence, would easily have escaped the clutches of the spell song. Numbed by the poison and lulled by the mildness of the Gentle Death, the shade put up no resistance whatsoever.

The hairs on the back of her neck shivered, and Ayleth

braced herself to maintain a steady flow of music from her pipes. Behind her, reality opened in a long, searing wedge. A gate to the Haunts loomed in readiness to reclaim the lost spirit. She closed her mortal eyes and concentrated on the spell melody, taking care to bind the shade tight. Deep down inside her stirred the unholy temptation to peer through the gate, to see that chaotic realm from which shades escaped to plague her world.

But Hollis had warned her long ago, when she was a young apprentice, that to gaze upon the Haunts was to gaze upon pure, unadulterated madness. She dared not turn, dared not look.

Instead, she lashed out with the spell song and sent the bound shade hurtling into the realm of its origin. The gate to the Haunts snapped shut, and Ayleth staggered under the shock of it. Yet she held onto the pipes and finished the melody before finally letting the drone fade back into silence.

Only then did she open her eyes and turn around to face Terryn.

The other venator had already removed the bracer from his left arm and was attempting to bind his wound one-handed. As though suddenly aware of her eyes upon him, he fumbled the swatch of bandages, which fell and unrolled across the ground. He bent to retrieve it.

Ayleth crossed the distance between them and plucked the roll from his hand. "Let me do that," she said.

"I don't need help."

"Never said you did."

Resentment simmered through his spirit, palpable to her shadow senses. Ayleth ignored it. After rolling up the unwound bandages, she tucked them into her belt before reaching for his arm. For a moment, he pulled back as though afraid to let her touch him. Then, with extreme reluctance, he let her take his arm and push back the sleeve, exposing the puncture wound from the spike.

Ayleth refused to let her face betray the shudder that rippled through her gut. She was used to blood, but this . . . this was ugly. The stink of iron poison slipped into her nostrils, making her dizzy, and Laranta growled and retreated further into the back of her mind. Ayleth steeled herself. "Have you any tuaflor salve on you?"

Terryn nodded. "In my saddlebags."

"Where's your horse?"

Leaving the dead shade-taken behind for the moment, they made their way across the sad little village to where Terryn's red mare waited patiently. Ayleth fetched the bottle of salve from Terryn's supplies and set to work applying it to his wound. At the touch of her fingers, he drew a sharp breath and his arm trembled in her grasp, though she tried to be as gentle as possible. The intense burn of his ice-cold eyes fixed on her as she worked; no doubt he watched for even the slightest mistake to criticize.

Ayleth set her jaw. She had some experience tending wounds, and she knew what she was doing. The iron spike on a venator's bracer served several uses, but its primary purpose was to suppress one's own possessing shade if it began to gain too much strength and ascendancy. In all her years serving under Hollis, Venatrix di Theldry, Ayleth had seen her mistress resort to the iron spike only three times. Ayleth herself never had; she'd never struggled to keep Laranta under her command.

But Laranta was not like the spirit Ayleth had just glimpsed twisting through Terryn's soul.

"How did you do that with the fire?" she asked

abruptly, glancing up from her concentration on his arm.

Terryn met her gaze, then quickly looked away, staring off into the night.

"I know you don't host an Elemental shade," she persisted, "so you don't command fire itself. Unless I'm much mistaken, you carry an Arcane, but . . . well, the truth is, I don't fully understand Arcanes."

More silence. Distinctly disapproving silence. Ayleth rolled her eyes. She should know better than to admit any gap in her knowledge in this man's presence. "Based on everything I've seen, I'm guessing your shade's particular magic pertains to light or the manipulation of light. So, did you . . . what? Draw the light out of the fire?"

His sharp profile was unreadable, from that high smooth brow to that stubbled jaw. Ayleth thought she saw a muscle under his eye twitch, but she couldn't say whether it was a contemptuous twitch or not.

Tying off the bandage, she stepped back and crossed her arms. "If you deprive fire of its light, it ceases to be fire. Without light, it cannot produce heat, without heat, it cannot be fire. Am I right?"

"Close enough, di Ferosa. Close enough."

Sometimes Ayleth had to fight the urge to prick him with a paralysis dart and leave him in a limp heap in the dirt. Him and his superiority and his perfectly spotless uniform.

"You know," she said, her voice edged, "if you didn't keep your shade so deeply suppressed all the time, it wouldn't rage so violently when you access its powers. If you gave it a little more freedom, it would—"

The look Terryn gave her cut off her words as effectively as any knife. For a moment, he held her gaze, and her words hung in the silence between them.

"Take care, Venatrix," he said at last. "Let that be the last time you speak heresy in my presence."

Ayleth's face burned with mounting heat. Turning abruptly on her heel, she left the venator behind, returning to the empty village street. A storm of protests, of arguments, even of accusations swelled inside her, but she knew better than to give them voice. This was a fight she could not win. Because he was right. According to the holy scripts of Saint Evander, all shades were nothing short of demonic. To allow one's shade freedom was to dance with evil itself. Even as she danced with Laranta daily.

She closed her eyes. The idea of binding Laranta as tightly as she saw Terryn bind his shade made her sick. Ayleth trusted Laranta more than she trusted any other spirit in this world. Did this make her a heretic? Did this make her unworthy of the Goddess's service?

These were not thoughts she dared pursue just now, however. Not while there was still work to be done.

She sighed, suddenly tired, and felt the back of her head with tentative fingertips. She'd hit the barn floor hard when the goat monster butted her in the chest, and a lump had formed. Her limbs were shaky now that the excitement had passed, and her skin was raw in places where she'd brushed too close to the flames.

The villagers had fled out into the surrounding fields and probably wouldn't return until morning. Ayleth was just as happy there was no one around as she approached the dead goat. She didn't need their accusing eyes watching her. Throughout this last week of hunting, she'd been utterly certain she was on the trail of an Anathema shade. And when she'd finally come upon this creature, Laranta had smelled blood magic all over it.

What an idiot she'd been, using the wrong dart like that! She'd been arrogant . . . and overeager. She hadn't bothered to search for signs of other shade presence. As a result, the whole village might have burned to the ground. If Terryn hadn't arrived in time . . .

As though her thoughts summoned him, Terryn approached from behind. She chose to ignore him, keeping her back carefully turned as she knelt to inspect the carcass. But Terryn was an effective loomer. She didn't have to see him to feel him looming behind her now from his great height, arms crossed, watching her every move.

"I'm sure there's a story here," he said.

Ayleth shot a glare over her shoulder. Rather than answer the question he didn't ask, she snapped, "What are you doing out here in the middle of the night, du Balafre? Were you following me?"

A faint, derisive snort. "I was following a lead."

"For what? That red-haired witch the prince has you hunting?"

"Maybe." Terryn took a step and bent over behind her where she crouched. She was very aware of his breath by her ear, the proximity of his broad chest at her back. He reached around her and, with long, dexterous fingers, plucked the Anathema dart from the goat's throat.

He said nothing as he straightened and stepped back. Ayleth coughed to loosen the breath caught in her chest and scowled up at him as he held the dart out before him, twirling it between finger and thumb. He looked at her, his expression meaningful. He'd seen that it was the wrong poison.

Ayleth hunched her shoulders. "He . . . smelled of blood magic." Her voice came out sounding more defensive than she liked.

"Perhaps you shouldn't trust your nose so implicitly."

With a huff through her teeth, Ayleth turned from the venator back to the dead creature. Narrowing her eyes, she concentrated her shadow vision. "You see what I see, don't you? This has the Warpwitch's fingerprints all over it. Look at those spines. An Elemental doesn't mutate like this."

Terryn shook his head and tucked the dart away into one of his quivers. "The Warpwitch is gone, di Ferosa. I saw her myself. She walked through the Great Barrier into the Witchwood. She can't come back."

"But are you sure?" Ayleth indicated the monster with a wave of her hand. "Tell me this isn't one of her curses."

A painful silence followed. Ayleth watched Terryn, watched how his eyes, glimmering with shadow-light, flicked back and forth across the monster. Of all people, Terryn ought to recognize Ylaire di Jocosa's curses. As a child, he had been cursed by her himself. And he had no doubt seen countless bodies broken by her magic and transformed into monsters. If nothing else, how could he not perceive the distinct similarity between the warping of this goat and the breaking and mutilation of Venator Kephan's body only a month ago?

"So . . . what?" Terryn said at last. "Is this what you've been working on all these weeks? When I thought you were riding the circuit trails, you've really been trying to find proof that the Warpwitch is still in Wodechran? Trying to make me into a liar?"

"No!" The coldness in his voice cut Ayleth to the quick. Shaking her head, she stood up and crossed her arms. "I'm not trying to prove or disprove anything, Venator du Balafre. I'm simply following the leads as I find them. This . . . this *felt* like the Warpwitch. And look!" On an impulse, she dropped back into a crouch and leaned over the goat, brushing back the fur on its cheek. There, invisible to mortal eyes but just visible to shadow sight, was the faint impression of a sigil. The sigil of Ylaire, a tattoo of blood-mixed magic.

It was the same shape as the circular scar on Terryn's cheek.

"See?" Ayleth said, her voice tight and eager. "This proves it."

Terryn, his face suddenly ashen, crouched beside her and touched the monster's cheek. A shudder ran up his arm, and for a moment he looked as though he would be ill. Then he drew a sharp breath through his nostrils and straightened, sitting back on his heels. "I agree. This is one of Ylaire's curses. But remember, she was loose in this borough for a good six weeks before we realized she'd escaped the Witchwood. She could have planted any number of curses during that time. It doesn't change the fact that she is beyond the Barrier now."

"But could she call a curse to life like this from the Witchwood?"

The venator shook his head. "Injecting the goat with the wrong poison might be enough in itself to jolt the curse to life." He stood again, wiping his hand on his vest, a grim line twisting his mouth. "I know what I saw. Ylaire is gone."

Ayleth stood up and backed away from the body. Her jaw hardened and her fists slowly clenched. She turned her back on Terryn and spoke sharply inside her mind: "*Laranta. Come to me.*"

Her shade rose up inside her head, sliding to the forefront of her consciousness. Ayleth felt Terryn's eyes fixed on the back of her head, watching how she commanded her shade without use of the Vocos pipes. But she had no time to bother with protocol now.

The shade is gone, Laranta said, looking out through Ayleth's eyes at the corpse.

"*I know,*" Ayleth answered. "*But I need you to search for a curse. It may be newly broken since the host body is dead, but I need you to try to find it.*"

Ayleth pushed her shade from her mind so it could manifest as a massive black wolf. This was not a physical manifestation; no shade could take physical form. But while attached by a soul tether to Ayleth's body, Laranta could move like a phantom in the outer world, invisible to all mortal eyes save Ayleth's.

Terryn, though unable to see the wolf shade, sensed its presence. His eyes flashed with shadow-light as he stared into the empty space beside Ayleth, and his mouth set in a grim, disapproving line. Ayleth ignored him.

"*Find the curse, Laranta*," she said, gazing into those strange, predatory eyes alight with magic. "*Find it before it vanishes.*"

Laranta sprang into action, searching the body first, and then moving out from it in an ever-widening circle. If there was a trace of curse to be found, Laranta would discover it. Ayleth reached out a hand to touch the shimmering soul tether connecting her to the wolf, feeling her shade's eagerness, feeling the sudden quickening of her senses.

Curse! Laranta barked.

"I knew it," Ayleth gasped, and sprang forward.

"Knew what? What are you doing?" Terryn demanded, falling into step behind her.

Without responding, Ayleth hastened to her wolf

shade's side. Laranta stood with her teeth closed around something invisible, and when Ayleth looked with her shadow sight, she saw the frayed edges of a broken curse thread, a humming filament of blood magic, almost more like song than thread, and not wholly like either. It glinted an ugly Anathema hue.

"This is it," Ayleth said, her breath quickening with excitement. She pounded her fist to her palm and whirled to face Terryn, her eyes widening as a surge of urgency coursed through her veins. "We've got to follow this thread, Venator du Balafre. It will lead us to the source, I'm sure of it. Then we'll know once and for all—"

Mistress.

Ayleth sucked a sharp breath at the sound of Laranta's voice. She turned just in time to see the curse Laranta held in her teeth fizzle into nothing with a last hum of sour, ugly magic. Not only was the curse broken, now it was gone. No leads left to follow.

Laranta twisted her head and licked her lips as though the curse had left a funny aftertaste. Standing up, she tilted her massive head to one side. *We hunt?* she asked, but not very optimistically.

"*No, Laranta.*" Ayleth sighed and beckoned her shade to return to her. Laranta obeyed, losing all trace of physical form and becoming nothing more than dark smoke and shadow, pouring back into Ayleth's head. She crouched down inside her mistress, still full of power, but her magic no longer active.

Ayleth turned her shadow sight back to the dead goat, searching for any other trace she might follow. Something about all this seemed . . . off. During the reign of Dread Odile in Perrinion, Ylaire di Jocosa had been one of the Witch Queen's most ferocious lieutenants, a figure of legendary terror. Yes, her time of imprisonment in the Witchwood had reduced her power, but she was still a formidable force, possessed of a formidable shade. The idea that she would escape her prison only to flee back into it . . .

Ayleth shuddered. She'd ventured into the Witchwood herself not long ago. Just a short journey, but one she would never forget. She couldn't imagine ever choosing to return to that hellish place. She'd rather die.

Glancing sidelong at Terryn, she caught him once more watching her closely. He had no doubt seen the curse thread dissipate as well. He knew she had no trace to follow now.

One dark eyebrow slid up his forehead. "It's late, di Ferosa," he said, his voice a deep rumble in the darkness. "You've fought hard tonight. Let's find shelter and rest. We can haul the carcass back to Milisendis in the morning."

Ayleth ran a hand down her face, breathing another curse through her fingers. Then she nodded and growled, "Fine, du Balafre. Have it your way."

CHAPTER 3

"THAT WAS TOO CLOSE."

Ylaire's eyes opened wide, staring into darkness. She lifted her hand before her face, twisting her wrist in a slow rotation. Blood streamed from her fingertips, but she didn't care about that. Blinking into shadow sight, she studied the gleaming curse threads that flowed from her fingers, extending into the ether for miles in five separate directions.

No. Only four now. The curse thread stemming from

her index finger was broken. Disintegrated into nothing.

Ylaire let out her breath in a long stream, ending with a curse. Closing her hand into a fist, she slumped and rubbed at her face, leaving smears of blood. That Haunts-damned venatrix! She was proving more and more difficult to throw off the trail. Three times now the girl had come too close, and three times Ylaire had only just managed to escape detection. This was the closest of all, however. Cabralet Village was a mere five miles away. If she hadn't placed a curse on that shade-taken goat, if the girl's Feral senses hadn't been distracted . . .

She cursed again, gnashing her teeth, and tasted blood on her tongue. If it were any other venatrix, she'd know what to do. She'd send a curse bolt straight through the girl's heart and leave her pinned to the ground as her soul wriggled free from its broken host body and her blood flowed to saturate the ground beneath her. The longing to fulfill this impulse was almost more than Ylaire could bear!

But this venatrix . . . this girl with her terrifying and so-familiar face . . .

Ylaire shook her head. She dared not kill this one. Not

yet.

Exhausted, she rubbed at her face, grimacing as she felt its heavy, ugly features. There was a time when Ylaire di Jocosa, Crimson Devil and Lieutenant of Dread Odile, would never have deigned to take a host body such as this crude farmwife. She had always worn beautiful hosts, strong and young and lovely. But these days, she was lucky to have a human body of any kind. Regardless, she dared not risk another possession just now. Not when word might easily get back to the young venatrix.

"We'll have to move again," Ylaire muttered, shaking her head. "Soon. The goat may have thrown her off the trail for the moment, but she'll be back." She lifted her heavy head to gaze across the dark little room. She dared not even light a fire on the hearth. This ramshackle hovel was believed to be abandoned, and a trail of smoke rising from its chimney might draw attention from the locals. The single room was tiny, one wall caving in, the chimney half-crumbled. It was as cold as a tomb, illuminated only by the moonlight shining through cracks in the walls and door.

One beam of moonlight fell on the face of a child

sleeping on a pile of woolen blankets across the room. Her round face rested on a skinny arm, and her hair fanned out from her head in long, limp snarls. Ylaire's heart twisted at the sight. The poor little mite! It wasn't fair that she should have to live like this. Hunted like an animal. She ought to be safe at home, nestled warm against her mother's bosom.

But her mother was dead. Killed by those Evanderians. If the child was found, they would kill her as well. They would build a pyre and burn her alive. And they would call it mercy.

Ylaire's lips pulled back from her teeth in a vicious, silent snarl. What a world this had become since the fall of Odile! But it couldn't last. No, such evil could not be suffered to survive. She would find a way to set things right again. She had to.

Crawling across the narrow space between her and the child, Ylaire took hold of one small shoulder and gave it a shake. "Wake up, little one," she said, trying to make her voice gentle, which was difficult to manage from this rough throat. "Wake up."

Long lashes parted, and a pair of jewel-like jade eyes

blinked up at her. "Auntie?" the child said, her voice quavering and small. Sitting up, she rubbed her eyes with the heel of one hand. "Auntie, I'm hungry."

"I know, sweetness," Ylaire said. She fumbled in the darkness until she found the sack of stale oatcakes she'd stolen a few days before from a village a few miles away. The same village where she'd left the decoy curse inside the shade-taken goat. She broke one of the cakes in half and handed it to the child, who gnawed at it hungrily like a little starving mouse.

Ylaire's stomach growled as she watched. She pressed a hand to her hollow middle, tempted to eat the other half of the cake. But she wouldn't let herself. She could push this body several more days without sustenance. She must save their meager supplies for the child.

Nilly must remain strong. She had work to do.

"I need to speak to Rasanala," Ylaire said as the child, still hungry, picked crumbs off her skirt and placed them on her tongue.

Nilly paused with her fingers in her mouth, and her eyes flicked up sharply to meet Ylaire's gaze. Her brow puckered. "Rasanala is sleepy," she said. "So sleepy."

"I know." Ylaire reached out and took Nilly's hand, giving it an encouraging squeeze. "But we don't have much time. Will you call Rasanala up for me? Please?"

The girl shook her head, and Ylaire wondered if she would have to resort to sterner methods to get what she needed. But then Nilly tucked her chin to her chest, and a ripple rushed through her soul and out into the ether. Watching with shadow sight, Ylaire saw how the mortal soul inside the girl gave way to the shade spirit rising from within.

The girl lifted her chin and raised her eyes once more. Only it wasn't Nilly peering out between those pale lashes now. The child's mouth moved, and a strange, mellifluous voice spoke. A voice like many voices blended into one. A shade voice.

"*My Nilly is afraid,*" it said.

"I know," Ylaire answered. "She is too young for all that I ask of her. She doesn't realize the danger she is in. But you understand, Rasanala, don't you?"

The child's head tilted slightly to one side. Then, slowly, she nodded. "*I understand. My Nilly needs my help. The hunters will kill her if they find her.*"

"Yes. So, we must do what we can to stop the hunters before they can hurt Nilly." Ylaire leaned forward and took the girl's hands in her long, bony, bloodstained fingers. She gazed earnestly into those gleaming eyes, and the shade inside the child gazed back. "I need your help, Rasanala. I need you to try again. Search for the vision."

"*I will try,*" the shade replied, its voice hesitant. Then it added, "*But I must have something to help me search. I must have a conduit.*"

Ylaire nodded. Letting go of the girl's hands, she reached into the front of her threadbare gown and pulled out a little black vial. Holding it up to the moonlight, she shook it, watching how the liquid sloshed inside. There was so little . . . and every drop worth a kingdom!

"Hold out your hand," she said.

The child obeyed. Ylaire pulled out the stopper and, holding her breath, tilted the bottle until a single drop poised on the lip. It fell; a gleaming red pearl landed in the center of that outstretched palm, bright against the pale skin.

Nilly's fingers curled tight. Without a word, she closed her eyes and bowed her head, cradling her hand against her breast. The shimmering jade glow of her shade fountained up from the center of her being and pulsed out from her in waves through the ether, visible only to shadow sight, but so brilliant that Ylaire had to shield her face and blink into mortal vision or risk being blinded. She felt the power of the shade as it channeled through the precious drop of blood.

That small body could be so easily overwhelmed by the force of magic flowing through her. Ylaire clutched the bottle tight, her knuckles whitening, and watched the child intently. Perhaps she'd asked too much. A Seer's powers were unpredictable at best, so rare and so little understood. Over the last month, Ylaire had worked to hone Nilly's abilities, but she was so young, so small. So mortal.

Ylaire's lips moved in silent pleading, like a prayer. "The queen. The queen. Find the queen . . ."

With no warning, Nilly's head tossed back and her eyes flared open. They blazed with jade light, the pupils and irises utterly consumed by the glow. She opened her mouth, and more light poured from her throat. The musical voice of Rasanala sang out, "*I see her! I see her! The queen! The queen!"*

"Where?" Ylaire couldn't stop herself. She lunged forward and caught Nilly by the front of her gown, nearly hauling the child off her straw mattress to the floor. "Where is she? Tell me!"

Nilly's chin dropped to her chest. The light magic went out like a snuffed candle. The girl moaned and covered her face with her hands.

"Rasanala!" Ylaire cried. She wanted to shake the girl in her desperation. Her hands trembled with need, with fear, with hope. "Rasanala, answer me! Where is the queen? Where is she?"

That little posy mouth moved several times before the shade's voice finally whispered, *"I saw her . . . I saw her kneeling before a black stone. I saw the man, the man dressed all in gold. He raised his sword and he . . . and he . . ."*

Ylaire couldn't breathe. "What did you see?" she pleaded. "Tell me."

"He cut off her head."

Ylaire let go of the child, leaving her to tumble back onto her mattress, and turned away sharply, striding across the room. Her hands flew to her head, tearing at

61

her hair, tearing at her scalp until streams of blood ran down her face and neck. So, it was true. It was true! The others had told her what happened, but somehow she hadn't believed it.

Odile. Her queen, her goddess. Odile was dead.

Beheaded.

But it couldn't be the end. No. Not for Odile. She had taken precautions. She had set protections in place . . . Ylaire clutched the vial of blood at her chest. Her heart pounded so hard, she half feared it would shatter the vial. Drawing long, careful breaths, she calmed herself. Odile's story wasn't over. Not yet. Not yet.

She looked over her shoulder at the little girl curled up in a ball on the mattress. The shade-light still gleamed ascendant inside her. "Rasanala," Ylaire said, turning to face the child, her voice rough and rasping, "did you see where they took her body?"

Those magic-filled eyes lifted, meeting her gaze. "*No. But . . . I may be able to find out.*"

A smile, swift and sharp, cut across Ylaire's face. She swooped down and picked up the little girl, swinging her onto her hip. Nilly gave a little squeak and tried to squirm free, but Ylaire gripped her tightly.

"Hush, hush!" she crooned. "We can't stay here, sweet girl. The venatrix got too close tonight. We must move on, find a safer place to hide. But then . . . then my little miracle child, we will find where my queen lies sleeping."

CHAPTER 4

AYLETH NEVER LIKED THE NIGHT AFTER A HUNT. IT was always difficult to bring her spirit back down from the thrilling heights of chase and battle to the earthy needs of the aftermath. Needs such as preparing and processing the shade-taken carcass, or writing down the necessary details in her logbook.

Needs such as suppressing her shade.

No, Mistress. No, Laranta whined piteously when she felt the first notes of the song spell winding toward her.

Ayleth braced herself and played on, her fingers moving with practiced familiarity along the double heads of her Vocos, both drone and recorder. It took all her strength of will not to apologize, not to soften the spell as it wound around her shade and dragged her down. But with Terryn's cold gaze watching her, she wouldn't dare. Everything must be done according to the law, every detail in place.

When the song was complete and the Vocos sheathed once more, she felt oddly hollow. Oddly alone.

Terryn sat a few yards away, feeding fuel to a campfire he had built to warm them against the deepening night. A shed with one sagging wall served as shelter for their two horses, who munched contentedly on the oats in their feedbags. The goat carcass, dragged from the village street, lay wrapped in sackcloth just to Ayleth's right, completing the less-than-idyllic scene.

Ayleth shuddered. All the aches and pains she'd been able to ignore while Laranta's strength was active in her system now sprang to the forefront of her awareness. In particular, the burn stretching from her neck to her shoulder and along her right arm. Not a bad burn, nothing she couldn't live with, nothing that wouldn't heal in a day or two. But . . . she grimaced, looking down her nose at the singed sleeve of her uniform. Parts were burned away entirely, revealing raw skin beneath. The price of tangling with an Elemental shade-taken.

"That looks painful."

The suddenness of Terryn's voice breaking the long silence startled her. Ayleth looked across the fire to find him watching her closely. He sat cross-legged, his right elbow leaning on one knee. His left arm, wrapped in its bandages, lay tucked close to his stomach, no doubt still throbbing from the wound he'd dealt it, despite the tuaflor salve.

He nodded at her shoulder. "You were burned in the fight."

"Maybe," she answered through clenched teeth, and moved to sit across from him. "It's not bad. I'll put alœu on it when I get back to the outpost."

"You didn't bring any with you?"

She could hear the unspoken questions underscoring his words: *You didn't prepare properly before setting out on the hunt? Are you or are you not a trained venatrix?* Her jaw tightened. Silence lingered, broken only by the crackle of the fire.

"I have some," he said at last.

Of course he did. Venator du Balafre would never dream of riding off on the circuit roads without an entire apothecary shop somehow miraculously shoved into his saddlebags.

She merely cast him a bland look.

His eyes narrowed, firelight gleaming bright in his black pupils. "It will help. You'll rest better tonight."

"I'll rest just fine, thank you."

A log broke, sending a spurt of whirling embers up into the night. Ayleth grimaced. Pain flared along her arm, becoming more difficult to ignore by the moment. When she hadn't known there was alœu available, she'd been able to push the pain back. But now, realizing there was relief close at hand . . .

Well, she wasn't going to ask for it. He could sit there with that knowing expression of his all night long. She was in competition with this man. She wouldn't give him anything he might use against her. So, she held her tongue, breathed deeply through her nostrils, and told herself the burns weren't so bad, they wouldn't keep her awake all night, the pain wasn't, in fact, getting worse by the second.

With a sigh, Terryn gathered his long limbs, got to his feet, and marched away from the fire to the shed where their horses rested, there to rummage through one of the saddlebags set off to the side. He returned a moment later, this time to Ayleth's side of the fire.

She glared up at him. "What?"

He lifted his right hand, displaying a small clay jar.

She looked at it. She raised her gaze up to his, eyebrows quirked.

"You helped me," he said, popping the lid off. "Let me help you."

"I don't need any—Oy! Hey!"

In one swift motion, Terryn scooped a dollop of slimy salve with two fingertips, crouched, and pressed it to her neck. Ayleth, surprised, leaned away so fast she fell back on one elbow. He followed, his fingers working in circles to rub the ointment into her skin. The effect was immediate. The pain didn't completely vanish, but the raw burning calmed to a dull, distant ache. A shuddering breath escaped her lips, despite her best efforts. Terryn's fingers were cool and quick, working with expert efficiency.

"You've got to rub it in thoroughly," he murmured. "You don't need a lot, but you need to work it in well."

Ayleth, still propped on her elbow, turned her head slightly. He leaned over her, his attention fixed on his work. Dark curls, getting a bit long these days but not yet long enough to tie back in a queue, fell across his forehead. The side of his face marred by the ugly scar was hidden in shadow, and Ayleth found herself noting other features instead. Firelight emphasized the sharp edge of his jaw, the prominence of his long, thin nose, the cut of his cheekbones. All hard as though chiseled by a sculptor's hand out of dark stone.

With a flash, those pale blue eyes lifted from his task to meet her gaze. Ayleth's breath caught in her throat, and she looked away, first to the fire, then up at the cold, starry sky. She felt his gaze still fixed on the side of her face, and his rubbing fingers slowed almost to a stop.

As though coming suddenly back to himself, he resumed his work. With each stroke, her pain decreased.

He scooped another small amount on the ends of his fingers and slid it under the neckline of her shirt onto her shoulder.

Ayleth sat upright and caught his wrist. She couldn't quite meet his eyes this time. "Um, I'll . . . I'll do it." Her voice sounded thin in her ears. She dared a glance his way, saw how his eyes moved from her face to her neck, to that place where his fingers rested under her shirt.

He pulled his hand back and held out the jar. "You should probably take off your outer garments."

Ayleth didn't answer.

He jerked his chin to one side, toward the darkness. "I'll step away. Find more firewood."

Ayleth nodded. "That's . . . Yes, good idea." She took the jar.

He stood, stepped back a pace, his lips parted as though to add something more. Instead, he gave his head a quick shake, turned, and stalked off into the night, leaving her alone by the campfire.

Ayleth waited until she could no longer hear his footsteps before undoing the laces of her jerkin and shirt, pulling her tender arm free. She worked quickly, partly because the relief was so great, partly because she didn't know how long she had before Terryn's return. Her heart thudded in her throat. Merely the leftover stress of the evening's hunt, of course. She looked down at her chest, bruised from where the monster rammed her with its goat-head. If Laranta had not been ascendant at the time, her ribcage would have been entirely crushed, her torso pulverized by that blow.

Plenty of reason for her pulse to throb. It was nothing more than delayed reaction to stress.

She finished applying the salve. If it didn't feel as soothing as it had under Terryn's ministrations, she told herself it was simply because she didn't work it in quite as thoroughly. She slid her arm back into her ragged sleeve, tied up the laces of her shirt, and buckled her jerkin, drawing long, calming breaths as she did so. Then she sat for some while, studying the fire, listening for sounds of Terryn's return.

She'd fed the campfire twice before he finally reappeared. She watched his shadowy form emerge from the darkness, his hood pulled up over his head so that she couldn't see his face. He dumped an armload of gathered fuel, then, without a word or look her way, stalked over to the shed again. She eyed him as he rummaged through another of his saddlebags.

When he returned to the fire, he passed close to Ayleth and tossed a little twine-tied cloth packet her way. As Terryn settled down on the far side of the fire across from her, she untied the twine, and the cloth fell away to reveal a hard lump of bread, a not-too-moldy wedge of cheese, and a strip of smoked beef. Once more she wondered if she should protest, insist that she'd brought her own supplies, that she didn't need anything from him. But she'd only packed a few dry barley cakes this morning before setting out. And she really hated barley cakes.

She felt Terryn watching her again as she gnawed on the smoked beef, tugging hard for each bite. Looking up, she caught his gaze just when she was in the middle of tearing at a particularly tough strip.

That hateful eyebrow of his slowly raised.

She froze, a flush of embarrassment heating her cheeks. "What?" she demanded around her mouthful.

"I don't believe I've ever seen a lady eat with such . . . vigor."

Ayleth blinked and forced the bite down to land in the pit of her stomach. "I'm not a lady. I'm a venatrix."

"Indeed."

"It's not as though I attend balls or frequent royal banquets, you know."

"Certainly not."

She scowled down at her meal. Venator du Balafre, with his perfectly pressed uniform and perfectly shined buckles, probably preferred lace-trimmed ladies daintily nibbling at crumpets or sipping soup from miniscule silver spoons.

Which was his problem and none of her business.

Ayleth ripped another huge bite from the strip of smoked beef.

They ate in silence for a while before Terryn cleared his throat, drawing Ayleth's attention back his way. "So," he said, twisting his neck and shoulders as though to loosen tension, "where did you undergo your indoctrination, Venatrix? I know you were not at Breçar, not when I was there."

Ayleth narrowed her eyes at him. "Why do you want to know?"

He shrugged, his mouth pulling a little to one side. "Curiosity."

She tilted her head. "I thought you didn't see any point in conversation between us." She watched his reaction closely. Did he recall their first meeting in the prince's office at Dunloch as vividly as she did?

Terryn lowered his eyes and shrugged again. "We have now served this borough together for a month. We have two more months ahead of us before this partnership, such as it is, comes to an end. It seems to me, in light of our current association, we might as well know something about each other."

He had a point, of course. Hunt brothers and hunt sisters had to form bonds to a certain extent. Their lives often depended on each other out in the field. The teachings of Saint Evander encouraged the creation of strong ties . . . although, not too strong. Never strong enough that a hunt brother would hesitate to put down his hunt sister at need, or vice versa.

Ayleth pressed her lips together. She really didn't want to tell Terryn anything about herself. It hadn't been that long since he'd accused her of consorting with witches.

Besides, how many times had he called her out for so-called heresy? No, Terryn du Balafre wasn't to be trusted. And he was such an ass besides.

Still, if she gave him something, perhaps she could get something from him in return.

"Castra Vielhir," she said at last. "I was orphaned during the Witch Wars and taken in by the Order as an infant."

He nodded. "Your people are from Campionarre, then?"

"So I'm told." She shoved a last bite of cheese into her mouth, letting the sharp, sour taste distract her from the sudden twist in her gut. The truth was, she had no memory of her life in Campionarre, no memory of Castra Vielhir, of her indoctrination, any of it. She knew only what Hollis had told her. That, and her suspicions that Hollis had never been entirely truthful . . .

She shivered and tossed her head, jutting her chin Terryn's way. "What about you? You were indoctrinated at Castra Breçar?"

"Yes."

She waited for what felt like a long interval, debating

the merits of probing for more information. At last she said, "And you were apprenticed under Fendrel, Venator Dominus du Glaive, right? That must have been . . . interesting."

"Yes."

Though her shadow sight was currently suppressed, Ayleth could almost see the icy wall going up around the venator's spirit. She'd picked up bits and pieces of his history over the last few weeks. She knew he was from Talmain, the southernmost of the five Gaulian Kingdoms. She knew that the woman who claimed him as her son had been lady-in-waiting to a Talmainian princess—Leurona di Taureau, who wed the Chosen King and gave birth to the Golden Prince before dying soon after.

Along with these facts, Ayleth knew something else as well—a truth which had been forming with more certainty in her brain for weeks now. She'd glimpsed a portrait of Queen Leurona in the prince's castle on the day she reported for duty, and she'd been struck at once by the queen's intense, pale eyes. Eyes which looked nothing like Prince Gerard's.

Eyes which seemed to gaze at Ayleth now across the campfire, peering out from beneath a venator's hood.

How many people knew? Was it common knowledge that Venator Terryn du Balafre was in fact the Golden Prince's bastard half-brother? If she had spotted the connection in just a few weeks, surely everyone else had figured it out long ago. It wasn't as if Terryn had been hidden away in some backwater borough throughout his upbringing. As apprentice to the Venator Dominus, he would have spent much of his growing-up years at the king's court in Telianor. Time enough to develop a close bond with the prince himself. Time enough to be recognized. Did everyone know and simply chose not to acknowledge the truth?

There was, Ayleth considered, a certain symmetry to the arrangement. Fendrel du Glaive served as Black Hood to his younger brother, the king. He could never be king himself, shade-taken as he was. But everyone knew how much power and influence the Venator Dominus wielded over King Guardin.

Now here was Terryn—also shade-taken, also the older brother. Trained since childhood to serve the

Golden Prince, primed to one day assume the role of Black Hood, the most powerful position a venator could hold in the kingdom. And on that rising path to rank and glory, he was meant to take over the outpost in Wodechran Borough.

But then, Ayleth had stepped in his way. She'd impressed the Golden Prince, convinced him to give her a chance at the position, and possibly thwarted Terryn's destiny in the process.

No wonder he despised her.

The silence lasted far too long for comfort, and the icy wall around Terryn only solidified. Ayleth brushed crumbs from her lap and pulled her cloak around her shoulders, wincing a little at the pressure on her burns.

"I'm going to sleep," she announced at length. "Wake me in two hours, and I'll mind the fire for a stretch."

Terryn nodded, his gaze on the embers smoldering beneath the flames.

Ayleth lay down on the cold ground, rolling away from the fire so that it could warm her cold back. She told herself she only imagined Terryn's gaze resting on her shoulders. Curling into a tight ball, she closed her eyes and willed sleep to come.

Terryn tended the fire, carefully arranging dry branches where they would best catch the blaze. On a night like this, so close to the edge of winter, they needed to keep a fire burning all night long. But Terryn had not anticipated a night on the road, and he'd certainly not carried with him firewood enough to last until daylight.

He stood, prepared to venture back out into the darkness in search of more fuel, but hesitated. His eyes moved almost against his will, dragging his gaze to Ayleth, curled up with her back to him on the other side of the fire. Asleep, he assumed. Ought he to wake her before stepping away? But no, most shade hunters worked alone. This certainly wouldn't be the first time she had slept out in open country with no one to guard her slumber.

Pulling his cloak close around him, Terryn set out into the darkness, away from the warm little camp circle. Shadow sight sparked in his eyes, illuminating his vision even in the depth of night. On his earlier foray, he'd found a dead tree fallen in a nearby field. The large limbs were too big to fetch without an ax, but the smaller branches were dry enough that he could break them off and gather them into a sizable armload. He set to this work with a will, his breath puffing between cold lips.

"Castra Vielhir," he muttered. The words slipped out unconsciously, but he paused when he heard himself, and his mouth twisted into a frown.

It was a good story, insofar as it went. Ayleth had already told him that she'd apprenticed in Drauval Borough, which was close to the border of Campionarre. Possibly her mistress—this Venatrix di Theldry she spoke of with such awe—had taken her apprentice to Vielhir each year for her annual examinations, rather than to Breçar. It made sense . . . .

But why did the uneasiness linger in his gut? That unwavering suspicion that Venatrix di Ferosa was not what she seemed.

His arms full, Terryn turned back to the camp, following the flicker of firelight through the shadows. His lips and nose seemed frozen solid, and the relief of stepping back into the warm reach of the campfire was so great, he dumped his armload and stood rubbing his hands and blowing on his fingers to get the blood moving again.

Through all this, Ayleth did not wake. But she stirred and turned in her sleep, her hood pulling back from her face so that the firelight illuminated her features.

Terryn added a few more crooked sticks to the flames, concentrating his attention on this task, watching how the fire licked at a stick's surface, blackening the outer bark, its heat lining the cracks with red, raging glow. He would not look at her.

But he was aware of her, nonetheless. Aware to the very tips of his fingers.

There was a simple explanation, of course. A reason why his senses were so attuned to her presence: She was dangerous. His hunter's instincts, finely honed over years of training, recognized her as a threat and thus refused to give him peace whenever she was near. This was why his eyes fought against his control, struggling to move from contemplation of the fire to contemplation of her face. It was perfectly natural, pure self-preservation: the need to keep a wary eye on the enemy.

Nothing more.

At last he gave up. Sitting back from the fire and huddling into his cloak and hood, Terryn allowed his eyes to swivel to where she lay. The harsh red glow of the fire sharpened her jaw and cheekbones. How stern she looked, lying there. Her brow was tense, her mouth hard. Somehow, even in sleep, she looked dangerous. Lethal.

His throat thickened. Terryn swallowed hard and dragged his eyes back to the smoldering embers, the flaking hot ash rising in glimmering spirals up into the sky. Yes, she was a threat, all right. This pseudo-venatrix, this heretic girl from nowhere, posed a greater menace to him than anyone, anything, he'd ever met. These feelings stirring deep down inside him . . .

He must be on his guard. As long as he remained aware of the danger, he could fight it. But he dared not let his resolve slip. Not for a moment.

"Goddess help me," he muttered, and rubbed a hand down his numb face.

She began to murmur. At first, her voice was so soft, Terryn couldn't hear it over the crackle of the fire. She turned her head sharply, first one way, then the other, the stern line between her brows deepening. She muttered again, this time louder, the words unintelligible. Her mouth twisted into a grimace, and she hissed as though in pain.

Terryn sat up straighter. "Di Ferosa?" he said.

Then she screamed.

The scent of pine filled her nostrils.

Ayleth moaned, squeezed her eyes tight, then opened them. Interlacing greenery appeared before her view, each sharp needle silhouetted against soft pale light. She blinked, and the image clarified.

"*I'm dreaming*," she whispered, and sat upright.

The vast, lonely acres of her own mental landscape stretched before her and on all sides. Miles and miles of pine forest and deep shadows, rolling hills and sheer mountain ridges. Ayleth wrapped her arms around her naked body. She was always naked here unless she took the time to envision clothing for herself. But the only other being that shared this world was Laranta, so she didn't bother covering her nakedness.

Ayleth got to her feet, swaying a little where she stood. A hum of song spell vibrated under her feet, the suppression song she'd used to bind Laranta. She would have no companion tonight for her dream wanderings. Sighing heavily, she took a step. And stopped at once.

A shadow flickered on the edge of her vision.

A shiver raced down her spine—a shiver not of fear, but of . . . familiarity. Why did she feel as though she'd seen that shadow before? As though, if she could have just caught a clear glimpse of it, she would recognize it, would even know its name?

Another flicker of movement. Ayleth turned swiftly in place, but not fast enough. Her eyes saw only pine boughs waving softly, though there was no wind to stir them.

She took a step. Then another. "*Wait,*" she whispered. "*Please.*"

Then she was running as hard and fast as she could. Chasing after shadows she sensed without seeing, so close, just on the edge of her peripheral vision. She knew what they were. She couldn't say how she knew, yet she clung to her certainty. They were her memories—her lost memories, those moments, those years, those faces that were so vital to who she was, but which she could not recall. But if she could catch them, if she could remember . . .

She tore through the forest, faster and faster, pushing through the low, prickly boughs. Her feet churned up pine straw behind her. More shadows appeared up ahead—three, four . . . six. A dozen. Names burned on the tip of her tongue, names she could not quite remember. She longed to call out, and she knew that if she could just make her lips form the right sounds, those shadows would stop, would turn back to her, would show her their faces.

She burst through a stand of pines and came to an arm-wheeling stop on the brink of a gorge. Her heart thudded in her throat, and she fell back hard onto the stone ledge, her feet scrabbling at the edge of that precipitous drop.

All around her, shadows streamed out of the wood and poured over the edge, vanishing into the darkness below. Slipping away from her.

"Wait! Please, don't go!" she begged. She pulled herself

up enough to crawl to the edge of the gorge. The dizzying fall loomed beneath her, and vertigo whirled in her head. Yet she stretched out one hand, reaching for those vanishing figures. "*Come back,*" she whimpered. "*Rotoro. Dulrudu. Rhadarka.*" Then, with soft desperation, "*Mother . . .*"

The ground broke beneath her. With a scream, Ayleth pitched forward into the abyss—

She felt the wind of a fall, felt the plunge in her gut, the jolt in her limbs as she tried to grasp at empty air. Then her flailing hands caught hold of something solid, and she gripped as hard as she could.

Only then did she realize she was screaming. She coughed, gagged, choked back her voice, and struggled for breath for what felt like an eternity, all the while convinced that her body must lie broken and pulverized on stone.

Gradually, her panic eased. She drew a long breath and then a longer one. Her frantic heart calmed its pace, no longer trying to break right through her ribcage, and her senses returned, one after another. First, smell—she inhaled the scent of fire, smoke, and another, a woodsy aroma, like fresh-chopped cedar. Her ears picked up the crackle of burning branches and the sound of breathing—her own breath, she thought. Her eyes were closed, but beyond her lids she sensed the flicker of warm red light.

A sensation of calm filled her. It was a dream. Only a dream. A dream she'd had before, which always faded with the dawn. She could try to remember, but she knew the images would slip away. Those shadows . . . those names . . .

She groaned and squeezed her eyes tight in an effort to keep from fully waking. Something cold pressed into her cheek, but otherwise her face seemed to be resting on something warm and solid. Something moving rhythmically in time to a heartbeat against her ear.

Was that an arm draped over her shoulders?

Ayleth's eyes flew wide, and she pushed back from where she had apparently been cradled against Terryn's chest. Her arms and legs caught in the long folds of her cloak, pulling her off balance.

He sprang to his feet and stepped back, both hands out. "Venatrix!" he said, his deep voice husky in his throat. "I'm sorry, you . . . You were dreaming, and then you screamed. I thought . . . I tried to . . . and then you clung to me . . ."

Ayleth stared up at him. She could feel the pressure in her hands where she had gripped the front of his leather jerkin, pressing her face against his chest. Her fingers moved to her cheek, touching the indentation left in her skin by his topmost buckle.

"I . . . I'm . . ." She couldn't find words. She brushed loose strands of hair out of her face and blinked stupidly up at her fellow venator. "I'm all right now. Th-thank you."

Terryn looked as though he wanted to speak. His eyes were questioning and a little frightened. He looked strangely helpless, vulnerable even, with his hands extended toward her in the empty air.

He swallowed hard and turned away abruptly, stalking round to his side of the fire. He busied himself for some moments, tossing a few more branches into the flames, giving her time to pull herself together.

Ayleth shuddered and rubbed both hands down her face. "You might as well sleep," she said, flashing a quick glance across the fire to Terryn. He met her look, his face an absolute blank. All that helpless vulnerability was gone so completely, she must have imagined it in the first place. "I . . . I can sit watch a while," she finished lamely.

Rather than answer, Terryn immediately wrapped his cloak around his shoulders, lay down, and turned away from her, becoming nothing more than a lump of shadow.

Ayleth scowled at the broad expanse of his back. Her heart pounded, and her fingers once more brushed the indentation on her cheek. What an idiot she was! Had she really held onto him like that? Like some frightened child or some swooning damsel . . . Her face heated again, and she buried it in her hands.

Darkness and silence extended endlessly before her. An hour passed and then another. She added fuel to the fire, but no matter how close she huddled to the flames, she could not drive out the shiver in her bones. Her stomach twisted in knots.

She pressed the heels of her hands to her eyes, her

fingertips tense against her scalp. Images burst into the darkness of her head. Long, low figures in the forest . . . ferocious faces, twisted in bloodthirsty snarls.

Her lips moved almost unconsciously. A whisper slipped out into the cold air, puffing on white vapors.

"Mother . . ."

CHAPTER 5

THE FOLLOWING MORNING, TERRYN RETURNED TO
Cabralet village and negotiated for the use of a cart, which
Ayleth hitched to Chestibor. Together they heaved the
hideous goat carcass into the cart's bed. The stench of
shadow blight already seeped through its canvas
wrappings. It would be a long ride back to the outpost.

Ayleth mounted Chestibor and guided him to the
nearest circuit trail leading toward Milisendis. These
narrow tracks winding throughout Wodechran Borough

were exclusively for Evanderian use, and denizens of the borough tended to avoid them unless they had need of a venator's services. Usually a circuit ride was a lonely affair. Ayleth didn't mind the loneliness. Chestibor was company enough for her, and when she was alone, she often allowed Laranta a certain measure of ascendancy.

But today, Terryn's red mare fell into step on Chestibor's right. The venator himself, silent and stone-faced as ever, watched the road ahead, saying nothing at all. Not exactly companionable.

Ayleth cast him several sideward glances as the morning progressed. An hour slipped past with neither of them speaking. Why didn't he ride on ahead? She could think of no reason for him to stay with her and the cart. It would be better if he put a little distance between them . . . if he gave her a chance to forget the feel of his fingers gently treating the burns on her neck. To forget the hard warmth of his chest, the weight of his arm across her shoulders . . .

Heat flooding her face, Ayleth ducked her head further into the shadows of her hood. Haunts damn it, would this ride never end?

Determined to fill the silence, she cleared her throat and pulled back her shoulders. "So, tell me about this red-haired witch you've been hunting, Venator du Balafre."

He glanced sideways at her, one eyebrow quirked. "Why?"

"I don't know." She shrugged. "Maybe . . . maybe I could help."

"I don't need your help."

And there was the Venator du Balafre she knew. Ayleth sighed, rolling her eyes heavenward. "As you pointed out last night, we *are* hunt brethren at least for the next two months." Cold silence answered this, but she persisted doggedly. "I've already picked up a little information here and there. Her name is Fayline, isn't that right?"

The icy, contemplative look vanished from Terryn's face. He glanced at Ayleth with some surprise. "You know about her?"

"Not really," Ayleth admitted. "I've heard no story. Just the name and other odd tidbits. I know that Fayline was . . ." She paused, strangely reluctant to say the words out loud. "She was . . . important to Prince Gerard. But she was lost. Shade-taken." She felt Terryn's gaze on the side of her face and turned quickly to catch his eye. "And now Gerard has you hunting this witch because he thinks it's Fayline. Or her host body, at least."

"There's more to it than that." Terryn drew a long breath and let it out slowly, as though deciding how much he should say. Ayleth waited, refusing to press him. If he was willing to tell her, she was willing to hear. If not, she'd find her own answers in her own time. She wouldn't beg him for scraps of information.

But Terryn continued at last: "Fayline was the eldest daughter of Duke Celestin d'Aldreda, one of the most powerful men in Perrinion. He was once enslaved to the Phantomwitch, Inren di Karel. When the Chosen King set him free, d'Aldreda helped to entrap the witch in a powerful spell. Then, before the venators could stop him, he slew her body. Violently."

Ayleth nodded. Some of this she knew already; Hollis had told her how Fendrel du Glaive and other Evanderians, including Hollis herself, had worked with a liberated witch's slave to bring about the fall of the Phantomwitch, one of Odile's Crimson Devils. She'd not known the name of the slave in question, though she had been told that he spoiled the trap by dealing a violent death at an untimely moment, thus enabling the witch to escape the ultimate damnation of the Haunts. Terryn's version of events fit with what she already knew.

"The spirit of Inren survived," Terryn continued, "bound up with her possessing shade. Just before d'Aldreda dealt the death blow, Inren swore that she would return and take from him that which he held most dear. She fulfilled that vow four years ago on the night of Gerard and Fayline's wedding."

"His wedding?" Ayleth's jaw dropped open. She hadn't known that the prince ever married. Drauval was so remote, and news from the kingdom was so rare, she'd never heard even a rumor of a wedding.

Terryn cast another swift glance her way, and Ayleth wished she could take back her gasped words. Mentally, she kicked herself for betraying more of her country-girl ignorance.

"Yes," Terryn continued. He adjusted his grip on his reins and faced the road again. "Inren's soul was hidden inside the body of a servant at Dunloch. The ceremony was hardly complete, and the prince and his bride were just stepping onto the floor to open the celebration ball. Everyone was distracted with music and cheering, and no one noticed when a servant stepped up quietly behind Fayline, took out a knife . . . and slit her own throat."

A sick sensation coiled in Ayleth's stomach. She could almost see the tragedy as it took place. The sudden violence of death rippling through the ether, propelling the spirits inside the dead servant into the nearest available host body. Into Gerard's bride.

"And . . . and what about Fayline's soul?" she asked after a moment.

"Lost," Terryn answered heavily. "At least, so we must assume. Mortal bodies were not meant to hold more than one soul. For a single body to carry three—a shade, a witch, *and* the original soul? Impossible. The red-haired witch is not Fayline anymore, no matter what Gerard wants to believe. It is Inren di Karel and her shade."

Silence fell once more. Ayleth chose not to break it for several minutes as she considered Terryn's story. When she first met Gerard, she hadn't known he was the prince. Yet even in that meeting, he'd mentioned Fayline, speaking her name with such heartbreak in his voice. It seemed so strange that the Goddess's promised Golden Prince could be allowed to suffer so. And the poor lady, poor Fayline, ousted from her body, doomed to oblivion. What a cruel fate!

Ayleth shook her head, her brows deepening into a scowl. She understood that the ways of the Goddess were often incomprehensible to mortal understanding. How can a mortal mind hope to grasp the complexity of the Divine? And yet the words returned to her again, words spoken by Gerard at their first meeting: "*Seems an ineffectual Goddess who cannot save the souls of her children.*"

Ayleth shivered, and the autumn wind blowing at her back seemed colder than before.

"What of the witch?" she asked at length. "What happened to her?"

"Fendrel pursued her to the Witchwood. She escaped across the Great Barrier, and he didn't follow."

"Have you found any evidence that she escaped through the opening Nane made? Along with the Warpwitch, I mean."

Terryn shook his head. "I've spent the last month

hunting for some indication that Inren has returned to Wodechran. So far, every rumor has led nowhere. I don't believe she escaped the Witchwood."

Ayleth didn't press him with more questions. Somehow, his assurance didn't ease her mind, but she kept her mouth shut and focused on the road ahead.

At long last, Milisendis Outpost loomed into view, its watchtower the tallest point in the valley below. A flash of color near the gate caught Ayleth's eye, and she peered ahead, half-wishing for Laranta's power to increase her vision. As it was, she had only her mortal sight to depend on and wasn't entirely certain what she saw.

"Is that the Dunloch livery?" she asked, the first words she'd spoken in some while.

Terryn lifted his chin, his eyes keen under the shadow of his hood. "I believe it is. A courier from the prince."

Ayleth's heart thudded. If the prince had sent a message all the way out to Milisendis, there must be shade-doings near to Dunloch. Terryn, obviously sharing that conclusion, spurred his red mare ahead of Ayleth to the outpost gate, hailing the courier with an upraised hand. Ayleth urged Chestibor to hurry after, and the cart rumbled and bumped down the stony decline.

The courier was little more than a boy, a skinny, freckled young fellow who puffed out his chest, trying to fill his oversized uniform and bravely face the Evanderians as they approached. By his wide-eyed stare, Ayleth knew he feared them as much as he would fear any other shade-taken he met out in the borough. His hand trembled as he handed a rolled scroll over to Terryn.

Terryn didn't wait for Ayleth to reach the gate before he opened and read the prince's message. She pushed Chestibor a little faster, sparing the skinny messenger a brief glance as she drew up beside Terryn. He seemed to reach the end of the message just as she approached.

Ayleth held out her hand. "May I?"

Terryn rolled the scroll again and tucked it into the front of his jerkin. "It's addressed to me. I am summoned to Dunloch. You are to remain here and see to the needs of the borough."

A stone dropped in Ayleth's stomach. Was this a sign that Gerard had chosen his favorite? But he'd said they had three months to compete for the post!

"When will you return?" she asked through gritted teeth.

"Why?" Terryn raised both eyebrows. "Do you think you'll need me?"

Ayleth glowered. Instead of answering, she turned to the courier, offering him a formal nod. "Do you require anything else?"

The boy shook his head, hair falling in his eyes.

"Very well." She dismounted and opened the gate. Leading her horse and cart through into the outpost yard, she did not look back, not even when she heard sounds of Terryn's mare and the courier's pony trotting back across the valley, heading west toward Dunloch.

"I'll see to the needs of the borough," she muttered as she unloaded the shade-taken goat carcass into the bonehouse. "I'll see to it all on my own, while you put your feet up at the castle. Enjoy your little holiday, Venator Terryn. You're going to need it!"

She rather wished she'd thought to say all of that to his face, just to watch him squirm. This was the opportunity she needed, after all: the perfect chance to prove to Gerard that she could handle the borough on her own, without Terryn's assistance.

Besides, she wasn't certain she was ready to face the beautiful prince again. Not so soon after learning the tragedy of his lost love.

"Terryn, Venator du Balafre, Your Highness."

Prince Gerard half turned from his contemplation of a portrait on the gallery wall to acknowledge the servant at the door. The servant stepped back, and Terryn filled the doorway in his stead, the top of his head nearly brushing the lintel. He offered a quick bow, more out of habit than deference, and strode into the gallery, leaving the servant to shut the door behind him.

"You're prompt, Terryn," Gerard said, resuming his study of the portrait, his arms crossed over his chest. "I expected you to be out on the hunt. Did Billin just happen to catch you at home?" His voice held an edge he didn't bother to hide. He knew Terryn sensed it.

After a pause that lasted a little too long for comfort, Terryn said, "I've not been idle, Your Highness, if that's what you're implying. I have followed every rumor and every whisper of rumor. I have yet to find any proof that she has returned to Wodechran Borough."

"Fayline, you mean," Gerard whispered.

Another pause. Then, quietly, "You know who I mean."

Gerard drew a long breath, his nostrils flaring. He felt the intensity of Terryn's eyes studying him, but he continued to gaze up into the face of the woman in the portrait: Queen Leurona, his mother. She had died before he could remember, and he often came here to look at her face, to study those features, to try to get a sense of the woman she had been. But the tall, dignified woman merely looked down on him through cold, piercing eyes. Eyes that were nothing like Gerard's.

The prince's jaw tightened. He turned away from the portrait to face Terryn, who met his gaze and held it.

"If she is near, I will find her," Terryn said. He took a step nearer, and his voice dropped an octave. "I swear to you, Gerard: You will have your vengeance. Inren's soul will be damned to the Haunts for what she did."

Gerard shook his head. "That's not why I summoned you here. Actually, I must ask you to leave that hunt alone for the time being and take up a new assignment."

Eyes narrowing with suspicion, Terryn turned his head slightly to one side. "Go on."

And here came the moment, the moment when Gerard must speak out loud the truth of the future about to descend upon him. "Hallow's Well Night is now a week away," he said, forcing his voice to remain level and calm despite the weight crushing his heart. "Duke d'Aldreda has written and demanded the fulfillment of the contract I made with his house. I am . . ." Gerard swallowed to wet his dry throat. "I am to take Cerine d'Aldreda as my bride during the Rite of the Holy Well."

Terryn blinked. He opened his mouth, began to speak, then stopped himself.

Gerard hurried to fill that silence before it became unbearable. "Lady Cerine is due to arrive tomorrow. Duke d'Aldreda too, of course. And my uncle. Fendrel is bringing venators and venatrices from Castra Breçar to see to the safety of Dunloch, so that . . . so that . . ."

So that history would not repeat itself. So that no witch or shade-taken would descend on the merrymakers and damn the prince's bride. He didn't need to say it.

Terryn knew.

"My father will join us for the night of the ceremony, along with a host of celebrants from Telianor, coming for the ceremony and for the wedding ball." Gerard gave Terryn a quick look but broke away again almost at once. "I want you to be on hand. I feel I may need your support in the coming days."

"You don't have to marry her, Gerard."

The words struck his gut like stones. Gerard winced but shrugged, his arms still folded tightly across his chest. "I must marry someone. I am the Chosen King's son. Our line is destined to rule Perrinion throughout a Golden Age. Hard to do that if I refuse to wed, if I refuse to sire children."

"It doesn't have to be Cerine," Terryn said. "You can choose someone else. When you're ready."

Gerard snorted. "Try telling that to my father. Or d'Aldreda, for that matter. I did, as they are quick to point out, sign a contract with the Aldreda family. And they have a daughter of marriageable age. To break that contract would be to break faith with the most powerful lord in Perrinion."

"You are the prince. You get to decide."

"I am the Golden Prince." Gerard bowed his head, feeling the weight of his dead mother's eyes looking down upon him from the portrait. "My future was decided for me long ago."

Another silence. Not even Terryn, his stoutest supporter, would dare to contradict the truth of Gerard's words. They both knew the prophecy—they had been raised on it since before their memories began. It had shaped their lives down to the very core. To try to deny the destiny of the Golden Prince would be to deny life and existence.

"I'd like you to stay on at Dunloch until everything is finalized," Gerard said. "Will you do that for me, Terryn?"

"Fendrel will wonder at my not seeing to the needs of the borough," Terryn answered, and Gerard heard the strain in his friend's voice. Terryn's first loyalty was always to the prince, but he had a role to maintain as well. The carefully crafted role Fendrel had molded for him over the course of many years. "I can't abandon the outpost."

"You'd hardly be abandoning it. Venatrix Ayleth is perfectly able to handle shade-doings in Wodechran on her own."

A complicated expression flashed across Terryn's face, a mingling of frustration and grudging acknowledgement. He said nothing, but Gerard took it as a sign that Ayleth was indeed, much to Terryn's displeasure, quite good at her job.

"I need an ally here with me," Gerard persisted. "One week, that's all. You weren't here when . . . four years ago. I've often wondered if things might have gone differently if you had been at my side. I trust you, and I trust your instincts." He drew a long breath, afraid of saying too much, equally afraid of saying too little. "I don't want anything to happen to Cerine. While I doubt that Inren would try the same trick twice, it's unsettling, to say the least, that these rumors of the red-haired witch have begun cropping up *now*. Just before the Rite of the Holy Well."

The puckered scar on Terryn's cheek twitched with tension. But he said only, "I will stay."

Gerard breathed a sigh of relief. "Thank you. I'll have

a room made up for you." With that settled, he took two steps toward the door before pausing and looking back over his shoulder. "By the way, how are things going with you and Venatrix Ayleth? In your competition, that is. You are working well together managing the borough, I trust?"

"Venatrix Ayleth is . . . capable."

From taciturn Venator Terryn, this was high praise indeed. Practically gushing.

"So, you like her?" Gerard said.

Terryn's nostrils flared slightly. "She is not wholly without merit."

Gerard's mouth quirked to one side. "So, you *love* her."

Terryn rolled his eyes and brushed past the prince without so much as a parting bow, only muttering, "Haunts damn you, Gerard." He marched through the door and away down the hall beyond, leaving Gerard chuckling behind him.

CHAPTER 6

EVENING DARKENED THE SKY BY THE TIME AYLETH finally stumbled from the bonehouse, a stench of vinegar and lye soap wafting in her wake. Preparing the warped goat carcass for shipment to Castra Breçar had been a longer and fouler procedure than she'd anticipated, and afterward she'd had to scrub the bonehouse down thoroughly.

Now, gore-stained and limp with exhaustion, she staggered across the outpost yard, making for the blockhouse. She'd hardly slept the night before during her little campout with Terryn, and her heart fixed with single-minded purpose on her bed.

The hum of her suppression-spell songs vibrated oddly inside her as she stepped through the blockhouse door, making for the stair. She really ought to pause and reassert them, take care to bind her shade thoroughly before she slept. But . . . why? She rubbed a hand against one weary eye, then the other. Laranta wouldn't hurt her. Evanderian law be damned, let her shade have a little ascendancy for once! They'd both rest easier as a result.

Besides, if Laranta was ascendant, she wouldn't be alone in her dreams.

Leaning rather heavily on the stair rail as she climbed, Ayleth paused on the landing of the second floor. There were two rooms on this level: Venator Kephan's, which was kept ready in anticipation of his return, and the other room, which formerly belonged to Venator Nane, and which Terryn had quickly claimed upon first arriving in Milisendis a month ago. Ayleth had taken up residence in the tower, and though she'd managed to acquire a lumpy mattress and something that might almost pass for a pillow . . .

Her gaze slid to Terryn's open door. The door to his pristine room, so perfectly ordered, without even a speck of dirt. To that bed of his, so invitingly made, the blankets crisp and neat as though he took pains to press them every morning. That pillow, so soft, so white.

Ayleth pushed through the door, stripped off her belt and sheaths, dropping them in a pile on the floor, then fell across the bed without bothering to shed her blood-stained, vinegar-reeking garments. She was asleep moments after her head hit the pillow, sparing only a passing thought that it smelled like Terryn, like crushed pine needles and fresh-cut cedar and smoke and . . .

Her snores soon echoed through the blockhouse.

Mistress. Mistress, wake up.

Ayleth groaned and rolled over, nuzzling into her blankets and squeezing her eyes tight.

Mistress. Bad smell. Bad magic.

With a snort and a mutter, Ayleth shook her head. "*Go away, Laranta,*" she growled inside her head. But her wolf shade was there, ascendant and insistent. She pawed at Ayleth's consciousness and whined softly. Ayleth swore and curled into a tight ball of blankets and resentment. *"I should have suppressed you!"*

Bad magic, Mistress, Laranta persisted. *Bad smell. Bad, bad, bad—*

Ayleth's eyes opened.

A splash of pale sunlight fell through the window and landed full upon her face. Morning already? Had she slept through the night? Groaning, she pushed herself up onto her elbows and somehow contrived to get her head up and blow strands of hair out of her face. For a moment she couldn't remember where she was, whose soft white pillow now bore the imprint of her head and stains from her bloody, mucky face. Then it came to her.

Ayleth smiled wickedly. Terryn would be so mad when he discovered where she'd spent the night. She tipped her head, straining her ears. No sounds of movement downstairs or in the yard. Apparently, he had not returned in the night. If he had, he certainly would have ousted her from his bed and room. He must still be off with the prince on some secret, important mission.

Her smile faded into a grimace. She shook her head hard and sat up, swinging her legs over the edge of the bed. As she did so, she drew a deep breath . . . and a putrid stench filled her head. "Ugh! What in the Goddess's name . . .?"

Clapping a hand over her mouth and nose, she slid out of the bed and stared around the room. Why had she not noticed such a horrible stink much sooner? How had she managed to sleep through it? Holding her nose didn't help at all. The smell seemed to permeate her skin.

Wait. She frowned as realization struck. This wasn't a stink at all. Whatever she experienced, it was a shade sense, not mortal. *Stink* was the best word to describe it, the closest thing her mortal mind could comprehend for something so foul, so disgusting.

"*Laranta?*" she spoke into her mind.

Deep down inside, Ayleth felt her shade tugging at relaxed song spells, moving toward the forefront of her awareness. Oh, right. She remembered now: She'd not strengthened the binding spells last night before falling asleep. For the last many hours, Laranta had been pulling at her suppressions, and the more she pulled, the more of her power and awareness rose in ascendancy.

Mistress, the wolf shade growled, creeping up inside her head. *Something . . . wrong. Close. Bad.*

"*What is it? And where is it?*"

Laranta guided Ayleth's eyes for her, directing them to the plain brass-fastened chest by the wall under the window. Ayleth stepped across the room, wincing and shuddering as the stench—for want of a better word—increased. It had to be something magical to strike her shade senses so strongly. Had another one of Venator Nane's curses gone off? The venator had set any number of curses throughout the outpost which, in the weeks after he died, began to set off or break, sometimes to disastrous effect.

This didn't feel like a curse, somehow. There was no aura of Anathema magic in the room.

Ayleth knelt before the chest and lifted the lid. A putrid cloud seemed to rise and strike her in the face, and she sat back hurriedly, clutching her stomach, only just keeping herself from vomiting right into Terryn's chest of belongings.

Bad, Laranta whimpered in her head. *Bad, bad, bad.*

"*Yes, I know,*" Ayleth snapped and, bracing herself, looked inside again. The chest contained Terryn's various personal belongings: spare shirts and trousers—how many spares did he own?—buckles, spurs, bits and pieces. Ayleth pushed these aside, little caring how she disrupted the venator's orderly arrangement, digging until she found a pouch at the bottom of the chest. The spirit stench came from inside.

Her fingers flinching as though about to touch a dead rat, Ayleth picked up the pouch. It was like the pouches she wore on her own belt when out on a hunt, used for carrying small oddments or collecting samples. This one was much finer quality than hers, of course, newer, judging by the stitching and freshness of the leather. Inside, she felt something hard and round, hardly more than an inch in diameter.

She frowned. Curiosity overcoming her revulsion, she flipped the pouch open and upturned it. A black stone fell with a crack and rolled across the floor. Once again, Ayleth gagged, clapping a hand over her mouth to try to keep down the heaving in her stomach.

The stone settled in the patch of sunlight on the floor.

Its faceted surface, rather than refracting the light, seemed to suck it inward and devour it, rendering the room darker than it ought to be. A miasma of sour, broken magic surrounded it.

"*Laranta, give me your sight,*" Ayleth said, and blinked into shadow vision. Now she could see the magic, all the writhing tendril-tentacles of broken enchantment, a dense, tangled mass around that tiny stone. "*Is it . . . dangerous?*" she asked.

Give me my head, Laranta answered, tugging at the last of the suppression songs winding round her. Ayleth got up and backed away from the stone to fetch her Vocos pipes from the pile of sheaths and belts on the floor. She flicked them into a V-shape and played a hasty variation of the Song of Unbinding. The moment the already-loose suppressions were relaxed even more, Laranta gave a great shake of her spirit substance and poured out of Ayleth's head to manifest in her wolf shape in the room. Though she was too large to fit properly in that space, being a creature of spirit rather than real physical substance, she didn't let that bother her but seemed to shape reality around her to suit her own needs.

Padding on enormous feet, she approached the faceted stone where it lay eating up the sunlight, its broken enchantment threads writhing like ravenous snakes in the ether around it. Laranta sniffed the stone. Then her lip curled, and she backed away, growling.

"*What?*" Ayleth demanded. "*What is it?*"

Dead, Laranta said, and shuddered, her black fur rippling into puffs of smoky spirit-stuff. *Broken. Dead.* She shuddered again. *Bad.*

Using her shadow senses as little as possible to avoid that terrible stink, Ayleth stepped to Laranta's side and crouched over the stone. As Laranta said, it didn't seem as though the magic surrounding the sphere was active. She picked it up carefully, holding it between finger and thumb as she lifted it to eye level.

It looked like a jewel. A huge, well-cut jewel. Ayleth was certainly no expert on gemstones, but she would be willing to bet it was oblidite. Memory stirred in the back of her brain. Some almost-forgotten tale heard years ago. Bringing the stone closer to her face, she peered through the facets, deep down inside.

And saw writhing, living darkness at its center.

Ayleth dropped the stone and lurched to her feet, backing away. Her heart raced with realization of what it was she had discovered. "An anchor," she breathed. "It's a curse anchor. It belongs to the Phantomwitch."

How many long hours had she spent as a child, poring over the endless notes and details Hollis wrote down for her? Details of the Crimson Devils, Dread Odile's lieutenants from the days of the Witch Wars, and the shades they carried.

Inren di Karel, the Phantomwitch, carried an Evanescer shade, a being which could open rifts between this world and the Haunts. As long as Inren maintained a connection to an anchor in this world, she could step in and out of the Haunts at will anywhere within a mile radius of the anchor itself.

Ayleth stared at the diamond-crusted eye where it lay inert on the floor. Her careening heartrate slowed. Whatever spells had been implanted in that anchor were broken. It could no longer be used by the Phantomwitch, so Ayleth needn't fear a sudden appearance in the room beside her.

But a hundred questions crowded her mind at once.

How had Terryn come by one of Inren's old anchors? Was it part of his investigation? He'd told her only yesterday that he'd found no evidence to support the rumors that the Phantomwitch had returned. Was this anchor not evidence? Or was this simply an old anchor, unimportant because the enchantments were broken long ago?

Ayleth didn't think so. If the connection between the anchor and Inren had been broken for more than a year, the enchantment would have dissipated entirely, leaving nothing but a black stone. These snarled spell threads were still potent and putrid. Recently broken.

Which meant Terryn was wrong. The Phantomwitch had escaped the Witchwood after all. What's more, if he had this anchor in his possession, he knew it.

An ugly sliver of suspicion slid down Ayleth's throat. She tried to argue it away. After all, it was entirely possible Terryn didn't realize what it was he had. If Ayleth hadn't neglected to reinforce her suppression spells last night, she wouldn't have noticed anything amiss in the room. Terryn kept his shade even more tightly bound. Maybe he hadn't sensed the rotten magic.

But no. She knew better than to believe it. If she could recognize one of the Phantomwitch's anchors, Terryn certainly could. And he had purposefully withheld that information. Why?

Ayleth turned away from the eye anchor, crossing her arms. She needed to think, needed to reason through all the dark uncertainties crowding her mind. As she turned, however, her eye was caught by something she'd overlooked the night before when first entering Terryn's room.

He had pinned a large map to the wall just to the left of his bed, a map of Wodechran Borough, and quite an intricate one. Not part of Venator Kephan's collection, which Ayleth had studied with much interest during her first few days at Milisendis, this was Terryn's own map, possibly one he'd drawn himself. It had that precise refinement to it, characteristic of Terryn's work.

But none of these details interested Ayleth as much as the strange red circle in the lower right of the map, not far from the stark line indicating the Great Barrier. She stepped in close and read the words within that circle— *Cró Ular.*

The Tower of Blood and Eyes. The onetime stronghold of Ylaire di Jocosa and Inren di Karel.

She stepped back again. While the rest of the map was neat and orderly, rendered in a deep brown ink, that red circle stood out glaringly, like a signal fire.

Glancing at Laranta, Ayleth saw her wolf shade's ears pricked. *Hunt?* she asked, her voice a deep growl in Ayleth's head.

Ayleth didn't answer. She chewed thoughtfully on the inside of her cheek, then, giving her head a sharp shake, shifted her gaze back to the map. Terryn had ridden out to Cró Ular with Venator Kephan three weeks ago when on the hunt for the Warpwitch, Ylaire. He'd told her they'd found nothing there of interest. Just piles of broken stone.

But what if both Ylaire and Inren, having escaped the Witchwood, had returned to the location of their former power? Could it be that Terryn had discovered more than he'd let on?

Ayleth glanced at the anchor on the floor. Obviously, he had.

Resolution firmed in her heart. She was in motion

before she quite realized it, catching up the anchor and stuffing it back into its pouch. Then she fetched her belts and sheaths and called back over her shoulder, "*Come, Laranta,*" as she hastened down to the main room below. There she set to work, gathering up a fresh supply of poisons, looping the quivers over her shoulder.

Her wolf shade watched her with interest, a shadowy spirit shimmering with eagerness. *We hunt now?* Laranta asked as Ayleth donned her cloak.

Ayleth pulled the red hood up over her head. "*We hunt, Laranta,*" she said.

CHAPTER 7

TERRYN GRIPPED HIS LEFT WRIST IN HIS RIGHT FIST, both hands pressed against the small of his back. His shoulders straight, his head high, he assumed an expression of perfect stoicism, ready to face whatever came. Standing on the front stone stairs of the castle keep, several steps above and behind Gerard, he watched the procession which even now passed through the gate and crossed the bridge to Dunloch Castle.

The Duke d'Aldreda rode at the head of the company.

And beside him on a tall black horse came Fendrel, Venator Dominus du Glaive.

It had been more than a year since Terryn last met with his former master in person, but only a few months since their most recent correspondence. Terryn had been serving as hunt brother at a borough in the far north when Fendrel's message arrived, bidding him make all haste to Wodechran to claim the newly vacant position at Milisendis. Although Fendrel had always intended Milisendis to fall into Terryn's keeping, Terryn hadn't expected the appointment for many years yet. The tragedy of Nane's death had created an unexpected opportunity, and he'd hurried to obey his master's bidding.

Only to find a certain stubborn venatrix standing firmly in the way of his destiny.

The company progressed around the white circular drive now, carriage wheels and horse's hooves clattering on paving stones. While other parties journeying to Dunloch for the wedding would set up pavilions on the wide green lawn outside the castle, d'Aldreda and his entourage would take rooms in the keep itself. As would

Fendrel. Fendrel may be a venator and used to a rough-and-ready lifestyle, but he was also the king's brother and Gerard's uncle. He would not be asked to sleep in a tent.

Terryn swallowed, trying to wet his dry throat. It was ridiculous to feel this tense about facing the Dominus again. Nevertheless, a part of him—a larger part than he liked to admit—suddenly wished he was anywhere but here.

The two men on horseback drew rein at the base of the castle porch. Terryn cast a glance at Gerard, seeing how the prince's jaw tightened before he forced a welcoming smile onto his face. Gerard knew how to play the games of court far more effectively than Terryn ever would. Lifting a hand in greeting, the prince took the last few steps down to the drive. "Welcome, my lord duke," he said. "Welcome, Uncle."

Both men dismounted and handed their horses off to stable boys before bowing solemnly to their prince. Gerard waved a dismissive hand at this and quickly stepped forward to clasp the duke by the hand in a far more familiar greeting. "I trust your journey was uneventful?"

"Indeed, we enjoyed fair weather all the way," d'Aldreda answered. Everything about the duke was the height of style and elegance, from his bright ginger hair, still perfectly coiffed after a long day's ride, to the engraved silver toes of his riding boots. Over his right eye socket, he wore an eye patch of black silk embroidered with the insignia of his house; it was said that d'Aldreda was perhaps the only man in Perrinion who could utilize a disfiguring injury to set a fashion trend among young noblemen. A tall, narrow man, the duke had once been handsome, but sorrow and bitter anger had hardened his face.

By contrast, Fendrel looked, as he always did, as though he'd just come from riding a brutal circuit trail. His hood was thrown back on his shoulders, and road dust grayed the long, pale hair confined in five tight braids that pulled at his scalp. His worn and faded venator's uniform hung on him so naturally, he might have been born wearing it. He wore no marks of his rank, and yet something in his bearing bespoke power and authority in a way the duke's silks could never match.

But Terryn's gaze fixed on one detail—the bracer on

the Dominus's left arm. Where most venators wore a single iron spike, Fendrel's bracer bore three.

Though not a muscle on Terryn's face so much as twitched, his stomach lurched. Too well he knew the final fate of all venators. As a man aged, as his body weakened, so too did his will. Eventually, he would lose the strength to suppress the shade inside him, no matter what songs he played on his Vocos, no matter how many spikes he drove into his arm. The day would come when he must choose a fellow venator to deal him the Gentle Death.

The surest sign of an aging venator was more than one spike on his bracer. When Terryn last saw Fendrel, he had worn only one. Had so much changed in a year?

"Ah, and is this Lady Cerine?" Gerard asked suddenly, his voice too bright and cheery to be natural. A stylishly gilded carriage drawn by four elegant chestnuts with matching white blazes rattled to a halt before him. A footman jumped down from the back to open the door, revealing the occupant within.

Sudden heat rushed up Terryn's neck.

Haunts damn him to death, what was *she* doing here?

"Cerine is traveling by a different road and will join us

later today," d'Aldreda said, his voice seeming to come from a great distance. "You remember the Lady Liselle di Matin, my ward? She has come to serve as lady-in-waiting to your bride."

Accepting the footman's proffered hand, the lady lifted the edge of her skirts, revealing one delicately slippered foot as she stepped down from the carriage. She ducked her head to clear the low doorway, and long golden curls escaped from under her traveling veil, draping across her shoulders. She wore a thick cloak trimmed in white fur which, despite its many folds, could not disguise the gracefulness of her womanly figure.

Terryn realized his mouth was open and shut it fast. Yet he could not tear his gaze away from the lady as she wafted to d'Aldreda's side and made a low curtsy before the prince.

"Lady Liselle," Gerard said, taking her hand and lifting her from her curtsy. "It's been some time since you graced Dunloch with your fair presence."

Behind her veil, Liselle's mouth curved in a gentle smile, and her lashes lowered briefly to cover her eyes. "Too true, my prince," she answered, and the sound of her voice stirred memories in Terryn's blood. "I hope I may serve your lovely bride well in the years to come. It is the least I may do for the sister of my dearest friend."

Gerard's face froze at those words, though his welcoming expression never wavered. He cast d'Aldreda a swift glance, his eyes flashing. Liselle had been Fayline's lady-in-waiting for years, since they were children together. For the duke to give her to Cerine now was yet another attempt on d'Aldreda's part to force his second daughter into the role of the first.

A role Cerine could never hope to fill.

But Gerard, ever the prince, acknowledged Lady Liselle's words with some courtly phrase of his own and offered her his arm. Liselle laid one hand on his wrist and allowed herself to be led up the stairs, with the duke and the dominus trailing behind. Not once did any of them look Terryn's way. Not even Liselle, not so much as a glance.

Terryn maintained his position on the steps. He knew Gerard would wish him to follow closely, to stand by his side through these early interactions with d'Aldreda, but for the moment he couldn't do anything but . . . breathe.

Breathe, and not let his memories venture too far back. Not remember those stolen glances, those stolen moments . . .

Three familiar faces swam before his vision, their heads covered in red hoods. In a blink, Terryn forced his attention back into the present, lifting a hand in respectful salute. "Venatrix di Lamaury," he said. "Venator d'Acelet, Venator du Gy."

The three most-trusted lieutenants serving under the Venator Dominus answered Terryn's greeting in kind. After turning their horses over to stable hands, they approached the porch steps. All wore armed scorpionas on their right arms, and their eyes gleamed with ascendant shadow-light. Everild, Venatrix di Lamaury, led the way as she always did. A broad woman with a face like a blunted battering ram, her hair cropped short for easy maintenance, Everild stood equal to Terryn in height.

She disarmed her scorpiona as she climbed the stairs, hawk-nosed Venator d'Acelet and lanky Venator du Gy following in her wake.

"Terryn du Balafre." Even when speaking a greeting, Everild's voice held an aggressive edge. "How is Fendrel's special boy these days?"

The muscle under Terryn's eye twitched. Everild made no secret of her disdain for him. As years passed, it seemed that the harder he worked, the more he impressed the Council of Breçar, the more he excelled with pipes or scorpiona or knowledge of poisons, the more Everild despised him. He could see it in her eyes now. He could see it in the way her gaze fixed on his scar. As though when she looked at him, she saw only a witch's slave.

Terryn maintained his cold mask, allowing no expression to reveal the thoughts flashing through his head. He inclined his chin ever so slightly and motioned for Everild to proceed up the stairs. Without pausing, she breezed by, her long legs taking two steps at a time. At the top of the porch, just before passing through the great door, she called back over her shoulder, "Venator du Tam tells me Wodechran has proven too difficult for one poor venator to handle on his own. I hope the new girl is proving a . . . *comfort* during this difficult time of transition."

Venator du Gy snorted and Venator d'Acelet raised suggestive eyebrows as they followed in Everild's wake.

SYLVIA MERCEDES

Terryn's lips thinned, and once more he squeezed his left wrist, nearly cutting off the circulation. Only after the three Evanderians had disappeared into the keep did he turn to follow. It would be a long week until Hallow's Night and the wedding. And he still had Fendrel's ire to face when he tried to explain to his former master how he'd ended up in a competition with—

Someone grabbed his forearm just as he stepped through the door, pulling him with surprising force. He felt a jolt of pain from his wound, but he had no time to react to that before fingers caught him by the back of his head, pulling him down so that his open mouth pressed against a pair of exceedingly soft lips.

Terryn startled back. "Liselle!" he gasped. "I mean . . . I'm sorry . . . Lady di Matin."

Shining eyes laughed up at him from beneath a tumble of loose curls. Her traveling cloak was gone, revealing a honey-colored traveling gown with a low, square neck, the front laces not done up as tight as they might be. The only ornament she wore was a gold chain strung with some heavy pendant, which hung between her white breasts. The V it created drew the eye with alarming precision.

"It's been some time, Venator du Balafre." Liselle cast quick glances from side to side. Servants approached up the stairs, carrying luggage from the duke's entourage, their faces blank, their eyes blind to all the doings of those they served, however intriguing those doings might be. But Liselle's eyebrow quirked nonetheless, and she gripped Terryn's hand in hers. "Come, this way," she said.

He knew he should protest. He knew he should pull free and run for it.

Instead, he let himself be led around a corner into an unused passage. "My lady—" He was cut off by a second kiss, this one fiercer than the first. He tried to pull back, but her arms were around his neck, and her soft curves were pressed up against him, and her lips tasted sweet, and . . .

He crushed her close, one hand pressed to the small of her back, the other slipping beneath her long hair to feel the skin of her neck, to discover the openness of the gown across her shoulders, down her spine. She shivered in response to his touch, molding her body against his. For a wild moment, reason deserted him, and he was aware of nothing but the warmth flowing from her mouth into his, sinking down into the very pit of his being.

Then her teeth nibbled sharply at his lip, and the pain startled him back into reality. With more force than gentleness, Terryn yanked the lady's arms free of his neck and pushed her away, his hands gripping her shoulders. One sleeve of her gown had slipped from its place, sliding down along her upper arm, and his fingers held onto bare flesh. He instantly let go and backed up into the wall, hitting so hard a candle rattled and fell from its sconce three feet away. He folded his arms tight across his chest like a shield.

"So glad to find your skills haven't faded, Venator," Liselle said, that irrepressible smile of hers slicing at him like the most delightful knife. "Nor your adorable discomfort at momentarily forgetting yourself." She indicated the fallen candle with a nod of her head. "You always were a satisfying quarry to run to ground." She took a step closer, her white teeth gently playing with her full lower lip. "How long has it been, exactly? Four years and . . ."

"Seven months," Terryn answered too quickly. He

grimaced at the flash of pleasure in her eyes and hastened to add, "We've . . . both changed since then."

"*You* certainly have." The lady looked him up and down, her gaze lingering and admiring as it went. "You're not the lanky lad you once were. Hmmm, but you've still got the same irresistible coldness that makes a girl wonder just how far she must go to light your fire."

She tilted her head and crossed her arms, mimicking his defensive stance. The gesture pulled her sleeve even farther out of place, and Terryn hastily averted his eyes. She laughed, but her next words lost some of that teasing note. "You never wrote."

"I . . . have been busy."

"Too busy to come to court? Telianor is quite dull without you, you know. I can never find a dance partner to suit me."

"I've been serving. In Nion first, then Campionarre, then—"

"All places without quills or ink, I imagine." Liselle shook her head with a reproachful *tsk*. "Or was there a sudden shortage of parchment, and no extra sheets could be spared? Do tell; I am eager to hear of your struggles."

Terryn found it hard to swallow. "I . . . I heard you were married."

"I was." She tossed a length of curls back over her bare shoulder. "To the Marquis du Matin. Such a dignified personage he was. Quite old, but, you know. *Experienced.*" A flash of sorrow crossed her face, almost too brief to be believed. It was gone in a moment, replaced by another of her saucy smiles. "He died, Goddess bless him. Not before teaching me a number of interesting things, however. Things I would be most happy to share with a willing student."

She took a step toward him.

"My lady," Terryn said, his voice coming out in a rush, "you know that as a servant of Saint Evander I cannot pursue . . . marriage with any woman, least of all the widow of the Marquis du Matin."

Liselle paused, one eyebrow rising. "Marriage? Do you imagine, Venator, that I have any interest in wearing that harness again? No, no." She took another step, then another, until scarcely a breath separated them. Placing one hand on his chest, she stood on tiptoe, her lips just brushing the lobe of his ear. The perfume of her hair filled his nostrils, and his eyes stared down at the enticing curve of her neck and shoulder, so near to his mouth.

"I know the rules that govern your life and harness your urges," she whispered. "And I know all the best, most *interesting* ways of bending those rules. If you'll let me show you . . ."

Every part of his body urged him to act. What could be the harm, after all? With the lady so willing, with the history they shared? The laws of Evander forbade marriage and the risk of a shade-taken venator producing inborn offspring. But they did not expressly require celibacy. It was common knowledge throughout the castra that various members of the Order—even among the domini—indulged in the needs of the flesh, using various protections to ensure the ultimate blasphemy was never committed, the laws of the Saint never flouted.

It was only between hunt brothers and hunt sisters that such indulgences were forbidden.

Something in Terryn's chest twisted, a sharp pain that seemed to ignite a fire. A fire he dared not face or even acknowledge. He stared down into Lady Liselle's wide blue eyes, oddly desperate to see them and not the flash

SYLVIA MERCEDES

of black eyes under stern dark brows hovering in the forefront of his mind. He wanted to grab her, to pull her close, to lose himself in sheer pleasure. Why should he not lower his mouth to that bare white skin, why should he not take what was so eagerly offered?

"Tell me," Liselle breathed, her lips close to the corner of his mouth, "is there a woman in this world who can find the beating heart of Terryn du Balafre? Or are you truly as unassailable as you like to pretend?"

He didn't move. A long, silent moment passed between them.

The lady pulled back, her fair brows puckering slightly. "Think about it, Venator," she said. With a deft gesture, she slipped her fallen sleeve back into place on her shoulder. "You know where to find me."

With that, she planted a last soft kiss on his unresponsive mouth before gliding down the passage. At the turn she looked back once, a puzzled light in her eye.

Then she was gone.

CHAPTER 8

THE FIRST THRILL OF THE HUNT FADED AFTER A FEW hours of hard riding. Though the sun rose high in the sky, Ayleth shivered in her saddle. Not even the warmth of her shade, called to higher ascendancy, could ward off the chill in the air . . . or the more profound chill that swept through her soul as they crested a rise and she found her view sweeping east.

East, toward the Witchwood.

Ayleth cursed softly. She pulled her horse to a halt,

watching how the sun cast pale autumnal light across the landscape before her and yet somehow failed to illuminate the forest. Its spreading branches, like a vast horde of ghoulish hands, caught at the light, clutching and dragging it down to their roots, there to devour it.

And only the Great Barrier of Fendrel du Glaive stood between that darkness and the rest of the world.

Could it truly be enough? When she first arrived in Wodechran, Ayleth had seen the Great Barrier up close, had felt the power of that mighty song spell woven by a true master of the Evanderian arts. But she had also passed through; she had walked in the darkness of the Witchwood. She had breathed its poisonous air and felt its potent wrath pulsing in the ground beneath her feet.

Ayleth grimaced, breath hissing through her teeth. For a moment, she almost thought her lungs were full of *oblivis*, her throat coated and thick and choking. Something in her head zapped like a bolt of lightning. Clinging to her saddle, she only just kept herself from falling headlong to the ground. Sweat broke out across her brow despite the coldness of the air, and she squeezed her eyes shut, bowing her head into the depths of her hood.

A word hovered on the edge of her conscious awareness . . . a name she had heard spoken by witches deep in the darkness of the wood. A name of the spirit realm, not to be spoken with mortal lips. Nevertheless, Ayleth's mouth moved, whispering into the cold air: "*Oromor . . .*"

The spell passed. Ayleth blinked back into herself, clinging to the saddle and gazing out across that landscape to the forest, which now seemed farther away than it had a moment before. Her mouth tingled oddly, as though she'd just bitten down on something strange, and her lips were frozen in the shape of a name she'd just spoken. But she couldn't now remember what it was.

Mistress? Laranta's voice in her head growled with concern.

"*It's all right, Laranta,*" Ayleth answered hastily. Her limbs shuddering, she spurred Chestibor back into motion. "*It's nothing. Be quiet now.*"

They started down the incline and were soon out of sight of the Witchwood for the time being. Then, Chestibor's hooves clopped on stone. The sound jarred

Ayleth out of her wandering thoughts. Grateful for a distraction, any distraction, she murmured a gentle, "Whoa," and drew rein.

Looking down over her horse's shoulder, she blinked in some surprise at the remains of a stone-paved road. By daylight it was difficult to discern, so broken were the stones, so overgrown with moss and grass. After nightfall she might have overlooked it entirely. But now that she'd seen it, she could almost *sense* how it must have looked back in the days of its establishment, cutting across this hilly country, a broad enough road for seven horsemen to ride abreast.

It led straight toward the Witchwood.

"Haunts damn," Ayleth murmured. No doubt now that she was headed the right way. This could be none other than the Queen's Highway, the vast road built during the reign of Dread Odile, one of the many wonders of her age. The Witch Queen had established this road using a combination of natural stone and oblidite. After her defeat and death, without her magic to sustain it, the oblidite had faded and flaked away to dust, the natural stone sank into the dirt or was carted away for other uses, and the Queen's Highway was ultimately lost, leaving behind nothing but this long winding scar on the landscape.

Ayleth followed the still-visible line of the ruined road with her eyes, searching. Cró Ular, her destination, had stood guard over this stretch of highway. She must be close to the Tower of Blood and Eyes.

Setting her jaw, Ayleth kicked Chestibor into a brisk trot. She would not let herself be distracted from the hunt at hand.

Following the scar of the road, her horse made swift progress, and soon the tower ruins appeared ahead, standing just outside the fringe forest. Like the road itself, Cró Ular had been built of oblidite mixed with natural stone, but large sections of the great edifice had fallen, leaving behind a pile of rubble.

A gust of wind blew in Ayleth's face, carrying with it a horrible scent that hit her like a blow. It took her a moment to realize that, as with the witch's anchor itself, what she perceived wasn't a smell. It was more like a chorus of discordant music striking her shadow senses and making her gag at the foulness.

Laranta shuddered inside Ayleth's head.

"What is it, Laranta?"

Curses. Many curses.

Chestibor stopped abruptly, shaking his head and pulling at his bit. Ayleth tried to urge him onward, but he balked again. He wasn't sensitive to magic, one of the qualities which made him a good venatrix's horse. But the sensations rippling through the ether around them were so strong that even sturdy Chestibor felt them.

Ayleth dismounted, looped her mount's reins up so that he could not step on them and do himself an injury, then proceeded on foot. Her stomach roiled as the sensation of broken magic continued to assault her senses.

"Laranta, go on ahead of me," she commanded. *"Make certain there are no witches lying in wait."*

Her wolf shade poured out of her mind, manifested on the ground, and raced toward the ruins, tugging on the soul tether connecting her to her mistress like a leash. While carefully picking her way down the incline, Ayleth sensed Laranta's frustration as the shade struggled to detect other scents beneath the stink of broken magic.

Roiling threads of broken curses clung to the fallen walls and the huge toppled gate. At least none of the curses seemed to be active anymore.

Ayleth climbed a pile of rock that had once been part of the wall. At the top she paused, gazing down into the circular yard at the base of the tower. A flickering passed before her shadow vision, an impression of memory, a ghostly trace of pain and trauma and fear. She almost believed she glimpsed the souls of the Evanderians who had fought and died here . . . and the equally present souls of the witches and human slaves who had laid down their lives defending this stronghold. The sounds of battle and hundreds of spell songs hummed in her core, echoing across the years.

Cró Ular was the site of the final great battle before the Chosen King marched on Dulìmurian itself. It was here, amid terror and bloodshed, that the tide of the war had turned.

Ayleth's hands clenched into fists. Her nostrils flared as she breathed in the foul air. So long as Dread Odile's lieutenants lived on in this world, the war was never truly at an end.

Mistress! Mistress, Mistress!

Turning sharply at the sound of Laranta's excited barks, Ayleth hastened down from the wall and into the yard. Navigating around fallen stones and pits in the dirt, she found her wolf shade circling a patch of what appeared to be empty earth. *"What did you find?"* she demanded, peering with shadow sight and seeing nothing.

Magic, magic. Not old. Not rotten.

Recent magic? Ayleth stepped closer and crouched to extend her hand over the bare place on the ground. As she concentrated her heightened shadow senses, a shape seemed to manifest beneath her fingertips. A shape that was more like sound than form. Ugly . . . and familiar.

"A sigil," Ayleth breathed. She stood hastily and backed away, her breath quick in her throat. Training her shadow sight on that patch of earth, she saw the ward planted deep down, etched in blood. Anathema magic.

She knew that sigil. She'd seen the same mark implanted in Venator Kephan's cheek. The same mark had been carved out of Terryn's face years ago.

Ayleth took another step back and another. Wards only affected those linked to them. Slaves of the

Warpwitch who fell within range of this ward would react to its compulsion and be obliged to fulfill whatever command it gave them. It could be a command to kill. It could be a command to forget. The ward probably couldn't touch her, but Ayleth chose not to risk it. Just in case.

"*Laranta,*" she said, "*how recently was this ward planted?*"

Her wolf shade sniffed hard, channeling her strange shade senses through her wolfish form. She looked up at Ayleth, red eyes glinting. *A moon ago. No more.*

Ayleth swallowed hard, trying to wet her dry throat. Kephan had been under the Warpwitch's influence a month ago. If he had stumbled upon this ward when he came here with Terryn, he would have succumbed to its powers.

But what about Terryn? His enslavement to the Warpwitch was supposedly broken. But was it possible . . . ?

Gritting her teeth, Ayleth pulled the anchor stone out from the pouch and held it out to Laranta, who flinched back from it, teeth flashing in a snarl. "*See if you can find a trace of this magic,*" Ayleth commanded her. "*See if this stone came from here, somewhere.*"

Laranta tossed her head and bounded off across the yard, following her nose. Within moments, she barked excitedly, *Mistress! I found it!*

Ayleth followed the pull on her soul tether and hurried after her shade. Her footsteps slowed as she drew near, however. As bad as the stink of broken curses was, Laranta had found a stench far worse. Ayleth recognized it at once: the stink of *oblivis,* the air of the Haunts.

A patch of dirt no more than a foot square lay festering beside Laranta. Dead earth, black with decay, damp with ooze. This was the effect pure *oblivis* had on the natural world. And in its center, an indentation. Just the right size.

Though she didn't want to come any closer, Ayleth crouched over the dead patch. Fetching the anchor from her pouch, she dropped it. She watched it fall perfectly into that notch.

There could be no doubt: This anchor had come from Cró Ular. It had been planted not long ago, had been activated and then discarded, the connection broken.

And Terryn had found it. He had carried it back with

him to Milisendis.

And he had lied.

CHAPTER 9

TERRYN HURRIED DOWN THE PASSAGE TOWARD THE Great Hall, straightening his uniform and running his hand through his hair on the way. Before stepping out of the passage, he pulled himself up short and drew several breaths. He could only hope his face betrayed nothing of his encounter with Lady Liselle. After a last tug at his uniform, he stepped between pillars, strode swiftly to the staircase, then climbed the treads two at a time.

His eyes were on his feet, so he didn't spot the tall

figure on the landing above until a familiar voice startled him: "I trust you have found more productive ways of occupying your time than trysts in darkened halls."

"Haunts damn," Terryn hissed. He paused halfway up, one foot ahead of the other. Then he planted both feet on the lower step, drawing his shoulders back at attention, and saluted smartly. "Dominus. I did not see you there."

"I gathered as much." Fendrel leaned against the banister, his iron-hard eyes lancing into Terryn. "Tell me, Venator du Balafre, did my eyes deceive me? Or did I just now catch you indulging in behavior unbecoming to a member of Evander's Order? I trust you have not forgotten the saint's teachings on the lusts of the flesh."

Another curse sprang to Terryn's lips, but he bit it back. He once again gripped his wrist behind his back and held his tongue. Fendrel raised an eyebrow and took a few steps down toward him. His appraising eye was far less appreciative than Liselle's.

"You seem sound of limb and sound of mind," he said. "In no way incapacitated, I trust?"

"I am well, Dominus. Thank you."

"And Venator du Tam . . . he has spent the last month in the phasmatorium at Breçar, undergoing treatment for a curse, I am given to understand."

"Indeed."

"In that case"—Fendrel drew to a stop one step above Terryn and fixed him with another lancing gaze—"explain to me why you are not in command of Milisendis Outpost."

Terryn's throat seemed to close. He cleared it and spoke with careful precision, not quite meeting the Dominus's gaze. "I am . . . I am in the process of assuming command. The prince has yet to make his final decision, but—"

With a growl, Fendrel turned and marched up to the landing, then turned and continued up the second flight of stairs, making for the floor above. Though he said nothing, Terryn knew his master intended him to follow, and he fell into place behind.

They proceeded to the west wing of Dunloch, Fendrel's riding boots leaving a trail of dirt behind him on the fine Suurian rugs. Sometimes it was easy to forget that Fendrel was, in his own right, a prince. He never used the title, never accepted any of the honors or advantages his rank endowed. He lived by a venator's code, which included sparseness and severity in all things. He was more comfortable sleeping under a tree by the open road than he could ever be in a dignified bedchamber with cushions and silk curtains.

With this in mind, Gerard had seen to it that a humble chamber was prepared for his uncle for the duration of his stay in Dunloch. The room was still grand by venatorial standards, but it boasted no more than a bed, a chair, a desk, a washstand, and a window. Fendrel led Terryn into this stark chamber now, taking the one chair with all the majestic grace of royal blood. In this, at least, he seemed a true prince.

"Shut the door, boy," he said. Terryn obeyed, then again stood at attention, awaiting his master's pleasure. Fendrel lowered his chin to his chest, studying Terryn from under his pale, prominent brows.

"Tell me about this Ayleth di Ferosa."

Terryn, prepared for this at least, answered promptly. "She is from Drauval Borough."

"So I've heard." Fendrel's left hand formed into a fist,

and he pounded it gently and repetitively on the arm of his chair, beating out a rhythm. "A young venatrix whom I do not recall being presented at Breçar. Unsupervised and untested. Do we even know who trained her?"

"Venatrix di Ferosa trained under Hollis, Venatrix di Theldry."

Fendrel's fist froze in mid-air. His entire face and demeanor went still. "Is that so," he said. His voice dropped to a lower register as he repeated, "Is that . . . so."

"She underwent her indoctrination at Castra Vielhir," Terryn continued. "I assume she completed her board examinations at Vielhir as well."

"Interesting." The word hung in the air, suspended on a silence like a silk thread ready to break at any moment. Terryn hardly dared breathe for fear of what would follow. His shadow senses were suppressed, but even so he thought he felt an intense vibration of spirit emanating from Fendrel's core.

At last Fendrel's mouth twisted on one side. On any other face it may have been a smile, but on him it was a snarl. "So, this girl, this Vielhir indoctrinate from Drauval

Borough, she has somehow convinced my nephew that *she*, and not you—not Terryn du Balafre, my own chosen and trained apprentice—is the right choice for the Milisendis posting."

"The prince has not yet made his decision."

Fendrel leaned forward in his chair, resting his elbows on his knees, his hands relaxed at the wrists save for a certain tension in his fingertips. "And yet it is she, and not you, who currently occupies Milisendis. While you, apparently, reside here. In Dunloch."

Terryn drew a long breath through his nose. He wouldn't stammer. He wouldn't hesitate. He wouldn't give Fendrel even an inch. "I'm here on a special assignment from the prince himself."

Fendrel's brows slowly rose up his forehead. "*Special* assignment? And does this assignment include chasing after silk skirts?"

Terryn drew himself straighter, setting his jaw hard. "Following the events of four years ago, Prince Gerard feels safer to have me on hand for his upcoming wedding ceremony."

The Dominus's eyes flashed, and Terryn realized, with

a jolt, the dreadful insult he had dealt his former master. Fendrel *had* been present four years ago, when all the Chosen King's court had come to Dunloch to celebrate the nuptials of Prince Gerard and Lady Fayline. He had been present, and he had not prevented the tragedy which took place. It was a failure that would mark his conscience for the rest of his life.

Fendrel stood. There were few men in all Gaulia who managed to tower over Terryn, but Fendrel dominated both in physical presence and in the potency of his spirit, a spirit augmented over the years by the presence of the shade stirring just behind his iron eyes.

"You need to start taking this situation seriously, *boy*," he said darkly. "Are you the man for Milisendis or aren't you?"

"The choice is Gerard's. I will honor his decision."

"You will make the choice for him."

Terryn felt the blood drain from his face. His chest constricted, and he couldn't quite make his lungs draw breath.

Fendrel took a step closer, his face drawing near to Terryn's. "You will do what it takes, Terryn. You will be venator of Wodechran. You are the man to carry on my work, to maintain the Barriers. To protect the legacy of the Chosen King. You are Gerard's closest confidante, his only friend."

"I am aware," Terryn answered. "I . . . I care for Gerard. And he knows it."

"But what else does Gerard know?" Fendrel persisted. His gaze slid from Terryn's eyes to the scar on his face. "He knows you were once caught under the same spell that so recently weakened and nearly destroyed Venator du Tam. He knows you were once nothing but a sniveling witch's boy. He's pondering that knowledge; he's considering that weakness. That vulnerability. And he's plotting how he might use any weakness and vulnerability to thwart *me*. To thwart the good plans I have for him. As though I were his enemy."

Fendrel's hand rose, his callused fingers reaching toward Terryn's cheek as though he would like to tear the scar away. Instead, he rested a heavy hand on Terryn's shoulder.

"You cannot allow for any weakness, Terryn. You cannot let Gerard compare you to Kephan, not even for a moment. In that comparison, you will suffer, and even this girl—this di Ferosa—will seem a worthy alternative in his eyes. But you are not some ensorcelled slave, not anymore. You are the worthiest venator ever to come out of Castra Breçar. And you are his . . ."

He didn't finish. But Terryn heard the unspoken words loud and clear: *And you are his blood.*

The weight of that truth threatened to crush him. The weight of responsibility which he had never chosen for himself, but which was ordained for him. Ordained the moment his mother looked with longing upon a man beneath her station. Ordained the moment she gave in to her love and lust. Ordained the moment Terryn drew breath in this world. The bastard brother of the prophesied prince.

He knew his role; he knew he had no place in the prophecy.

But he also knew, from the deepest core of his being, that he must do everything in his power to protect the Goddess's chosen one. And without this purpose to guide him, what was his life? Nothing but emptiness. Nothing but the monstrous spirit inside him, waiting to devour and damn him the moment he relaxed his guard.

"You must fight for your future, Terryn," Fendrel said. His knowing gaze watched Terryn too closely. "You must prove your worth to the prince."

"I am fighting." Just saying the words made him sound weak, but he forced them out anyway. "I am proving myself."

"But have you asked yourself the hard question yet?" Fendrel turned his head, studying his former apprentice, not with mortal vision, but with eyes flashing with shadow-light. "Have you asked yourself how far you are willing to go to prove your worth?"

Terryn looked down, staring into the unlit fireplace, studying the pattern of smoke stains on the grate.

Fendrel shook his head. "I thought not." He stepped around Terryn, making for the door. He opened it, paused in the doorway, and said without looking around, "Start asking, Terryn. And decide your answer before it's too late."

With that, the Dominus left the room, slamming the door behind him.

Terryn stood several moments, still staring at those

smoke patterns, seeing shapes in the random stains of darkness—twisted spirits struggling in torment at the clutching, dark-fingered edges of the Haunts.

CHAPTER 10

WHAT IN THE GODDESS'S NAME WAS SHE SUPPOSED TO do now?

The cold wind stung Ayleth's eyes, drawing tears that streamed from their corners as she rode back along the circuit trail. She tried to pull her hood lower, but it only blew back over her shoulders at the next big gust, and her hair escaped from its braid to flutter in loose wisps behind her. The sun was setting fast as she left Cró Ular behind. It was a four-hour ride back to Milisendis, and she knew she'd be out after dark. She'd have to pray for a little moonlight to help Chestibor find his way. Otherwise, she'd be reduced to seeking shelter in this remote part of Wodechran. Perhaps she could find some farmer willing to allow her a bed in his hayloft, perhaps . . .

Perhaps she should stop dwelling on such mundane matters and face the actual problem at hand.

Ayleth's whole body tensed. Chestibor, reacting to that tension, shuffled sideways, tossed his head, and snorted uncomfortably. Pulling him to a halt, Ayleth patted his shoulder and murmured a few wordless sounds of comfort.

Then, with a short huff of breath she said out loud, "Should I confront him?"

Chestibor shook his head and pulled at his bit. She gave him his head, letting him nibble at the long grass alongside the circuit trail. The echo of her unanswered question vibrated in the air around her.

What else could she do? Having made these discoveries, having found proof of Terryn's falsehood, she ought to ride to Dunloch at once, pound at the gates, demand to see him, and present her findings. Let him defend himself if he could.

But then what? Would he acknowledge his lies and step down from the competition? Would he report his error to the castra? Unlikely.

Besides, Terryn was clever. He probably had reasons for his choices, and this, coupled with his longtime friendship with the prince and his good standing at Breçar, would be enough to counter any paltry evidence she had accumulated.

And really, what proof did she have? The oblidite curse anchor and her testimony that it *probably* came from Cró Ular and Terryn *probably* picked it up there a month ago. Not exactly damning evidence.

"What then?" she demanded of Chestibor's bowed neck, grabbing a fistful of his mane. "I could go to the prince directly, tell him what I've found, let him draw his own conclusions. But how could I make him believe me? All I've got are accusations."

It wouldn't work. Without solid evidence, there was no way Gerard would believe ill of Terryn. Which, Ayleth acknowledged even amid her frustration, was to the prince's credit.

So, if she couldn't confront Terryn or go to the prince . . . should she contact the castra? It wasn't as though she could package up something as terrible as the oblidite anchor and entrust it to a little courier boy in bright-colored livery! That would be begging for trouble, especially with two of the Crimson Devils possibly on the loose. No, no. She'd have to ride to Breçar herself.

"Because that's how I want to present myself to the castra," she muttered. She threw her head back to stare at the heavens as though seeking heavenly aid. But, as usual, the Goddess had no spontaneous wisdom to offer. Ayleth glared at the thin moon gleaming in the purpling sky, opposite the setting sun. "Am I seriously supposed to walk into Breçar waving a Haunts-damned anchor and spouting slander against my own hunt brother? The darling of the castra, Fendrel's favored boy? And what happens when Terryn denies it all? They'll run me out of Perrinion."

Or they'd kill her. If they deemed her untrustworthy and a threat to other members of her Order, the council would not hesitate to deal her the Gentle Death, just as they would any other shade-taken.

She inhaled, then let her breath out in a long steady stream of white vapor. She was being overly dramatic, surely. At worst, the castra would deny her the posting at Wodechran and send her back to Drauval or on to some remote borough in Campionarre or Nion.

But this didn't matter. What mattered was two witches rampaging unchecked across Wodechran Borough. She had to find them and stop them. Somehow.

"I'm going to have to confront him," she whispered. "There's no other choice."

The sun completed its descent behind the western horizon, and the long shadows of night swarmed in. Gazing out across a shallow valley, Ayleth saw fires springing to life. Campfires, she guessed. A merchant caravan, perhaps, traveling up from the southern boroughs to trade in Wodechran. Easy enough to skirt around on her way back to the outpost. She turned Chestibor's head and nudged his ribs, urging him back into motion.

Suddenly, Laranta growled long and low inside her head.

Ayleth halted her horse. *"Laranta? What is it?"*

Laranta growled again, then whispered, *Shade.*

"What?" Ayleth looked around, half expecting to see some treacherous figure lurking in the shadows just off the road. But there was nothing. Only rolling hills, twilit sky, and those campfires burning across the way. *"What shade, Laranta? Where?"*

Laranta strained at the suppressions holding her inside Ayleth's head. She pressed against the backs of Ayleth's eyes, eager to spring free, to manifest in the mortal world. *Shade,* she said again, loudly this time. Then she surged with power, taking momentary control of Ayleth's gaze and turning it toward the campfire in the distance. *There!*

Ayleth's eyes widened. Before she could even draw breath, the first terrified scream reached her ears, sweeping across the valley on the night breeze.

His dressings needed changing.

Terryn grimaced as he slipped out of his shirt and looked down at his throbbing arm. A small patch of blood had soaked through the bandages, leaving a stain on his sleeve. He must apply fresh wrappings if he didn't want another such stain on his formal dress shirt.

Muttering to himself, Terryn carefully unwrapped the bandage and pulled it away from his skin. It stuck a little, then came away all at once, revealing the puncture wound from the iron spike. An ugly wound with blackened edges. Not large, but his shade-taken body reacted strongly to the iron. It would take time to heal properly.

He touched the sore spot gingerly with one finger, wincing at even that light touch. Then, setting his teeth, he set to work, applying tuaflor salve and rewrapping his arm, taking special care not to wish for an extra pair of hands to help him. Not to think about the dark-eyed venatrix who had treated this wound two nights ago. Not to wish she was in his room now, with her gruff voice and her stern face and her surprisingly gentle hands . . .

Haunts, how he hated her.

He finished the awkward business, tying off the bandage and tucking the ends under so it would all lie flat. Then, moving carefully, so as to jar his arm as little as possible, he slid into the white linen undershirt of his dress uniform. A welcome banquet was scheduled tonight for Duke d'Aldreda and his daughter. Gerard had specially requested Terryn to attend and would hear no protests.

He must endure a night of merrymaking. Trying not to look at Liselle, all golden-haired and smiling and voluptuous in the candlelight. Trying not to feel Fendrel's hard gaze watching his every move. Trying not to notice Gerard's silent misery or the duke's stone-hard resolve. Trying to focus on his plate and his wine and nothing else, nothing else at all.

It was going to be a long few hours.

Terryn hadn't worn his formal uniform in several years now. It fit him like a glove, every pleat crisp, every button and buckle shined. But he felt odd wearing it. As if he'd shrugged off his own skin and now tried to wear someone else's. His left hand was a little numb as he did up the lacings and slid into the brass-fastened jerkin.

He was just pulling his red hood into place when a knock sounded at the door, followed by a voice. "Terryn? Are you in there?"

"I'm here," Terryn answered, turning as the door opened and Gerard looked into the room. The prince was clad for the banquet, regal in scarlet and gold, his hair slicked back from his high forehead. But the elegance of his apparel did nothing to soften the lines of stress around his mouth. "What's wrong?"

"Nothing," Gerard answered quickly. Then he rolled his eyes and leaned one shoulder against the doorpost. "Everything. But at the moment, nothing overt. It's only that . . ."

"What?"

"According to d'Aldreda, Lady Cerine's company should have arrived several hours ago. They're coming by the south road, crossing the Sangcòr River at Grimaud."

Terryn shrugged. "Any number of things may have delayed them."

"True. And I'm sure Cerine will have sent a rider on to tell us if that is the case. Only no rider has come, and . . . well . . ."

"The duke is getting impatient?"

A strange expression crossed Gerard's face. "The duke doesn't seem to have noticed. But I have. And I'm concerned."

Terryn's brows drew together ever so slightly. "For

Lady Cerine."

Gerard blinked, and the expression Terryn had glimpsed vanished entirely, replaced by a mask of calm disinterest. But he couldn't disguise the tension underscoring his voice. "That road from Grimaud passes within a mile of the Cró Ular ruins. I know you've found no trace of the Phantomwitch in the last month, but. . . ."

He didn't finish. He didn't have to.

Turning abruptly, Terryn caught up his cloak from where he'd draped it across his bed, pulling it around his shoulders. Then he snatched up his scorpiona and bracer, his quivers of poisons. Gerard watched him without comment. When Terryn approached the door, the prince moved to one side, giving him room to pass.

"Thank you," he said quietly. "It will put us all at ease if we just . . . if we know."

"Of course." Terryn entered the passage with long strides and spoke over his shoulder while striding away: "I'll return with word soon. Don't hold the banquet for me."

CHAPTER II

"LET ME SEE IT AGAIN, CERINE. PLEASE? JUST A LITTLE peek."

Cerine sighed as she pushed back the entrance flap to her pavilion and stepped inside, Sister Ducette trailing in her wake. Servants had worked swiftly to set up this shelter for the duke's daughter, including a pile of blankets and furs to serve as a bed, and a wash basin with which she might try to clean away some of the day's travel grime.

In one corner sat the huge trunk, a gift sent from Aldreda along with instructions for his dutiful daughter.

Ducette fairly danced up to the trunk, touching its brass fastenings with eager fingers. She turned a hopeful expression Cerine's way.

"Very well," Cerine said reluctantly. "Help yourself."

With a happy squeal, Ducette opened the lid and gazed with dreamy eyes at the mounds of pink brocade so carefully folded into that trunk. She ran her fingers along a bead-trimmed bodice and delicately touched filmy sleeves. "It's so beautiful!" she breathed. "Why didn't you wear it today, Cerine? Isn't this the one your father intended for your presentation to the prince?"

Cerine let the satchel on her shoulder slide down onto the makeshift bed before tucking her hands deep inside the sleeves of her novitiate robe. Grand Mother Didienne had tried to convince her to give up her Sivelinian garb for the journey from the temple to Wodcchran Borough, but Cerine had insisted on wearing it. She was far more comfortable in these garments than in those her father had sent for the journey. Especially the pink confection that so captivated Ducette's fancy.

"A gown like that is completely impractical for travel," she said. "It would be sure to get caught in the wheels or splattered with mud. Besides, it's just as well I didn't wear it. It'll take the sisters several hours to replace that broken wheel, and by then it will be much too dark to keep traveling. We won't make it to Dunloch until tomorrow."

"But you *will* wear it tomorrow, won't you?" As though handling a holy relic, Ducette lifted a bejeweled, veiled headpiece out of the trunk, holding it up to admire how the silk hung.

Cerine's mouth twitched in a half smile. She stepped across the little space, took the headpiece from Ducette's hands, then pushed back her fellow novice's hood and placed the jeweled band on her head. Ducette gasped with delight as the silk fell about her shoulders. "Oh, Cerine! You shouldn't!" she protested, but didn't try to remove the pretty decoration. Her hands played with the folds of silk, her face aglow. "How do I look?" she asked, turning this way and that. "Do I pass for a proper lady?"

Cerine tilted her head to one side. Ducette was a plain, skinny sort of girl with large apple cheeks and a contagious smile. No amount of finery would transform her into a beauty, and the jewels and veils did not disguise the dome of her shorn scalp at the top of the headpiece. But at least she wore it only in play; no one expected her to try to pass for a courtly beauty in real life.

"It suits you better than it does me," Cerine said with sincerity.

Ducette laughed at this and spun in place so that the silk trailed behind her. "I wish I were about to become a princess!" She turned an irritable glare on Cerine. "Why do you have to look so glum all the time? One would think we were on our way to your funeral, not your wedding."

A shudder ran down Cerine's spine at this. She took care not to glance at the satchel lying on her bed, the satchel containing Sister Ilda's heretical translation of sacred writ.

The penalty for heresy was the chopping block . . . a fate that seemed rather too close for comfort these days.

Cerine shrugged and forced out a laugh. "Maybe I just prefer wearing itchy holy robes and hoods." She stepped briskly forward and plucked the headpiece off Ducette's bald scalp.

"Well, you're a goose," Ducette responded, trailing the silk between her fingers one last time before letting go. "I'd trade places with you in a heartbeat!"

"And I with you," Cerine whispered. But Ducette didn't hear her. The young novice flounced across the pavilion and sank down on Cerine's bed.

"Oh, my feet!" she groaned. "We must have walked a hundred miles today. And now we must spend another night on the road rather than in proper beds." She flopped back on the blankets, propping her feet up and lacing her fingers behind her head. "At least you get to sleep inside. The rest of us will have to crawl under carts and pray it doesn't rain."

"You're welcome to sleep in here tonight, Ducette." Cerine stuffed the veil down beside the gown and dropped the lid of the chest. "There's space enough for more than one person." That had been another argument with the Grand Mother when setting out on this journey. The last thing Cerine had wanted was special treatment: a pavilion of her own, as grand as that used by the high priestess herself. It only separated her further from her fellow novices.

Ducette's smile faded a little at Cerine's invitation, and her brow puckered sadly. She glanced around the draped pavilion, which really was not very big, then shook her head. "No, no. If I stay, Sister Albina will flay me alive in the morning. She'll make me sing a string of penance prayers until my voice is sore. Best not to tempt her wrath." With those words, Ducette sat upright and scrambled off the bed. As she did so, the satchel Cerine had dropped there fell over, and something fluttered out and landed on the floor.

Cerine's heart nearly stopped.

"What's this?" Ducette swooped and picked up the small parchment, which was well worn around the edges. She turned it over and, seeing the bit of broken seal still clinging to one end, caught her breath. "Is that . . . Is that the royal eagle? Oh!" She looked up, eyes shining and crooked teeth flashing in a knowing grin. "Is it a love letter from the Golden Prince?"

"No, give that to me!" Cerine dove across the room and snatched the letter from Ducette's hands. Realizing how harsh her voice sounded, she glanced up and hastily softened her tone. "I'm sorry, Ducette. It's a . . . an important communication from Dunloch, um . . . details of legal importance."

Ducette, for all her outward masks of smiles and lightheartedness, was no fool. She raised an eyebrow, opened her mouth, but for once thought twice and shut it again. "I'll see to your supper, my lady," she said rather coldly instead, and slipped out of the pavilion, leaving Cerine behind.

With the words "my lady" burning in her ears, Cerine grimaced and hung her head. She shouldn't have spoken to Ducette like that. But the idea that anyone might see what this letter contained . . . particularly someone like Ducette, who couldn't hold her tongue if her life depended on it . . .

She looked down at the parchment clutched against her breast. She should have destroyed this letter a long time ago.

Stifling a curse, Cerine fell to her knees beside the bed and pulled the satchel toward her. How stupid she was, how careless! So distracted by Ducette's prattle that she hadn't realized the flap was open. She slid the letter back inside, down to the bottom. Her hand brushed the leather binding of Sister Ilda's book as she did so. As though to reassure herself, she touched the book, ran her finger along the rough edges of its pages. Just to reassure herself they were all still there.

She could almost feel the power contained within that binding. Power to change the world . . . But only if it fell into the right hands at the right moment in history.

A lump formed in her throat. Cerine swallowed painfully and hastily closed the satchel, tying its leather thongs tight. Then she rose from her knees and sat on the bed. It had grown quite dark inside in the last few minutes. The sun had mostly set, and the only light came from flickering campfires shining through the tent flap. The air was frigid, but she couldn't quite work up the nerve to leave the seclusion of her tent and join her sisters around the fire.

Instead, she wrapped herself in her cloak and simply sat. The satchel lay against her hip, a weight both comforting and disconcerting.

They would reach Dunloch tomorrow.

At first, she'd been glad when the wheel came off the cart carrying the grand and dignified personage of Grand

Mother Didienne. The high priestess's swearing had caused much secret mirth among the sisterhood, and the delay of getting the spare wheel in place meant an extra night on the road. An extra night during which Cerine could still half pretend she was nothing but a Siveline Sister, a scribe devoted to the Goddess and to her work. An extra night during which she could ignore the prospects of all the wedding pomp and ceremony awaiting her in the next seven days.

An extra night during which she need not face humiliation.

"A queen may whisper in the ear of her king." Sister Ilda's voice came back to her, an echo in the darkness. *"A queen may say things in the safety of the marriage bed that a holy sister dares not speak aloud in public places."*

Cerine bowed her head and drew the satchel into her lap. "It's . . . it's not for my sake that I do this," she whispered. Her words were like a confessional prayer. "I do this for Perrinion and all the Gaulian nations. I swear, Fayline, I would never have agreed to this marriage otherwise. I would never have—"

A scream ripped through the air.

Cerine started to her feet, her muscles jumping with dread. Another scream, then another, a whole chorus of terror. Cerine took a step forward, then back, uncertain whether to stay where she was or burst out of her tent. The curiosity of fear won out, and she pushed back the tent flap, the satchel still clutched under one arm. As she stepped outside, a gust of wind blew her novice's hood back across her shoulders, exposing her shorn head.

A mayhem of panic flashed before her vision. She saw sisters running, heard horses screeching. Too many flickering forms rushed between the fires, shadows shifting wildly. But her gaze was drawn, almost against her will, to the center of the camp.

To a cloud of twining, living darkness, deeper than the night itself. And to the figure standing in the center of that darkness, a figure wearing the stained tatters of a wedding gown.

Cerine's lips moved soundlessly, trying to speak a name, trying to breathe a prayer.

The spectral bride stepped out of the void and looked around at the screaming nuns. Her face was ravaged and almost unrecognizable, one eye covered by a hideous growth, the other hollow and staring in its socket.

"Where are you, Cerine?" A raw, savage voice poured from that straining throat. "I know you are here. Show yourself!"

"I'm here."

The creature turned. Her lips curled back in a snarl, and firelight gleamed on the sharp points of her teeth. Her one-eyed gaze shot across the campsite and fixed upon Cerine standing in the doorway of her pavilion.

All else seemed to fade into the background. The screams of the nuns, the stamping and squealing horses. There was no one here but the two of them alone. Cerine gazed into that hellish face that wasn't her sister's and yet somehow, impossibly, still was.

"I'm here, Fayline," she said. Her feet taking one slow footstep at a time, she crossed toward the campfire flickering between her and that phantomlike form. From somewhere far away she heard Sister Ducette scream her name, but the voice may as well have come from another world entirely. Though her knees trembled so hard they could scarcely support her weight, she took another step and then another.

The creature studied her, its one eye gleaming strangely. Was a human soul still to be found behind that gaze? Or was it completely overtaken by the possessing spirit inside?

"So, you have come after all, Cerine." The voice that reached her across the crackling fire was low, like an animal's growl. "I'd heard rumor of your imminent arrival. I didn't want to believe it. I didn't want to think that you . . . that you . . ."

Her mouth twisted with pain, and her two skeletal hands clapped against her cheeks, pressing hard, nails tearing into her delicate skin so that black blood ran in tiny rivulets. "She wants out!" she cried, her one eye squeezed tightly shut. "She wants out, and she wants me to kill you! She wants me to kill all of you!"

Though the words were terrible, hope surged in Cerine's soul. This was Fayline. It had to be. If the witch were ascendant in this body, she would have killed them all by now. But her sister was fighting back, her sister wanted to spare her. Maybe . . . maybe . . .

Cerine licked her dry lips and, while Fayline's eye was closed, shifted the satchel from under her arm, slinging it over her shoulder by the strap.

At that movement, Fayline's eye flared open. The pale blue iris was lost in an oblivion of pure darkness. "What is that?" she snarled. Two strange voices echoed behind hers when she spoke.

The next instant, darkness burst around her, and she vanished, only to reappear a mere hand's breadth from Cerine herself. Her claw-like hands tore the satchel from Cerine's grasp.

"Fayline, no!" Cerine tried to snatch it back, but the demonic thing that was her sister turned away, presenting Cerine with a view of her emaciated back, shoulder blades piercing like knives through the red snarls of her hair. Cerine saw her tear open the flap, her spider-like hands plunging inside and rooting among the books and papers.

As though guided by the will of fate itself, she latched hold of the prince's letter and pulled it out. Firelight glowed on the broken eagle-head seal.

"No, please." Cerine choked on her own words and almost sank to her knees. It took every ounce of will she possessed to remain upright. "Please, give that back to me. Fayline, it doesn't mean any—"

But it was too late. Her sister opened the letter. Cerine couldn't see her face, but she didn't have to. She saw the spasm of excruciating pain that shot down her arched spine.

With a savage cry, the monstrous girl tore the letter to shreds, using her long, twisted nails and her teeth. She spat out chewed pieces of parchment, then whirled around, gnashing those blackened teeth, her lips pulled back from her bruised gums.

"You have betrayed me!" she cried.

"Never." Cerine lifted both hands. Through her mind's eye flashed images of four years ago . . . of all the bodies slain by her newly possessed sister's hand. She knew what magic roiled within that frail host. She knew how brutally Fayline could end her life.

But she reached out anyway and caught her sister's hand. "I would never betray you," she said. "I only want to save—"

Fayline shrieked and yanked herself away. "You cannot save me," she roared. "No one can."

Cerine leapt back just before another burst of darkness enveloped her sister. Her vision momentarily stunned, she staggered several paces, rubbing her eyes, but looked up in time to see Fayline reappear at the edge of the camp. Her red hair and ruinous wedding gown trailing behind her like pennants, she ran into the night.

With the satchel containing Sister Ilda's book clutched in both hands.

CHAPTER 12

With the unfamiliar valley ahead of them cloaked in darkness, Ayleth could not run her horse, but she urged him on as swiftly as she dared, using her shadow vision to help guide the way. Laranta loped at the end of the soul tether, straining with desire for the hunt and yanking so hard that Ayleth was almost pulled from her saddle by sheer spirit force.

The screams had faded. Somehow, this struck her as more ominous than reassuring. She cautiously approached the campsite, her shadow vision dazzled by the gleam of many mortal souls. Switching back to mortal vision, she reined in Chestibor.

A tumult of activity filled her gaze, highlighted by the glow of the campfires. Horses neighed and reared, hands scrambled for lead ropes, carts lurched and halted and lurched again. The air was a storm of gabbling voices. A dozen or more bodies rushed and shouted and swore, so that at first Ayleth thought she must have come upon a band of cutthroat mercenaries. But two blinks later, her mortal eyes adjusted enough to realize that everyone rushing about was clad in pristine white with hoods over their heads. And they were all women.

Nuns. She'd come upon a party of nuns. Screaming, terrified, hysterical nuns.

"*Laranta,*" she called out with her mind, "*any sign of a shade?*"

Before Laranta could answer, one of the nuns spied Ayleth on her horse at the edge of the firelight. She pressed both hands to her cheeks and shrieked, "Red Hood! Red Hood!" It was not a welcoming greeting.

Ayleth raised one hand. "I'm here to help!" she cried.

"Tell me what has happened!" Her voice was nearly swallowed in the mayhem.

Someone must have heard her, however. A ripple of purposeful movement passed through the milling throng as nuns parted to allow one of their number through. Before Ayleth's vision appeared an exceedingly short, impressively fat, and utterly intimidating person wearing full high-priestess regalia as though in preparation for a holy day. She waddled with dignified purpose through the crowd, her face a mask of disdain for the displays of hysteria around her. She was possibly the oldest person Ayleth had ever seen, the oldest person she could imagine ever seeing. Without the support of a carved rowan-wood cane gripped in one hand and the assistance of a stout young woman holding her by the other arm, she must surely have toppled over under her own weight and age.

Ayleth swiftly dismounted and made a low bow. She had never met a Grand Mother before, and she wasn't entirely certain of the proper mode of address. A bow seemed safest.

Laranta, still manifest on the ground beside her mistress, growled. *Rowan!*

"*Hush,*" Ayleth hissed, and the shade crouched low at her feet. She couldn't suppress a shudder of her own. The rowan-wood cane the priestess carried served not only as a support to her frame, but also as a ward against shade influence. No shade could bear the scent of the holy rowan tree, dedicated to the Goddess.

These must be Sivelinians, Ayleth realized—a high order of devotees founded under Saint Sivella of the Rood. Holy women who detested all things shade and shade-taken, they viewed the Order of Saint Evander as little better than a horde of demon-possessed heretics.

The priestess gave Ayleth a look of such severity, she half wanted to mount up and ride away again, leaving the sisters to their own business. But if word were to reach Gerard that she'd abandoned a party of distressed nuns in the middle of the night, it certainly wouldn't help her convince him she was right for the Milisendis posting.

Ayleth steeled herself under the Grand Mother's gaze. "I am Ayleth, Venatrix di Ferosa. Tell me what has happened here and how I may help you."

"Witch," the priestess spat. Ayleth bristled, thinking the holy woman aimed the epithet at her. But the priestess continued: "Appeared out of nowhere, a female, right in the middle of our camp. Frightened my girls out of their minds . . . which, granted, doesn't take a whole lot."

With this last, the old woman scowled around at the company, who, recovering from their terror, folded their hands beneath the long sleeves of their robes and bowed their heads in demure shame, faces covered by the folds of their hoods.

The priestess turned that formidable scowl back on Ayleth. "Is it or is it not the professed duty of your order to protect the kingdom from witches and the like? I'll have a word with your superior and let him know what I think, young woman."

Haunts damn. Just what she needed. "Good Mother—" Ayleth hastily put in.

"*Grand* Mother," the young nun supporting the priestess's arm corrected severely.

Ayleth flicked an uneasy glance from the old woman to the young one and back again. "Grand Mother . . . if you could describe for me this witch and tell me what she did and where she went, I will see that she is dealt with. Is it . . . is it possible that she had red hair?"

The priestess's eyes, already small behind wrinkles and folds of fat, narrowed. "Darkness," she murmured. "A cloud of darkness surrounding her, like a devil's shroud."

"And her hair?" Ayleth pressed. "What color was her hair?"

"Couldn't say about the hair. Just the darkness." The old woman shivered, and then, with an effort, lifted her cane and pointed it at Ayleth's heart as though she'd like to run her through. "Stole one of my novices, she did."

"*Stole* one?" Ayleth's attention twanged like a taut bowstring. "How did she steal her? A curse? A binding?"

"No, no, nothing like that." The priestess shook her heavy head and brought her cane sharply back to ground, leaning on it heavily. The young nun at her side adjusted her grip under the old woman's flabby arm. "Beguiled the girl somehow. The witch fled that way, and the fool-headed little short-wick ran after it like a creature possessed." So saying, the priestess nodded off to her left.

Nodded in the direction of Cró Ular.

Ignoring the priestess's subsequent diatribe about the idiocy of novices and the disintegration of the noble

Sisterhood of Siveline, Ayleth faced the tower. Although darkness and the intervening landscape hid it from view, she felt its presence looming just beyond range of both mortal vision and shadow sight.

Part of her wanted to run away, to resist the fate that seemed to draw her back to those cursed ruins. But such feelings were unworthy of a venatrix.

Ayleth turned back to the priestess. "I'm going to recover your novice," she said, pulling the red hood off her head even as she spoke, and tucking it into the front of her jerkin. "I'll deal with this witch. Here." She tossed Chestibor's reins to a nearby nun. "Hold him for me."

"Red Hood!" the high priestess called as Ayleth turned on her heel, prepared to march out into the night. Ayleth looked around. "Bring the girl back whole and un-taken, or it is the Goddess's own judgment you must face."

"We all must face the Goddess's judgment," Ayleth answered grimly. "We all must make an accounting for ourselves in the end."

With that, she set off at a run, Laranta at her heels, and they left the Sisters Siveline and their flickering campfires behind in the darkness.

"Any trace of a shade, Laranta?"

The wolf shade stalked along the winding ruins of the Queen's Highway, nose to the ground and sniffing intently. Ayleth followed, one hand resting on their connecting soul tether. Her eyes flared with shadow vision as she navigated the broken paving stones. Though rutted and somewhat treacherous in places, the old highway was still the smoothest route across this rough countryside, especially after dark.

Laranta growled an answer, the sound rippling back along the soul tether. *Shade. This way.*

Apparently, the shade-taken had also chosen to use the Queen's Highway as she fled from the Siveline campsite, drawing the novice behind her. Was it truly a witch, as the Grand Mother stated? Given the fact that it had enticed one of the young nuns to pursue, it was more likely a Lure, a shade-taken given to enticing prey with siren calls and illusions of the mind. Recently Ayleth had rescued the Golden Prince from a Lure, and she knew how dangerous they could be. As to the priestess's raving about a dark cloud, that could easily indicate a Lure illusion.

Ayleth gritted her teeth. She had made the mistake before of preparing to fight one type of shade when she faced another. She needed to take care, to make no assumptions . . .

But in her gut she knew: She now hunted the Phantomwitch.

It must be nearly a mile back to Cró Ular. At every turn in the road she expected to come upon the witch or the missing novice. But both had a good head start on her, and she didn't catch up with them. A crescent moon rose high but shed little light on the landscape below, and she depended almost entirely on her shadow sight to guide her. How the novice managed, she couldn't guess. Perhaps she was ensorcelled somehow.

Ayleth climbed a rise that felt familiar to her. When she reached the summit and gazed down into the valley below, she saw the ragged remains of the tower.

Her stomach clenched. If she was right, if the Phantomwitch truly waited among those ruins, she was woefully outmatched. She wasn't even carrying the right variety of poison on her for an Evanescer shade-taken. She should not engage this enemy alone. She ought to return to the outpost, get word to Terryn.

But if she backed down now, she doomed the missing novice. By the time she returned with Terryn, the poor girl would be dead. Or worse.

"You don't *know*," she reminded herself, grinding the words between her teeth. "You don't know what's down there."

Ayleth firmed her jaw and drew a steadying breath. She was a venatrix, trained to face shade-taken alone. She'd fought her fair share of foes in the past month and had always managed to walk away more-or-less triumphant. She could do it again.

Moving with expert care, she began her descent, placing her feet so as not to send even a single loose stone skittering down the incline. With Laranta currently running at the far end of their soul tether, she didn't have access to supernatural strength or stealth. But Hollis had trained her hard over the years, and she walked with the grace of a predator under that thin moon.

Laranta stopped up ahead, snarling and shaking her

wolfish head. *No shade,* she said, looking round at Ayleth, her strange eyes flashing. *No trace. No scent. Gone.*

Ayleth frowned. While there were many potential means of throwing a Feral hunter like Laranta off a trail, one seemed more likely than the others. "*Oblivis?*" she asked. If the shade-taken had *evanesced*, she might leave a trace of *oblivis* behind from where she stepped onto one of her malicious paths through the Haunts.

Laranta shook her head. *No shade. No trace. No scent.*

That didn't mean anything for certain. The shade could still be near. It could still be . . . anything.

She slipped her scorpiona from its holster and mounted it on her arm. But she hesitated to load the Gentle Death. The poison was so deadly, and what if she missed? The novice was out there, already at risk from the shade itself. While Ayleth liked to think herself a better markswoman than most, there were too many variables in this scenario. She'd be wiser not to load her weapon yet.

"I need to get a sight on the witch," she whispered. "Get a sight on her, then take the shot." With this decision in mind, she looked to Laranta once more. "*What about mortal blood? Can you find a trace?*"

Laranta drew back her lips. *I smell mortal.*

"Follow that scent," Ayleth commanded. It was as good a trail as any. If they found the novice, presumably they would find the shade-taken.

Laranta flowed on down the hillside, making for the ruined walls of Cró Ular. Ayleth followed, her mortal senses prickling and wary. She spied no sign of life among the fallen stones of the tower, and she knew Laranta would warn her if she sensed someone near. But something in the air felt . . . wrong. It was like walking into a trap, knowing it was a trap, yet all the while trying to convince herself otherwise.

Laranta reached the wrecked gate and instantly solidified into her wolf form, hackles raised. *Mortal,* she said, eagerness lacing her voice. The edges of her shape wafted and shivered like tendrils of smoke. *Mortal.*

Ayleth crept to her shade's side and peered through the broken gateposts into the courtyard of Cró Ular. Everything looked more ghoulish by moonlight, and that sensation of ghostly presences she had felt earlier in the day intensified, so sharp, so keen that she could almost swear she saw the revenant phantoms of dead warriors drifting between the fallen stones.

Then one of those phantom images stepped into a clear space, and the moonlight shone down upon white robes and a pale hood.

Ayleth's heart turned over. The novice! Her robes hung only as far as her knees, cinched with a wide belt at her waist, and her legs were clad in baggy trousers, the straps of her sandals wrapping the fabric tight around her calves. She walked with her head tilted back, gazing up and around as though expecting something to descend from the empty skies above.

Ayleth stifled the impulse to get up and run to the girl, grab her by the arm, and drag her away through the gate, back up the Queen's Highway. There was no sign of any witch, and her first duty surely must be to rescue this young idiot.

But could this be part of the trap? Was the novice being used like bait, to tempt Ayleth into rash action? She dared not act so impulsively. She must fall back on Hollis's careful training and secure the area before engaging with the girl.

"*Laranta, to my right,*" she commanded, motioning to

her wolf shade. *"Go around the ruins, watch for a shade. Meet me on the far side."*

Laranta's tail swayed once in response before she set off. Her wolf shape melted into subtle shadow. Part of Ayleth's awareness went with her shade, but with the rest she concentrated on her own path, moving clockwise around the ruins. Sometimes she lost sight of the novice through the tumbledown walls. Sometimes she caught a glimpse of her again, still within the courtyard. At least the fool girl didn't approach the tower itself. Ayleth sensed nothing along her way—no tingle of magic or curse, no sign of shade or even of another life anywhere near.

Then a crumbled part of the wall blocked her way, looking as though it had suffered an explosion. Possibly the work of an Elemental shade, twenty years ago. Ayleth climbed to the top, still moving softly, soundlessly.

Just as she was starting to descend, Laranta's voice rippled back along the soul tether to her. *Shade. Magic.*

Ayleth gave a start, and her hand knocked a stone loose. It fell, clattering and clashing, to the ground. She winced with each crash, a curse slipping through her clenched teeth.

The novice down in the courtyard turned abruptly toward the sound. Crouched and hidden among the stones, Ayleth watched the girl take three steps, then stop and peer up at the ruined wall.

A soft, tremulous voice called out, "Fayline? Fayline, is that you?"

Ayleth blinked. Why did the novice know that name?

Oblivis! Laranta growled along the soul tether.

Ayleth grimaced, her attention painfully divided. She concentrated on Laranta, too far off to see with her physical eyes but always perceptible in spirit. *"Oblivis? Like what we saw earlier today?"*

Yes. Shade magic too.

"Is the shade near?"

No. But despite her answer, Laranta growled, deep and vicious.

"Finish securing the perimeter and come to me," Ayleth said. Her mortal eyes blinked down into the courtyard where the novice still approached, her steps cautious but determined in the near-darkness.

As though to improve her line of vision, the girl threw

back her hood, revealing an almost bare scalp. Novices devoted to Saint Sivella always gave up their worldly possessions and shaved their heads as a symbol of relinquishing all claim to mortal beauty. This girl's hair had been shorn again recently, from the look of it, and rather badly at that.

"Fayline," the novice called out, "I know it's you. I won't hide from you, I swear. I'm not afraid. Please, come out."

Who was this girl? Ayleth's mind raced, trying to understand, and for the moment she was too baffled to shift into better hiding.

The novice took another step and stopped. With a sharp intake of breath, she drew back several paces. "Who . . . who's there? Who are you?" she cried.

No use in hiding now. Frowning slightly, Ayleth stood, raising both hands. The fastenings of her scorpiona gleamed, but it was obviously not aimed at anyone. "It's all right," she called. "I am Ayleth, Venatrix di Ferosa. I'm an Evanderian."

The novice gaped up at her. Her eyes were pale and very large, and for an instant she looked gentle, vulnerable. Then her expression hardened, her mouth twisting into a ferocious snarl.

"You shouldn't be here," she said. "Go away! You'll frighten her."

"Frighten who?" Ayleth asked, taking several careful steps down the pile of rubble. "Do you mean Fayline? Is she near?"

The novice's eyes narrowed. She drew back from Ayleth, but as she did so, her boot struck something, which skittered off to one side, flashing reflected light. The novice turned toward whatever it was, and her mouth dropped open.

"I'm here to help you," Ayleth said, sliding down a last incline to reach the same level as the novice. "You might be ensorcelled. I'm going to take you back to your people and—"

"Get back!" The novice whirled around, both arms outstretched in a gesture of warning. "Get out!" She broke off with a scream as the world erupted in a blinding flash. Not of light, but of pure darkness.

Ayleth staggered, throwing up her arms to protect her vision. She landed hard in the rubble, blinking painfully through the whirling shadows before her eyes, trying to force herself to see.

A figure stood not five paces from the novice: an emaciated woman clad in rags, her hair long and tangled. Her skin, so pale as to seem translucent, was webbed with a complex network of black, pulsing veins. A fungus-like growth sprouted from one eye socket and crept down her cheek and neck. Shadow-light flashed in her one eye, and darkness shed from around her like a cloak falling to the ground. Where it landed, the earth itself boiled and pussed.

The Phantomwitch.

For an instant, the witch stared into the face of the novice. An instant that seemed to stretch on and on, so that Ayleth's mind, whirling from that flash of darkness, confused by the impossibilities she saw before her, realized with a terrible jolt that—aside from the growth, aside from the gauntness—the witch and the novice looked strangely alike.

"Fayline," the novice said, reaching out both hands. "Fayline, please give that to me."

Only then did Ayleth see that the witch clutched a

satchel in her hands. She lifted it high over her head, baring her teeth at the novice.

"Why? Are there more of his letters inside? More evidence of your slatternly betrayal?"

Ayleth blinked. What in the Goddess's name were they talking about?

"No, Fayline. Don't say that." The novice took another step, her face full of entreaty. "You must hand it over. It's nothing to do with me, or you, or . . . or Gerard."

"Do not speak his name, you bitch!" The witch threw down the satchel, and it skidded across the ground. Then she raised both hands, and spittle flew from her lips as she screamed, "I'll tear out your festering throat—"

Ayleth grabbed the Gentle Death and slammed it into her scorpiona. The sound of the dart notching into place made the witch stop in mid-stride and turn. She saw Ayleth. Her lips peeled back from her teeth in a hissing snarl. She changed direction and hurtled at Ayleth, her arms outstretched, her fingers curved like claws.

"*Laranta!*" Ayleth cried out along the soul tether. "*To me! To me!*"

Her shade responded at once. Her power flowed back along the soul tether, but she was on the far side of the ruins, seconds away, while the witch covered the distance between her and Ayleth in mere moments.

Ayleth whipped her bone knife from its sheath. She had no time to brandish it, but ducked to escape the first swiping stroke of the witch. She lost her balance, fell, and rolled, but pulled up again in a crouch just in time to spring to one side as the witch brought both fists down at her head. The blow struck Ayleth in the shoulder instead, with surprising force coming from such a delicate host body.

It didn't matter. In the next breath, Laranta was with her, and shade power flowed into Ayleth's head, down through her limbs. She sprang upright, her mouth twisted in a wild smile she could not repress. As the witch hurtled at her again, aiming a blow at the side of her face, Ayleth ducked easily and drove her own fist deep into the woman's gut.

The witch doubled up without a sound and fell to her knees. For a split second, Ayleth's hand moved to deliver a killing stroke with her knife. It would have been easy enough to plunge the blade deep into that exposed neck.

But such a violent death would surely empower the spirits inside to escape and find a new host body. They might enter the novice herself, standing so near. No, she could not deal a violent death. She must try to subdue the witch, knock her unconscious before pricking her with the Gentle Death.

Ayleth cast aside her knife and sprang for the woman's throat, intending to strangle her until she passed out. But that moment of indecision was too long.

Another flash of darkness blinded her. Her arms grasped at empty air. She staggered, helpless, coughing and gagging as she fell to her knees. Two long arms grabbed her from behind, wrapping around her neck like a living noose.

A voice hissed in her ear, "It's been far too long since I killed a venatrix."

Someone screamed, "Fayline, *no!*"

Another clap of darkness. Only this time, it did not end . . . .

Chaos. Horror. Ruin and pain.

Ayleth's spirit screams and screams, first stretching so thin that it begins to tear, then constricting so small that it must crush itself under its own weight.

Light, darkness, madness. Meaningless, meaningless! She struggles for reason, struggles for one thing she can latch onto, one thing she can understand. There is only pain, unending, unendurable pain.

She clings to that pain as her only lifeline.

A face appears before her. A woman's face, one-eyed, surrounded by a cloud of fiery hair. The single eye widens with horror. The mouth opens, and two words emerge, slicing through the chaos.

"My queen?"

A bolt like a blast of lightning, searing her soul to the core.

Ayleth landed hard upon the broken pavement of the courtyard, coughing, gasping, choking. Inside her head, she heard Laranta scream, *Mistress! Mistress!*

She couldn't move. The world swam around her, black shadows creeping in on the edges. She thought she saw a flutter of white robes, thought she saw two sandals, then a pair of knees sinking to the ground before her. From a faraway, unreachable place a voice said, "Venatrix? Venatrix, can you hear me?"

Ayleth closed her eyes and gave in to what must be death.

CHAPTER 13

CERINE CROUCHED OVER THE VENATRIX, HER HANDS hovering in the air just over her shoulders, afraid to touch her. She thought she heard a sound at her back and turned sharply, expecting to see her sister manifest out of the darkness, hands outstretched to tear out her throat. But there was nothing. Only shadows and faint moonlight.

What could she do? What could she do? Her heart thundered in her throat, and wild fear crashed inside her head, drowning out all rational thought.

Then her eye landed on an indistinct shape a few yards away.

Cerine sprang to her feet and stumbled across the broken pavement. Her shaking hands caught up her satchel, which Fayline had tossed so carelessly to one side. She felt the weight of Sister Ilda's book inside, and her whole body sagged with such relief, she sank to her knees, whispering, "Goddess be praised!"

But she couldn't stay. Fayline might return at any moment. It seemed foolish to even try to flee from her sister, but worse still to wait like a mouse in a trap. She must try to get away, must try to fulfill the mission for which she came.

Her limbs shaking with mingled relief and terror, she returned to the venatrix. She couldn't see the strange woman's features clearly, but something about her gave an impression of youth. She might not be any older than Cerine herself. So young to be so ferocious!

But all her ferocity had been as nothing compared to the power bursting inside Fayline. The power of Inren di Karel.

The Venatrix moaned, and her eyes flared open. For a moment she was silent. Then her mouth dropped open and released a scream that echoed off the stones, ripped into the sky, and made Cerine cover her ears and crouch down into a shivering ball, hiding her face in her knees. The scream lasted an unnaturally long time, raw and savage and terrible.

But when at last the sound ceased, the venatrix's eyes were still open. She lay panting, not exactly awake, but not unconscious either.

Cerine pulled herself upright, forcing some small measure of courage into existence by sheer willpower. "Come on, Venatrix," she said, and took hold of the woman's upper arm. The venatrix tensed, and Cerine half expected her to lash out with one of her many weapons. But instead she submitted to Cerine's urging and allowed herself to be pulled to her feet. When she swayed heavily and almost fell, Cerine ducked under her shoulder, holding her upright as best she could. "Come on then," she said, and took a step.

To her relief, the venatrix took one step alongside her. Then another. Then another. Staggering and very nearly toppling on more than one occasion, they somehow made it out from among the ruins and into the open valley beyond. Cerine stared into the night, uncertain from which direction she'd come. When she chased after Fayline, she'd simply followed the ghostly image of her sister. But now . . .

Well, she couldn't just stand here, waiting for the witch to return and finish them both off. She took a step.

The venatrix pulled up short and shook her head, muttering wordlessly. Then, somehow, she managed to lift a hand, pointing. "Th-tha . . . that . . ." Her head sagged to her chest, and her long braid flopped over one shoulder. But there was no mistaking her meaning.

"All right. I understand," Cerine said. She changed direction, and, following the route the venatrix indicated, they set off across the valley.

Terryn took the circuit trail leading south as the sun disappeared behind the horizon. Now that he was beyond Dunloch's walls, beyond the gardens, back into the countryside where he belonged, he found he could breathe again.

Was there truly a need for him to dash out into the coming night? Probably not. Most likely a cart had lost a wheel, or a horse had gone lame. Maybe the ferry across the river was delayed. But if it would ease Gerard's mind for him to discover the whereabouts of the absent Lady Cerine, so be it. It was an excuse to get away, and he was grateful.

He bent over Fleeta's neck and urged her into a canter. The night was cold, and for this he was grateful. He let that cold drive into his face, drive into his lungs. Fleeta carried him nearly a mile from the castle before he let her slow and catch her breath. They continued at an easy trot as the sky above them darkened and the stars appeared one by one.

Terryn felt the gleam of moonlight on the back of his head, and . . . and it stirred something deep inside. Down in the place where his shade crouched, caught in its Vocos chains.

Terryn grimaced. Moonlight always had this effect on him—filling him with a strange, maddening urge to loosen those bindings with which he held his shade captive, to let its power flow through him, to feel magic swell and swell until it burst out from him in waves. He pulled his hood up and over his head as though somehow it could block out the influence of the moon.

But the urge remained. The deadly urge he must fight with everything he had.

"*She* doesn't fight it," he whispered, the words curling in white vapors before his lips. "*She* doesn't bind her shade, and yet it doesn't overwhelm her."

Heresy. He teetered on the ragged edge of heresy. And why? Because some ragged, poorly trained, back-borough country girl came dancing into his life with her devil-may-care recklessness? She made it look so easy, that bond she shared with her shade. She drew on its powers without so much as a thought, and barely took time to bind them back. It was impressive and terrifying and wrong and . . .

And he wished he could do the same. He wished he could trust his shade so implicitly.

Murmuring to his horse, he rode on, slowly eating up the miles. As long as he stuck to the circuit trail, Fleeta was confident even after dark, and eventually they shifted to the broader road stretching from the riverside town of

Grimaud toward Dunloch. An hour into his ride, he began searching for signs of the Siveline traveling party up ahead, but he suspected they had stopped for the night in Grimaud itself. He'd find them there, exchange a few words with Lady Cerine, then ride at a leisurely pace back to Dunloch to report to the prince.

It was odd, though. As the second hour trailed by, Terryn couldn't stop his mind from nudging curiously at the question: Why was Gerard so worried about Cerine? Yes, the prince was generally a considerate fellow who wished well to all those in his circle. But to send Terryn out in the middle of the night like this hinted at more than mere consideration. Gerard was worried. Truly worried.

Was it possible that he actually . . . *cared* for Lady Cerine?

Terryn frowned at this thought, uncertain how he felt about the concept. On the one hand, he wanted Gerard to be happy. If he could find happiness in this forced marriage, so much the better.

But . . . Cerine? Freckle-faced, solemn-eyed Cerine? She used to follow the prince and her older sister around like a devoted lapdog, eager for any spare attention either of them tossed her way. Terryn hadn't seen her in years, but it was hard to get this picture of her out of his head. Even harder when he compared that memory to the lively and vivacious memory of Fayline. Perhaps when he met her again, he would—

Terryn pulled up sharply. All other thoughts vanished from his mind, and a strange sensation prickled along his spine, a sensation for which he had no name. There was a *taste* on the wind that burned and froze and made the heart shiver. He couldn't quite describe it, but neither could he deny it.

A scream shredded the night's stillness. His eyes went wide.

"Ayleth," he whispered.

Digging his spurs into Fleeta's ribs, he galloped his horse down the road without a thought for the danger. Within minutes they rounded a bend, and he saw the flash of swinging lanterns on poles, at least a dozen of them, indicating a sizable company. They progressed in an orderly line despite the second bloodcurdling scream that shot up from among their number. Terryn recognized the cowls of the Siveline Sisterhood.

"Who's there?" one of the lantern-bearers on the edge of the company called out, her voice trembling.

Terryn reined in Fleeta, walking her into the torchlight. The sisters, seeing him, screamed and drew back before recognizing the red Evanderian hood. "I come from Dunloch Castle," he declared, his gaze sweeping across the traveling party. There were seven on foot, three on horseback, with one supply wagon. Everyone he saw wore the garments of the sisterhood. Surely this couldn't be the whole party from Siveline.

"Is Lady Cerine d'Aldreda among you?"

"I am Cerine."

A young novice on foot stepped away from one of the supply carts and approached Terryn's horse, peering up at him from under her hood. Her eyes were so like Fayline's, they made his stomach jolt. He'd forgotten how alike the two sisters looked. How alike, and yet how utterly different.

"Greetings, Venator Terryn," she said gravely, making a respectful sign of blessing according to the Sivelinian way. "It's been some years since last we met. I trust you are well."

Terryn opened his mouth, but before he could answer, a third scream shattered the air, coming from the cart near which Cerine had been walking. He was out of his saddle in an instant, striding past the lady without a word. His heart pounded in his throat as he grabbed hold of the side railings and climbed up on a wheel to peer inside.

Lying among the sacks and bundles, her hood thrown back, her dark hair a mad tangle around her face, lay Ayleth. She stared up into the night sky, unseeing. Darkness crawled through the whites of her eyes. Darkness crawled beneath her skin, pulsing in time to her frantic heartbeat.

The world seemed to fade to nothing around him. There was only that vision, that horror, lying before his eyes. He knew what this was. He knew what she suffered.

"*Oblivis.*" The word rasped on his tongue. "She's *oblivis* infected."

The next moment, he was down from the wheel and round the back of the cart. The knots of rope securing the end were too tough for his trembling hands to untie, so he whipped out his knife and slashed the ropes, letting sacks of food and barrels of spring water slide out onto the ground. Only vaguely aware of Cerine on one side and some scolding old woman on the other, Terryn reached into the cart and caught Ayleth by her arm, pulling her toward him. She recoiled and struggled before lapsing back into her stupor.

"Young man!" the scolding woman cried as Terryn slid one arm under Ayleth's shoulders, the other under her knees, and hauled her out. "Young man, you'll do her an injury with such rough handling!"

"We can carry her to Dunloch, Venator Terryn," Cerine protested, reaching a hand toward the venatrix but not quite daring to touch her. "We can—"

"There's no time," Terryn growled, pushing his way past both women and the lantern-bearers gathered round. "No time, no time! I've got to get her to Fendrel *now*."

Staggering under the awkward, inert weight, he returned to his horse. "Easy, Fleeta," he said, and heaved the venatrix up into his saddle. She moaned, but some instinct made her reach out and catch a fistful of mane. One of the nuns hurried to the horse's other side, lifting strong hands to steady Ayleth as Terryn swung himself into the saddle behind her.

Cerine appeared at his side. "She risked her life for me," she said, her face white and ghostly in the torchlight. "Save her, please."

Terryn nodded. Then, wrapping an arm around Ayleth's waist and holding her tightly to him, he spurred Fleeta into motion, galloping down the center of the road to Dunloch.

The banquet lasted late into the night. The midnight bells had long ago struck, and Chancellor Yves nodded off over his fifth chalice of wine. One of the ladies in the duke's party actually put her head down on the table and snored, but as the duke continued a stream of lively conversation and Prince Gerard seemed content to sit and listen, his guests felt obliged to remain where they were.

Fendrel sat silent at the prince's right hand as the hours rolled by. He watched the duke and the prince make strained conversation, but as he himself had nothing to contribute, he held his peace, offering answers only when they were directly asked of him.

He studied Gerard most closely. He'd known his nephew since the day of his birth, had watched him grow into a fine, strong, handsome man. The fulfillment of every dream, of every promise. The Golden Prince.

Shadows gathered across the Venator Dominus's brow. In all his twenty-two years, Gerard had never demonstrated such a strange willfulness as he had in this last month. What could possibly have motivated him to betray Terryn? To refuse to hand over the borough which was Terryn's right? The two of them had been raised in close proximity—like brothers, or as near to brothers as was possible for a prince and a venator's apprentice. Fendrel had labored long and hard to instill in Terryn a loyalty to Gerard that went far beyond the bond of blood, and he knew that Gerard loved Terryn.

Snatching up the chalice before him, Fendrel took a swig of dark wine. He wiped his mouth with the back of his hand and leaned back in his chair, studying the chalice as he turned its stem with his fingers. But his unfocused gaze did not see the fine silverwork catching the candlelight.

Who was this venatrix? This Ayleth di Ferosa?

Hollis's former apprentice.

Hollis . . . of all people.

He took another great draught of wine and gritted his teeth as he swallowed. Several red drops spilled over his lips and through the pale hairs of his beard. Something was not right here. Where Hollis went, only trouble could follow. A muscle pulled at the corner of his mouth, the faintest quiver of a long-forgotten smile. "Hellion Hollis" they'd called her during the Witch Wars. For her recklessness, her utter disregard for her own safety while on the hunt. And yet, he'd never met a venatrix her equal.

At this thought, he felt a pair of eyes upon him. Glancing up, he met Everild di Lamaury's gaze. She sat at the lower end of the table, away from the prince and his mighty guests, opposite Lady Liselle di Matin. No contrast could be greater than that between the weather-beaten venatrix and the lovely widow.

Everild, obviously bored with Liselle's attempts to draw her into conversation, raised an eyebrow at Fendrel. He offered her nothing in return, instead focusing once more on the contents of his cup. Everild was a fine venatrix, skilled with her pipes, a good shot with the scorpiona. She knew how to control her shade well enough. And she stood by her Venator Dominus no matter what. No questions, no bullheaded rebellion.

But she could never be Hollis's match. No one could.

The door of the banquet hall opened, drawing Fendrel's eye. A servant rushed through—a young boy, his face pale with fright. From the head of the table, Gerard looked up and saw him as well. "Billin, what's wrong?" he asked.

"Your Highness!" The boy hastened round the table, darting behind Fendrel's seat to fall on his knees beside the prince. "The venator's here. And the venatrix! And she's bad sick, Your Highness!"

"What? Ayleth?" Gerard stood instantly, his chair's legs scraping on the floor. "Where are they? What did they say?"

"Venator du Balafre told me to . . . to . . ." The boy's gaze flashed Fendrel's way but could not settle there. "He told me to fetch the Black Hood!"

Fendrel rose. "Where is Venator du Balafre, boy?"

"In the front courtyard," the lad gasped, and Fendrel

was in motion before he'd finished speaking. Everild, Venator du Gy, and Venator d'Acelet all leaped from their seats and hastened after him as he strode from the banquet hall and along the passage to the front entrance.

The door stood wide, an open view to the courtyard beyond. Fendrel saw Terryn's horse standing below in the thin moonlight, its head low, sides heaving. Terryn himself knelt on the ground, holding a woman upright against him, her limbs limp, her head thrown back across his arm.

"Terryn," Fendrel called out as he descended the porch steps, "what's happened here?"

Terryn looked up, his eyes bright with shadow sight. "She's infected. *Oblivis.*"

Fendrel paused. A shot of horror passed through his spirit. *Oblivis?* He'd not seen *oblivis* infection since the wars.

No . . . wait. That wasn't true. He'd seen it again more recently. Four years ago. On the night of the prince's wedding.

Which could only mean . . .

He shook himself hard, grinding his teeth. Now was

not the time to give way to baseless fears. "What happened?" he growled, hastening the rest of the way down the steps. "Who did this to her?"

"I don't know." Terryn shook his head, his face strained and tight. He gazed down at the venatrix, and Fendrel didn't like what he saw shining in the boy's eyes. "I wasn't there, I didn't see what took place. But I think . . . I'm afraid . . ."

"I don't want your speculation," Fendrel growled. He crouched beside the young woman and took hold of her arm, heaving her up so that he could get his own arm under her shoulders. "Come on, Terryn. Let's get her inside. I need to inspect her, to see how far—"

The words died on his lips.

The world seemed to stop turning. The blood in his veins congealed, and the breath in his lungs died. He stared down into that girl's face as though he would never be able to look away.

It was the face of the woman whose head he'd mounted on a pike twenty years ago.

CHAPTER 14

TERRYN WATCHED HIS FORMER MASTER JERK AWAY from Ayleth's still body. The Venator Dominus landed hard on one elbow before scrambling upright and backing away, his eyes round with horror so that the whites stood out bright in the darkness.

"Fendrel? Fendrel, what is it?" Terryn demanded.

Fendrel shook his head. Then he shook it again, his mouth opening and closing without words. Terryn's heart plummeted. She must be too far gone. The *oblivis* infecting her blood must already have filled her with its darkness. Otherwise, his former master wouldn't react so violently. Any moment now, the infection would pour out from her mouth, her nostrils, from the corners of her eyes, streaming into all those near.

Movement flashed in the corner of Terryn's eye, and someone else appeared opposite him, crouched on Ayleth's other side.

"I'm here, Terryn," Gerard said, slipping his arms under her shoulders. "Let's lift her up."

Terryn nodded, the sight of the prince's face momentarily filling him with relief. He pulled his feet underneath him, braced to stand. Together, he and Gerard got Ayleth upright. Their arms behind her shoulders, each holding her under one knee, they lifted and carried her up the porch steps, through the door, and into the entrance hall.

Faces and sounds flashed through Terryn's senses. He heard Gerard shouting for Fendrel to follow, then questions, so many questions. He couldn't answer. He scarcely heard anything Gerard said. He was aware of nothing but Ayleth limp in his arms and the pulse of *oblivis* pounding through her veins.

"This way, this way," Gerard said, guiding them toward the stairs and up to the private chambers in the east wing. Away from the banquet, away from Duke d'Aldreda and the other guests. "There's a room down this hall we'll put her in."

Terryn nodded without comment. Everild stepped from the shadows, silent as a sentinel gargoyle before a shrine-house door. With quick strides she moved to the door Gerard indicated and flung it open, then stepped aside to give the men room to carry their burden through. The bedchamber must have been prepared for one of the coming guests, for the bed was made and fuel stacked on the hearth.

Gerard and Terryn dropped Ayleth on the bed more roughly than either intended. She took that moment to let out another blood-chilling scream, her hands clutching and tearing at the bedclothes. Her eyes bulged wide, so black with *oblivis,* they looked as though they would burst. Gerard recoiled, but Terryn leaned in. He caught her by the hands. She shifted her grip from the blankets to his fingers, squeezing painfully. Thank the Goddess her shade was not ascendant, or she certainly would have broken every bone in his hand.

"You're all right," he said, his voice underscoring another piercing, ongoing scream. "We're safe now. You're all right, di Ferosa. Breathe, breathe."

Perhaps she heard him. She choked on the scream, and her eyes closed. Her head turned from one side to the other, the cords of her throat tight and straining.

"What happened to her?" Gerard asked, not for the first time.

"That is *oblivis* infection," Everild answered from somewhere behind Terryn.

Still holding Ayleth's hands, Terryn looked around at Gerard, met his gaze. "She must have encountered the Phantomwitch."

Gerard stared at Terryn. "I thought . . ." He put a hand to his forehead, pushing back the hair falling in his eyes. "You said you'd found no sign of her!"

"I didn't." Terryn gazed down at Ayleth's tormented face once more. "But she did, Goddess help her."

A figure appeared in the open doorway: Fendrel, jaw set, his cheeks deathly pale. He strode into the room, brushing past Gerard without a word, and stood behind Terryn, studying Ayleth.

"Report," he said.

Old habits immediately took hold. Terryn let go of Ayleth and stood up straight. He almost saluted. "I encountered the traveling party from Siveline Temple, Lady Cerine among their number."

"Cerine is here?" Gerard put in. But Fendrel silenced him with a swift motion of his hand, his eyes flashing for Terryn to continue.

"They had Venatrix di Ferosa with them," Terryn said in a rush. "She was already hurt when I found her. I don't know how."

Fendrel nodded and turned his attention from Terryn back to Ayleth. This time there was no sudden flinching, no pulling away. His inscrutable gaze searched her from head to toe. He sat on the bed and leaned over her, holding her chin with one hand while with the other he pulled open her eye to study it more closely. His own eyes flared with shadow-light.

"She's breathed it in," he said at last. He let go of her and drew back from the bed. Ayleth moaned and shook her head wildly, her eyes rolling. "Pure, unfiltered *oblivis,* straight from the Haunts."

Everild moved on the far side of the bed, catching Terryn's attention. "Sir," she said, "shall I send for a transfer host?"

"No," Fendrel answered, standing up. "No, she's too far gone now. It's too late."

"What?" Gerard said from somewhere behind him.

Terryn didn't hear whatever else the prince said. Thunder pounded in his ears. He caught Fendrel by the elbow. "She's not too far gone," he growled. "You can save her."

"Let go of me, boy." Rage sparked behind Fendrel's iron gaze.

Terryn's fingers tightened. "You can save her," he said. "How many did you save from Dread Odile's curses during the wars? Those were direct hits. They were worse than this."

Fendrel's jaw worked. "It's been hours. It's too late."

"It's not too late." Terryn leaned in closer, his voice scarcely above a whisper. "I'll not take Milisendis this way. I'll take it, but not with her death." Fendrel's eyes knifed into his, but he didn't back down, not for an instant. "Save her, Fendrel. Save her."

"You don't know what you're asking." Fendrel yanked his arm free and turned away from the bed. He took a step for the door.

But Gerard moved to block his way.

"Is Terryn right?" the prince demanded. "Can you save her? Have you saved others similarly afflicted?"

Fendrel lowered his chin to his chest in acknowledgement. "During the Witch Wars."

"How?" Gerard persisted. "Explain to me how it works."

"The ways of Evander's followers are—"

Gerard put up a staying hand. "I'm not asking for Evanderian secrets, Uncle. Just tell me, in simple terms that I can understand, how you saved others."

Fendrel's gaze swiveled from the prince to Terryn and back again. "A curse of *oblivis* always takes a life. Death is unavoidable. But it can be driven into another host."

"Another *human* host?" Gerard asked.

When Fendrel didn't answer immediately, Everild spoke up from across the chamber. "An animal host will do, so long as it's of comparable weight."

Fendrel did not look around at his lieutenant. But Terryn saw how the muscles in his jaw tensed at her words.

Gerard nodded. "A pig then?" he asked. His face was white with tension. "Or a sheep? Will either of those serve?"

"Yes," Everild answered.

Fendrel took another step. Gerard did as well, holding out both arms to block the Dominus's way.

"Uncle," he said, "you've got to try."

A moment of silence held the room captive, broken only by Ayleth's moans. Her agony increased, rising in intensity until she let loose another scream, this one worse than the others. Her body convulsed on the bed, and dark patches spread beneath her skin.

Terryn leapt to her side, catching her right before she rolled off the bed. Her flailing fist struck him in the jaw, not hard enough to make him let go, but enough to hurt. He shifted her so that her back was to his chest, put both arms around her, and held her tight, so that she couldn't hurt herself in her convulsions.

The episode passed. Ayleth lay panting in his arms. Her chest rose and fell unnaturally fast, and her mouth hung open. Terryn looked up at the other three and found them watching. Everild, with a grimace. Gerard, his face tense with concern, his hands clenched into fists.

And Fendrel. Stone-hard Fendrel gazed down at him from behind his inscrutable mask.

"Do something," Terryn urged through clenched teeth.

Fendrel's nostrils flared. He opened his mouth, but before he spoke, the prince rounded on him. He drew himself up to his full height. "Fendrel, Venator Dominus du Glaive," he said, "you will use whatever means and powers you have to save this young woman. By order of your Golden Prince, under the sovereign will of your master, the Chosen King."

Fendrel met his nephew's gaze. A sensation of pure power rippled through the air, striking both Terryn's and Everild's perceptions so that they flinched away. Fendrel's shade, stirred to life by its host body's fury, flexed inside him, and Terryn saw the edges of it rippling out from the Venator Dominus's spirit in dark hues of Anathema

241

magic.

But Gerard could not sense it, un-taken as he was. So he did not back down.

At last, after a terrible interval measured only in heartbeats, Fendrel bowed. "Your Highness," he murmured.

Gerard turned from the dominus to Everild. "Bring a sheep from the kitchens. Or a pig. Go now." Everild looked as though she would protest being used as a pig-fetcher, but at a swift glance from Fendrel, she saluted sharply and hastened from the room.

Fendrel strode past Gerard, moving to the other side of the bed, opposite Terryn. "Lay her down," he said as he began stripping off his outer garments. He wore the same rough garb he'd worn on the road, refusing to change into his formal dress for the banquet as Terryn had. He lacked only the quivers and scorpiona to be ready for a circuit ride. He undid the ties and buckles of his outer jerkin, stripping down to his undershirt. He even removed the left bracer with the three iron spikes and rolled his sleeves up over his elbows, revealing ugly scars scoring the skin of his arm. Only then did he take up his

Vocos pipes and begin to play the Song of Summoning.

A shock went through the air as the Venator Dominus loosened the intense bindings he'd placed upon his shade. The raw power of magic was so great, it made Terryn dizzy. He had grown up around this Anathema, observing Fendrel's control over it through the years. But he'd never sensed it so potent. So dangerous.

So close to taking ascendancy.

But Fendrel was a master of the Vocos pipes. He played a complex variation, weaving in strains of other spells as he went, so that the shade remained carefully bound as he accessed its power. He finished the song with a complex flourish that Terryn could not quite follow, and when it was through, the magic no longer felt so treacherous. Dangerous, yes, but a danger that could be channeled.

Fendrel folded up his Vocos and handed it to Everild while Terryn carefully laid Ayleth back down on the bed, her head on a pillow. She was quiet for now, save that her limbs shivered uncontrollably. Her eyes mercifully were shut, not bugging with terror as they had been.

"Strip her down," Fendrel said, pulling his knife from

its sheath.

"What are you going to do?" Gerard took a quick step forward as Terryn moved to obey. "Are you going to . . . hurt her?"

Fendrel cast the prince a dark look even as he set the knife at the ready on a side table. "There will be plenty of blood flowing tonight. It won't be a pretty process, and if you prefer not to get your fine raiment splattered, I would suggest you leave."

Terryn's hands trembled as he undid buckles of Ayleth's jerkin and gently slid her out of it, rolling her body to get her arms free. He knew the process Fendrel used for this transference of the *oblivis* curse, knew the theory. But he'd never seen it done.

"I'll stay," Gerard said behind him. Though Terryn hated to admit it, he was glad. He didn't want to face what was about to happen alone.

He untied the laces of Ayleth's undershirt, pulling the fabric open. There could be no preservation of modesty. Not that she would care under the current circumstances. Yet he hated that he should see her like this. She looked so small, so vulnerable, so . . . horrible.

Spider-web veins of deadly black stretched beneath her skin, all the white spaces slowly filling in.

Fendrel stepped forward and pressed his index finger against the hollow space at her throat. A faint imprint of Anathema tainted her skin, invisible to Gerard's eyes but visible to Terryn's shadow sight. Fendrel pressed each of Ayleth's shoulders, her heart, her navel. She shuddered at his touch, but the convulsions didn't return, not yet.

A snorting and snuffling at the door drew Terryn's attention. Everild stepped into the room, followed by a kitchen boy with a large sow in tow. The pig was huge and incongruous in this elegant chamber, and the boy looked as if he'd rather be anywhere else in the world.

"Out," Fendrel snarled at him.

The boy handed the pig's lead off to the reluctant Everild and dashed through the door. Everild's perpetual sneer deepened, but at Fendrel's command, she dragged the sow toward the bed. Fendrel knelt beside the animal and, after a quick study, pressed his finger against its throat, over its heart—all the comparable places on a pig's body which he had touched on Ayleth—leaving behind stains of Anathema magic. Then he drew open his own shirt, shrugging it off so that it hung from his trousers around his waist. In short order, he'd marked himself as well.

His eyes snapped up to meet Terryn's. "Hold her down," he said. "It's about to get messy. If she fights me too hard, I won't be able to do anything for her, so hold her down. No matter what."

Terryn nodded. He placed both hands on Ayleth's bare shoulders, gripping hard enough that he could almost ignore how badly his limbs shook. Fendrel took up his knife, pressing the blade lightly to Ayleth's pulsing skin. The dominus took a long, shuddering breath.

At the first cut, her eyes flared open. Ayleth looked directly up into Terryn's face and screamed.

CHAPTER 15

"IT'S MUCH BIGGER THAN I THOUGHT IT WOULD BE."

The sound of Ducette's voice jarred Cerine out of her reverie. She blinked, startled to discover that she was still on her feet, still walking determinedly down the night-darkened road. Ducette took hold of her arm, slipping a hand through the crook of her elbow. She nodded up ahead. "Look," she said, her fingers squeezing.

Cerine unwillingly lifted her head and peered out from under the shelter of her hood. The night had reached its heaviest hour, cold and heavy on the world, and a distant shrine house rang out three dolorous bells, the notes drifting through the sky. The moon had set long ago, leaving only starlight to gleam on the dark waters of the Holy Lake and the white towers of Dunloch Castle. But flickering torches illuminated the gate and silhouetted the tall guardsmen at their posts.

"Come on, Cerine," Ducette urged, pulling her along a little faster. "We're almost there. We'll soon have proper beds. I don't know about you, but I intend to sleep a good hundred years at least!"

Cerine grumbled wordlessly, yet she was thankful for Ducette's grip on her arm. She was ready to drop with exhaustion. This had to be the longest night of her life.

Her hand moved quietly to grasp the shoulder strap of her satchel. Feeling the weight of Sister Ilda's book bump against her thigh, she breathed a little more easily. She'd been mad to run after Fayline alone into the darkness. She knew that well enough. She shouldn't even be alive now after such a rash act.

But when she considered what could have been lost . . . no. Rash, mad, or whatever, she'd made the right choice.

Someone must have alerted the gate guards to expect their arrival. They allowed the little cavalcade to pass through, requiring no identification other than the well-known blue hoods of the Siveline Sisters. Cerine and Ducette passed under the gate arch last of all, behind the rattling cart. After crossing the bridge lined with torches, they stepped onto a gleaming white road that split to loop around a circular lawn and rose garden. Taking the torchlit right branch, they followed the road toward the steps of the main castle keep.

Cerine dropped her gaze to her feet. She had last journeyed to Dunloch four years ago, riding in a coach along with her parents and sister, who'd been bursting with plans for the wedding and the weeks of celebration to follow.

She remembered sitting in her seat corner, nodding, smiling, and making her own quiet plans for her own quiet future. The Siveline Sisterhood had already agreed to accept her for initiation. She only needed to convince her father, but she didn't think that would be too hard. He was successfully marrying his eldest daughter off to the Golden Prince of Perrinion. If his younger daughter chose to enter a life of holy devotion, the house d'Aldreda wouldn't suffer for lack of a second well-connected marriage.

How the world had changed in a few short years!

The three horseback escorts had already dismounted, and sleepy stable hands, rubbing their eyes, came out of nowhere to take the horses and the cart. Someone in velvet robes appeared as though by magic, asking where the Grand Mother was. Leaving Ducette to explain that this was only a small part of the cortege traveling from Siveline, that the rest would arrive tomorrow after the high priestess's carriage was repaired, Cerine approached the porch steps, lifting her eyes to the looming castle keep.

Though most of the household must be asleep, light gleamed behind various windows, mostly in the east wing. Cerine gripped her satchel like a lifeline. Who would come down to greet her? Would anyone? Perhaps she would be able to slip away with the other Siveline sisters. No one had realized yet that she was the duke's daughter, and if Ducette held her tongue for once . . .

The front doors of the keep opened, and her father descended the steps.

At sight of his face, each feature distinct in the torchlight, a chill ran down Cerine's spine. She hadn't seen her father in years, and their exchange of letters during that time had never been pleasant. Although she felt like a quivering little girl inside, she drew herself up straight, determined to reveal no timidity.

His gaze traveled over the cluster of nuns, seeking his daughter, failing to recognize her. Better not to wait until he succeeded.

Squaring her shoulders and lifting her chin, Cerine deliberately stepped away from Ducette and the others. "Father," she said in a clear voice.

His one eye darted to her face, and she watched his lip curl. As always, his appearance was in perfect order, from his coiffed hair to the cut of his jacket to the gleaming embroidery on his slippers. All the finest, most elaborate trappings of his position, including the silk eye patch concealing his disfigurement. Celestin d'Aldreda spared no expense to ensure that no one who looked at him would ever guess he had once been a witch's slave.

And he would be damned before he let a mere daughter embarrass him.

"I should have known," he announced in the affected accent Cerine knew only too well. "Of course you would arrive in rags. Did the gown I sent not fit? Or was it simply not to your liking?"

Cerine's mouth was so dry, her voice emerged as a croak. "The gown was lovely, but . . ."

In four quick steps, d'Aldreda crossed the distance to Cerine, caught her by the elbow, and dragged her up the stairs. "Get inside, girl, and don't bother with your excuses or your pious protests. I don't want anyone seeing you like this, certainly not the prince. Liselle is here, and you will let her make you presentable before you come down from your rooms tomorrow morning, do you understand?"

Cerine stumbled on one of the steps, and her hood fell back across her shoulders. Turning to adjust his grip, the duke saw her bare head. "Haunts damn!" He dropped his hold on her and recoiled as though he'd been bitten. "What happened to your hair?"

Straightening to her full height, Cerine clutched the

strap of her satchel. "When you sent me to Siveline Temple, I gave up all rights to my mortal life, including all claim to beauty. My head was shaved before I passed through the inner doors."

D'Aldreda folded his arms. "I informed you three years ago of my intention to wed you to the prince in your sister's place. All that time you've known that you would not be joining the Sisterhood. Are you telling me you couldn't grow your hair back in three years?" Before she could answer, he reached out and caught her by the back of the head to examine her scalp more closely. "Shades take you, you shaved it just days ago, didn't you? You look like a plucked fowl ready for the game pot. What were you thinking?"

Cerine didn't try to respond. She couldn't begin to explain her choices. Not to him.

Gripping her by the back of her neck, the duke shoved her on up the stairs. "Liselle will have a head covering or veil. She'll make you presentable if anyone can." While servants held the door open, he hustled her inside. "Heaven help me, at least the contract is ironclad! Goddess willing, Gerard won't take one look at you and—"

"Father." Cerine twisted in the duke's grip. So few lights burned in the cavernous front hall that she could scarcely see his face beyond the gleam of his one eye. "I saw Fayline."

For an instant, d'Aldreda's fingers tightened. He stared down at Cerine, no longer seeing her ravaged hair, no longer seeing her at all. "You . . . you're certain?"

At the sound of his voice—his real voice, without the affected accent—Cerine's heart flinched. Her father loved no one in all this world as he had loved his oldest daughter. Fayline had inherently possessed that effect on people. Nothing could fill the hole left in her absence.

"I'm certain," Cerine answered quietly. "I spoke with her. And it was—"

The duke's hand dropped as he turned away, leaving Cerine where she stood. "It was Inren," he said, bitterness lacing his words. "The Phantomwitch, Haunts damn her to oblivion."

But Cerine shook her head. "I know who I saw."

"You know nothing, girl. You know what you wished to see. But *I* know Inren. I know how she works, and—"

The duke broke off, his head whipping sharply about. Cerine, following the line of his gaze, saw a figure descending the great front staircase, a candle in his hand. The candle's small flame could hardly combat the heavy gloom of the vast entry hall, but it was bright enough to illuminate the strained features of the man carrying it.

Cerine's stomach plunged. Her lips moved in a breathless whisper. "Gerard."

The prince paused and blinked, frowning, peering ahead through the shadows. "Lady Cerine?" His voice echoed in that lofty space.

"Don't say anything. Don't do anything," d'Aldreda hissed, rounding on Cerine. His long arm darted out to haul her hood back over her head. "Cover yourself, for saint's sake!"

Gerard hastened down the last several steps, shielding his candle flame with one hand. Cerine hunched beneath her hood, her elbow firmly grasped in her father's hand. The prince's pace slowed as he drew near, and he offered a solemn bow. Cerine hesitated, uncertain what her response ought to be. Then, with a quick shake of her head, she offered him a Sivelinian bow, bending slightly at the waist, her fingers pressed to her lips.

D'Aldreda growled, and his fingers pinched her arm painfully. "My daughter has arrived safely at last. But she is wearied from her travels and needs to rest. You two may reacquaint yourselves in the morning."

"Of course, of course," Gerard answered. Cerine felt his gaze on her but dared not meet it. "I, um . . . your rooms are upstairs in the west wing, my lady. I'll have a servant escort you."

Cerine nodded. It had been too much to hope that she'd be allowed to spend the night with Ducette and the other sisters. She knew better than to make any such request.

A serving girl was soon summoned. Only then did the duke release her arm, and Cerine hastened after the girl toward the stairs, passing by Gerard. She heard her father speak to the prince and heard the prince respond, but her heart hammered in her ears so hard, she could not discern their words.

Gripping her satchel tightly, she climbed the stairs. The passage on the next level was illuminated only by a few candle sconces, which cast the serving girl's shadow like a flickering dark phantom on the opposite wall.

"Cerine."

When she turned sharply, her hood fell back from her head, exposing her close-cropped hair just as Gerard appeared at the top of the stairs. A hot flush burned her cheeks. She'd made the conscious decision to maintain her appearance according to the strict, unlovely guidelines of Siveline's Order because she didn't want Gerard to believe she either hoped or intended to step into her sister's place.

Gerard, still shielding his candle, looked beyond Cerine to the serving girl. "Leave us a moment, Kella, if you please."

The girl curtsied and slipped on ahead without a word. The heavy shadows of Dunloch seemed suddenly to drop onto Cerine's shoulders. She lowered her gaze to Gerard's shoes as he approached.

"I heard you had some adventure on the road," he said, his voice tight and tense. He moved in close, so close she could easily have reached out and touched him. "Terryn told me what he knew, but that wasn't much. He says that Ayleth—Venatrix di Ferosa, that is—

encountered . . ."

"Fayline." Cerine spoke the name softly. "Yes. We both saw her. Talked with her."

He was silent for a moment. She heard him swallow hard. Then: "Tell me."

The pain in his voice struck her to the core. But she couldn't withhold the truth. Not from him.

"She appeared first in the middle of our campsite. We spoke briefly, and when she fled, I ran after her."

"Alone? Are you mad?"

"Perhaps," Cerine acknowledged with a mirthless half-smile. She rapidly summarized the events of her strange evening. Gerard listened closely to her description of the witch's appearance, of the venatrix's arrival, and of the battle.

"I believe I glimpsed one of her curse anchors just before she appeared again and attacked the venatrix," Cerine said. "I stepped on a stone, and it looked very like what my father described the Phantomwitch using. Like a diamond, but black and living inside."

Gerard drew a long, long breath. Her story complete, Cerine could not resist the opportunity to study him by the glow of his candle. In the four years since she'd last seen him, he'd grown from a handsome boy of eighteen into a man. She recognized those strong cheekbones, those full lips, and those eyes, sweet and warm as honey. She recognized that high, pale brow, a few stray curls escaped to fall across it in a manner that reminded her keenly of his wilder boyhood days. But everything about him had matured.

And there were lines between his eyebrows and at the corners of his mouth, lines she had never seen there before. Sorrow played harshly with even the most beautiful of faces.

The impulse to take his hand was almost more than she could bear. A foolish part of her thought perhaps he felt it too, that his hand moved toward hers.

She turned away abruptly, wrapping her arms about herself. Gerard pulled back a step.

"It was the Phantomwitch you saw," he said quietly. "In Fayline's body. Neither of us wants to believe it, but—"

"You know that's not true," Cerine said.

Gerard winced.

"You know as well as I do," she persisted. "Fayline would never let go. She was too strong for even a witch to oust. I know my sister. The Evanderians can say what they like. She's not gone."

Gerard didn't answer. She glanced up at him. His eyes were tightly shut, and she saw how the muscles in his jaw tightened as though he fought back words he dared not say. But when he looked at her at last, still without speaking, she saw hope in his face.

She knew then what she had known all along: He would never stop loving Fayline. No matter what he claimed, no matter what he tried to make himself believe, he would never see anyone else.

Hastily, Cerine shoved these thoughts to the back of her mind. "What became of the venatrix?" she asked hastily. "Is she all right?"

Gerard shook his head. "She . . . is still alive. They're with her now, and I ought to go back. I don't know what will happen to her. I don't know if she'll even wake up." Gerard ran a hand down his face, pulling at the skin around his mouth. "I can't believe Fayline would hurt her, would hurt anyone! To see Ayleth like that, to think that

Fayline might be responsible . . ."

What could she say? No witch would ever look at her with such hatred as Cerine had seen simmering in her sister's eyes. Such hatred, such sorrow, such rage. Inren would not feel those things, and her shade would not care. Only Fayline would feel that bitter betrayal.

Cerine pressed a hand to her chest, as though she could ease the jolt of shame in her heart.

"You're tired," Gerard said, his voice concerned. "I'm sorry, I shouldn't keep you. You must rest while you can."

"Yes, Your Highness," Cerine murmured, and curtsied. A proper curtsy like a lady, not like a novice scribe. In this setting, in his presence, old habits began to reemerge.

Gerard turned to go, but paused after only a few paces and looked back. "Your letters stopped," he said.

Cerine swallowed hard. She couldn't speak.

"I . . ." His eyes were very large, illuminated by the candle. "I was sad not to hear from you. It's been . . . hard."

"I know," Cerine said. She cleared her throat. "I miss

her too."

"That's not what I—" His brows drew together, and he opened his mouth. She waited for whatever he might say. But he shook his head and turned away. "Good night, Cerine," he said, and left her alone in the passage.

The serving girl, Kella, materialized seemingly from nowhere. "My lady?" She motioned politely for Cerine to follow her. With a last glance at the prince's retreating back, Cerine adjusted her satchel and followed the girl to her new set of rooms. She was surprised, when she stepped through the door into her chambers, to find a fire already lit and someone sitting in a chair drawn up close to the flames.

Liselle stood, her face glowing in the warm firelight. "Cerine!"

With a little "Oh!" Cerine dropped her satchel and flew across the room to wrap her arms around the other young woman. "You're here! Father said he'd bring you, but I still can't believe you're here!"

"Of course I'm here," Liselle said, giving Cerine an extra squeeze before she stepped back and gazed into her face. "You're like my sister, Cerine. You always have been."

"I know." Cerine shook her head, disbelieving. "But you were Fayline's lady, and I thought . . . I thought it might be—"

"You thought it might be too painful for me to serve you like I served her?" Liselle smiled again, that bright, warm smile Cerine knew so well. Except now there was a trace of sorrow and even solemnity in it. "Cerine, dearest, there is nowhere I would rather be than by your side."

Embarrassed but pleased, Cerine tucked her chin, lowering her eyes. "I . . . I was so sorry to hear about your husband," she said quietly.

"Don't be." Liselle tossed her head and laughed. "He never really needed me anyway. And you certainly do, my poor little waif! Goddess love you, whatever have you done to your hair?"

Suddenly, all her exhaustion, all her sadness, all her disappointment and hurt and terror seemed to well up and spill over. With a little choking laugh that was more of a sob, Cerine bent her head onto Liselle's shoulder and wept. And her friend could do nothing but stand there and hold her, murmuring, "I know, dear. You love him, don't you? I know it hurts. I know, I know . . ."

CHAPTER 16

AYLETH FLED THROUGH THE PINE FOREST OF HER mind.

All around her the trees caught flame, black flame without light, hungry tongues of darkness devouring everything within reach, ravenous for more.

"*Laranta!*" she cried. Where was her shade? Hiding somewhere in the forest, vulnerable to this spreading inferno? "*Laranta, come to me!*"

No answer. Only the fire's roar.

And somewhere, far away, her physical body bled.

Ayleth felt it all, the cuts across her skin, the flow of blood, the weakness. But that reality was nothing compared to this. Her own mind had become a hell from which she could find no escape, and though she ran, the black flames were ever at her heels.

Hold her down.

Ayleth screamed, forcing her heart to strive harder, her legs to pump faster. In another world entirely, her limbs thrashed beyond her control, but she didn't care. The flames gained on her. She couldn't escape them, not trapped here inside her own head. But if she could force herself to wake up . . .

I've got you. I've got you, Venatrix. Breathe, breathe.

Smoke filled her lungs, only it wasn't smoke, she realized, but madness, pure madness. If she breathed it in, she would be lost forever, driven to raging insanity. She would never escape this place. Death itself would not liberate her, for her soul would remain trapped here.

She had to wake up.

Her feet stumbled. She fell to her knees. The flames nearly caught her, biting at her back, burning her skin so that it bubbled with heat, and the smoke of madness rolled in over her head. Terror and pain shot through her, a bolt of pure power, and she sprang up and plunged forward, breaking through the smoke to a small space of clarity.

Ahead, ahead, there was a break in the trees. If she could reach it, she could wake up; then she would escape this torment.

Give her the dose, Everild. If she wakes up now, she'll ruin the work. Give her the sòm, *make her sleep.*

"NO!" Ayleth screamed. Somewhere far away she felt her own mouth open, felt her own throat constrict. She latched onto those sensations, willing her physical body to respond. "*No, no, no! Don't make me sleep! Don't leave me here! Let me out, let me out!*"

She tried to fight, tried to regain control of her body. But it was in that other world, that waking world. And she was here, surrounded by flames. She couldn't fight whoever grabbed her mouth and held her jaw open. She couldn't spit back the burning bitterness of the liquid as it trickled down her throat.

No way out. No escape from the burning. Except . . .

The gorge opened suddenly and horribly before her. Her projected image skidded to a stop, hair flying, eyes wide. The flames roared behind her, consuming the forest, reaching for her with hungry, thrashing hands. She had mere moments before it would envelop her.

With a cry, Ayleth leapt. She plunged down into the gorge, down into the darkness, into the cavernous gully far below. Down where the fires raging through her mind could not reach her.

Thread upon thread upon thread of magic stretched from Fendrel to Ayleth and back again, a terrible cobweb shimmering with Anathema glare and humming with pulses of darkness. Of poison. More threads reached from Fendrel to the pig lying in a drugged heap on the floor, breathing heavily.

The magic Fendrel weaved was a grim sight. Terryn tried to observe it closely, tried to pay attention to his former master's skill. He had never before seen this particular working; he'd only heard stories. He ought to be fascinated, ought to be taking advantage of the opportunity to learn from a true master of the craft.

But Terryn couldn't bear it. He blinked out of shadow vision back to mortal sight and looked down at Ayleth. Her blood flowed red once more, which was a relief. No longer the black ooze which had bubbled up from her skin as Fendrel made his shallow cuts. Perhaps they hadn't started too late. Perhaps the poison could be purged out of her after all.

The door to the bedchamber opened and closed softly. Terryn, who stood at the head of the bed, glanced up to see Gerard slip into the room. The prince nodded silently, then took a place by the wall, alongside Everild. They all watched the Venator Dominus at his work.

Fendrel sat on the edge of the bed, one hand pressed against Ayleth's sternum at the point where all his long slits converged. His torso bled from the marks he'd carved on himself—marks made over the top of long-ago scars. He'd performed this procedure more times than Terryn could guess.

Around the dominus pulsed the crackling power of his shade, straining at the song-spell bindings.

The pig died. Terryn felt the shudder when its animal

soul burst from its poor, poisoned body. Blood clotted with shadow blight seeped from its mouth and eyes, and from the cuts Fendrel had carved in its body.

Was that it then? Was the job complete? Terryn watched his former master's face, willing Fendrel to open his eyes.

At long last, Fendrel released an exhausted sigh. He lifted his hand from Ayleth's chest and stood up from the bed. "It's done," he said.

Terryn swayed on his feet. Unsure of his balance, he caught hold of one of the bedposts. Feeling Gerard's gaze upon him, he again glanced the prince's way and met an encouraging smile. He couldn't smile in return.

"Is she safe now?" he asked instead, turning his attention back to Fendrel.

The Venator Dominus shrugged. "It's difficult to say." He wiped his hand down his face, smearing dark blood on his cheek and forehead. "If she wakes in the next few hours, she will live. If she doesn't . . ." His voice trailed off as he nearly lost his footing, his knees buckling. Everild stepped out of the shadows and caught him by the arm, but he shook her off. "My Vocos," he said.

"Give me my Vocos."

The venatrix nodded and fetched the pipes from among Fendrel's garments and supplies piled carefully in a corner of the room. Fendrel snapped the Vocos into position and played the Song of Suppression. His shade immediately responded, first lashing out angrily and then diving down inside him, fleeing the spell song. No need for iron spikes this time. The oppressive pulse of magic faded, leaving the air more breathable than it had been.

Fendrel finished the spell and sheathed his pipes, the hum of magic quivering in the air around him. Everild produced a clean rag, and the Venator Dominus set about wiping away the blood on his torso. His eye caught Terryn's, and he nodded at Ayleth.

Terryn sprang into action. There were no bandages at hand, so he used one of the blankets from the bed, dabbing at the blood smeared across Ayleth's chest, between her breasts, pooling at her navel. His fingers brushed bare flesh, and he pulled back sharply, his heart leaping into his mouth.

She would kill him. She would absolutely kill him if she knew—if she even guessed—he'd seen her so vulnerable. Naked. Weak. Helpless as a kitten. Not the proud, wolfish huntress he knew.

Yet there was something so real about this girl lying here before him. It was as though he'd been offered a glimpse of the deeper layer of truth beneath all her brusqueness, all her bravado. She was a huntress, yes, and a formidable one at that. But she was also a girl. A woman.

He applied the cloth again, gently dabbing at the dark stains marking her skin. Caught up in the task, he didn't hear Gerard's approach behind him, and he jerked when the prince touched his shoulder.

"I've sent for someone to tend her, Terryn. She needs a proper wash and bandages."

Terryn grunted, his brow constricting. Forcing his hands to be steady, he took the stained blanket and draped it across Ayleth to cover her nakedness. Then he stood and faced the others in the room just as the door opened to admit serving women with bandages and clean water.

Fendrel winced as he shrugged into his jerkin, his undershirt sticking to the cuts on his chest. His iron-hard eyes fixed on Terryn. "Come," he growled. "Our work isn't done tonight."

Terryn nodded. He didn't permit himself a last glance back at Ayleth, but fell into line behind Fendrel and Everild, Gerard just at his heels. They filed out into the hall, only to find Duke d'Aldreda waiting for them, candlelight from the wall sconce glittering in his one eye.

"I heard there was an attack." His lips stretched in a snarl. "Inren."

Fendrel grunted and beckoned. "We must set out at once. Where are d'Acelet and du Gy?"

"I sent them to prepare horses and gather our weapons, sir," Everild answered at once. Terryn should have given that order himself. A venatrix had been wounded in the field, and the shade was still at large. They must act at once . . . but he had been too distracted, not thinking straight, not thinking like a venator.

Fendrel hastened down the passage toward the stairs, trailing the others behind him. Everild put on speed, inquiring, "Sir, do we know where we are going? Do we have any idea where the venatrix encountered this shade-taken?"

"The Tower of Blood and Eyes." It was Gerard who spoke.

Fendrel paused at the stair landing and looked back up at the prince, his brow stern and questioning.

Gerard hurried to explain. "Lady Cerine was present. She saw the battle between Ayleth and the witch. It happened in the ruins of Cró Ular, and Cerine believes she saw the anchor itself."

Duke d'Aldreda shook his head and scoffed. "Cerine wouldn't know one of the anchors."

Gerard fixed his gaze on the duke, his eyes like two knives. "She described it as a diamond filled with living darkness." He raised a brow. "Sound familiar?"

The duke opened his mouth to respond, but Fendrel shook his head and continued down the stairs. "Once an anchor has been planted," he said, "the witch can step in and out of this world anywhere within a mile radius."

"So that's how the venatrix breathed in so much *oblivis*," Everild said, realization dawning. "The Phantomwitch must have caught hold of her and . . ."

And Inren had dragged her into the Haunts. Held her there for some time. Gasping in terror, drawing pure madness, pure evil into her body. Terryn shuddered.

But it was curious . . . Fendrel had told Terryn stories about the Witch Wars and battles with Dread Odile's lieutenants, including the Phantomwitch. Inren had slaughtered many venators over the years by dragging them physically into the Haunts and leaving them there. If she brought them back out, it was only after they'd breathed in so much *oblivis* that their bodies were blackened from the inside out, beyond recognition.

Why had she not done the same to Ayleth?

"We must make for the ruins." Fendrel tossed the words back over his shoulder.

"I'm going with you," Gerard put in.

At this, Fendrel paused and glared round at his nephew. "No. It's too dangerous. I'm leaving d'Acelet and du Gy behind to stand guard over Dunloch, and you should remain here under their watch."

"I'm as safe with the Black Hood of Perrinion as I am with anyone," Gerard replied. "And I may be able to help."

For a moment, Fendrel looked as though he would argue. Then he shrugged and, without another word, continued out the door.

D'Acelet and du Gy met them in the front hall, offering the weapons and equipment they had gathered for the hunt. Terryn, seeing his own gear in the mix, armed himself with scorpiona and poisons. Fendrel had carried a full supply of Evanescer poison with him from Castra Breçar, and he distributed the darts among the venators, including d'Acelet and du Gy. D'Aldreda's man assisted the duke out of his fine banquet garments and into a hunting jacket, equally fine but sturdier. Gerard called to a servant to bring him his sword.

"In all likelihood," Fendrel said, checking the triggering mechanism on his scorpiona with a practiced hand, "the witch removed the anchor and relocated hours ago. But an activated anchor leaves a strong trail of magic in its wake. If she carried it with her, we should be able to track her down."

"And we'll end her," d'Aldreda said with a bitter smile. He strapped a sword to his belt and took a crossbow from his servant. "I'm ready."

Armed for the hunt, they moved to the door. But Terryn hung back a moment, catching Gerard by the shoulder. "Are you certain you want to be along for this hunt?"

Gerard met his gaze. "I will be there. For the end."

Horses were brought round from the stables, and in the blue gloom of impending dawn, the party prepared to mount up. Terryn was just putting boot to stirrup when he heard Cerine's voice call out from behind him. He turned and saw the lady, still wearing her novitiate robes, descend the porch steps. Lady Liselle followed, wrapped in a long fur-lined cloak over a soft white shift, her hair loose about her shoulders. Her eyes were puffy, as though she was not yet fully awake, but Cerine's face was alert with apprehension.

"I saw the horses from my window," she said, approaching the prince, who stood holding the reins of his black stallion. "Are you setting out for Cró Ular?"

Gerard nodded, opened his mouth, then seemed to think better of whatever he was going to say. He gave his head a quick shake and didn't meet her gaze. "We all must do what we can."

Her hands gripped her upper arms, squeezing hard. "Please . . ." she began, but broke off when her father stepped suddenly to her side. She glanced up at the duke, then down again. "Be safe," she finished softly.

"Stay inside until we return," d'Aldreda told her sternly. "The Dominus has left two of his best to guard you. You should be safe enough."

Cerine nodded silently. With no other word of farewell, the duke strode to his horse and mounted. Gerard lingered a moment longer before swinging into his saddle.

Movement at his elbow drew Terryn's attention away from this tableau, and he looked down into Lady Liselle's face. She looked strangely solemn, an unnatural expression for so merry and lighthearted a spirit.

"You take care of your prince now," she said, resting a hand on his arm. "And I'll watch over our soon-to-be princess. Deal?"

Terryn nodded and swallowed. Then, on impulse, he blurted, "Take care of yourself as well, my lady."

The smile that broke across her face was brighter than the rising sun. Terryn hastily ducked away from it and mounted his horse, unwilling to look at her again. Nevertheless, the warmth of her smile burned in his head even as he nudged Fleeta into position beside Gerard's horse.

Gerard gave Terryn a look, the ghost of a grin on his lips. "Did she give you a token to carry on the hunt? A silk handkerchief, perhaps?"

Terryn growled and pulled his red hood up over his head.

The hunting party set out from the courtyard, and Terryn fixed his attention on the road ahead. As the horses trotted around the circular drive, he refused to let his gaze slide off to one side. Refused to look up at a certain window in the east wing, behind which Venatrix di Ferosa lay drugged in her bed.

CHAPTER 17

AYLETH SCRAMBLED TO HER FEET.

She didn't bother to imagine clothes for herself. Not here in the world of her mind. She stood naked and small in this dark place, with only her long hair for covering.

Sheer walls rose on either side of her, cliffs of stone she could never hope to climb, not without Laranta's strength. But Laranta wasn't here. She was far away in the pine forest above. Even their soul tether was too slack for her presence to do Ayleth any good, so she walked along the gully alone. Step by step, placing each foot purpose-fully, she forged on through the darkness.

Ahead, a light pulsed.

Why did this feel so familiar?

The pulse grew stronger, and in it she heard the hum of a song spell. As she followed the light, she soon saw the spell itself, a delicate webbing of music placed over a hole in the ground. Ayleth stopped. She knew that song. She knew the signature of that spell better than she would know her own face in a glass.

This magic could only belong to Hollis.

And what lay on the other side of that web? Her memories . . . her lost memories . . .

As a savage cry tore from her spirit, Ayleth threw herself at the spell. Her imagined hands caught hold of the webbing, and she pulled, pulled, pulled with all the strength of her will. When this didn't work, when the song didn't falter, she shrieked again, clasped her hands together into a tight ball, and pounded the center of the web.

The song shuddered.

The walls of the cliff high above groaned, then

crumbled.

Ayleth looked up in alarm and flung her arms over her head just as a massive ton of rock crashed down on her from above.

Cerine stood in the cold, her hands folded deep into the long sleeves of her robe, the morning wind slicking tears from the corners of her eyes. She watched until the company was out of sight, beyond the bridge and through the gates. Only when they were gone did she turn to face the castle.

Liselle, standing a few steps above her on the porch, huddled into her cloak and smothered a yawn in her hand. Hastily she swallowed the yawn and offered a tired smile instead. "Come inside, dearest. It's much too cold out here." She put out a hand as Cerine climbed the stair, taking her by the elbow and pulling her through the door. "There's nothing you can do now," she said, her teeth chattering. "I know it's hard, but you must try to sleep."

"I can't sleep," Cerine whispered, letting Liselle lead her through the entry hall toward the stairs. "Not while they're out there. Not while they're . . . hunting . . ."

"There's nothing you can do," Liselle said gently. "We've all known for years now that Fayline is gone. Let them find her. Let them put her to rest. You must move on with your life, Cerine. We all do."

There was no use in protesting. Cerine climbed the stairs beside Liselle, making for the west wing. At the landing she cast a glance back toward the east wing, where she believed they were keeping the poor poisoned venatrix. Was anyone tending the young woman? Or had they left her alone with her wounds?

Cerine was half inclined to find out for herself, but before she could take a step in that direction, Liselle firmly led her on toward her own rooms. For the moment at least, Cerine lacked the energy to protest.

At her door, Liselle reached for the latch, but Cerine placed her hand over the top of her friend's. "No, no. You've done enough for me, and you're exhausted. Go sleep. I'll be fine for a few hours."

"Are you sure?" Liselle gave her a narrow-eyed look. "It's not healthy to weep alone, you know. Much better you dampen my shoulder again than make your pillow all waterlogged."

Cerine tossed her head, half smiling despite herself. "I've cried enough to last me a week, Liselle, I swear! I'm going to sleep, and you should as well. Come find me in a few hours if it'll make you feel better."

Stifling yet another yawn, Liselle nodded and, with a last squeeze of Cerine's fingers, floated away down the hall and around a corner to her own room. Cerine waited till she had gone before stepping through the door.

It was so strange, an entire room to herself! Standing just on the threshold of the chamber, still wearing her travel-stained robes, Cerine felt wholly out of place. This was a room fit for a princess, with an absolutely enormous canopied bed, a bureau painted with stylized roses and hummingbirds, heavy brocade curtains to ward off the chill trying to creep through the diamond-paned windows, and a hand-knotted Suurian rug, thick and plush, almost too beautiful to walk on. Elegant white moldings framed the hearth, and a fire blazed behind a scrolled screen.

She would certainly never be able to rest here. Not without Ducette snoring in the next bed over, their two cots crammed in a room with three other young novices. But the Siveline Sisters had been given quarters in the servants' house, a separate building from the main keep of Dunloch. Cerine dared not seek them out.

She was a princess now. Or as good as one.

With a sigh, she paced to her window and pulled back the curtain. The shining waters of the Holy Lake nearly dazzled her vision. She looked beyond it across rolling landscape, east, toward the shadow on the horizon which she knew to be the Witchwood. Her sister's prison for the past four years.

What horrors had Fayline experienced in that place? Imprisoned in her own body, at the mercy of a witch.

Pulling back from the window, Cerine began pacing the room. Her eyes burned with fatigue, but her mind was such a chaotic storm, she dreaded trying to lie down or close her eyes. After the twenty-second lap of her room, she clenched her fists and muttered, "Get ahold of yourself. You've got to sleep, or you'll be no good to anyone."

Turning a resolute face toward its dainty luxury, she marched to the bed. Her satchel lay beside one of the snowy pillows, looking very dirty and worn. Without bothering to change or even shed her outer garments, Cerine climbed into the bed, hugged the satchel close to her chest, and sank into the soft pillows. Her eyes closed.

And saw Fayline's face in the darkness. Her tortured face, one-eyed, covered in growths. Mad with pain, with rage. With betrayal.

Cerine rolled onto her back to stare at the decorative canopy overhead. Her heart pounded in her throat, and she couldn't make her lungs draw a full breath.

This was no good. She couldn't just lie here waiting for the hunters to return, waiting for them to bring Fayline's broken body draped across one of their horses. No, no . . .

"No!" she growled and sat up, clutching the satchel hard enough that she felt the contours of the book pressing through the leather. Her legs swung over the edge of the bed, and her feet hastily slipped back into her sandals.

She would follow her first impulse. She would find the poor venatrix and see if she needed anything. It was the least she could do.

Utter darkness surrounded her, crushed her.

For some while, Ayleth could neither feel nor perceive anything but darkness and weight. Eventually, however, her alertness returned. Enough for her to begin questioning whether she was dead or not. Ultimately, she decided she was probably still alive. If she'd died, her soul would have flown to the Haunts. This current situation was bad, but it didn't seem quite bad enough to be the Haunts.

Still, she couldn't move, couldn't even feel her arms and legs. No, wait . . .

Memory clarified. This was the realm of her mind. She didn't *have* limbs here unless she made the effort to envision them. It was her mind being crushed, not her physical body. Which was not a terribly comforting thought.

Pulling herself together a little bit more, she tentatively called out in the darkness. "*Laranta?*"

No answer.

Ayleth felt around in her consciousness until she

found the soul tether connecting her to her shade. It was flaccid, unresponsive, but still whole. Sliding her awareness along this tether as far as she could go, she felt Laranta's presence. Still in her mind, but separated from Ayleth as though by a dense, impenetrable curtain.

Ayleth slid back down the soul tether, back to where her center of being rested under that vast weight. The *sòm*, she thought. The drug they had dosed her with to make her sleep, despite all her protests. The main use of this concoction brewed up by Evanderian phasmators was to suppress shades while their host souls lay unconscious. It was intended for protection.

But it also meant that, for now at least, Ayleth was alone in this darkness. She'd have to find her own way out.

With an effort she pulled her self-perception back into a physical shape. As soon as she'd done it, she wished she hadn't. The crushing seemed much worse now, and panic threatened to take hold. Slowly, carefully, she tested how the weight and pressure on top of her shifted as she slid first an arm, then a foot. Rocks moved, groaned, grated. At one moment the weight on her chest increased, and she thought for certain she was about to be crushed to oblivion.

One more fractional shift, and the weight rolled away. She was able to get her arms in place, to brace them against the stone directly over her chest and head. She pushed, pushed, *pushed*. More growling of rock against rock, distant crashes and clatters. She applied more power, reminding herself with every strain that this was not the physical world, that here she was not bound by physical laws. This was her own mind. She was in control here.

The tendons in her neck strained, both here and in the physical world. She opened her mouth and roared, putting everything she had into one last great push. A huge rock shifted overhead, rolled, fell . . . and all the weight above her fell away. She lay free, staring up and up at a distant gray sky.

"*A counter-protection,*" she whispered. "*Hollis laced her spell with a counter-protection, triggered when I tried to break through.*"

The fact that she was still alive was a miracle.

Ayleth stood, brushing dirt and gravel off her

shoulders, and picked her way down the pile of rubble. She was still in the deep gully, far below her pine forest. The glow of Apparition magic caught her eye.

The spell-webbing remained in place, apparently unharmed by her attempted assault. It was partially buried, but Ayleth required no more than a few moments to unearth it again. She stood above the hole, trying to peer between the shimmering threads of magic, trying to glimpse what lay beyond.

But Hollis's spell was impenetrable.

"*Haunts damn*," Ayleth whispered, and sank back onto her heels. Pressing her palms against her eyes, she drew a long breath.

Suddenly, her soul tether jerked, snapping tight along its length. It pulled so hard, so fast, that it yanked her up onto her feet and then over onto her face. She gasped. The tether twanged like a plucked bowstring, and in those reverberations, carried even through the suppressions of the drug, came a voice.

Mistress! Mistress! Danger! Shade!

"There you are! What in the Goddess's name are you doing in here, Cerine?"

Startled, Cerine looked up from her folded hands. Liselle stood framed in the doorway of the venatrix's sickroom, her eyes very wide and uneasy as she peered into the shadowy chamber.

"Oh. You found me," Cerine said and tried to smile. "Come in, if you like. She's asleep. I think she's been drugged."

"Drugged? Well, I suppose in that case . . ." Liselle warily entered the room, her silk skirts rustling softly with each step. The gown she wore was every bit as sumptuous as the pink confection the duke had shipped to Siveline Temple for Cerine to wear. Only on Liselle's graceful, shapely figure, the flounces and jewels and pleats somehow made sense. She lifted the edge of her petticoats delicately and wrinkled her nose. "Does it smell like blood in here?"

Cerine shrugged and dropped her hands into her lap. She sat in a chair near the head of the venatrix's sickbed. The room was dark with the heavy curtains drawn, presumably so the sleeping venatrix could rest. Very little light crept through, just enough to emphasize the greenish tinge to the poor woman's skin. Blood-soaked bandages wrapped around her torso, and a blanket concealed her lower half. She hadn't received those gory wounds during the fight in the ruins last night. Cerine could only guess what had happened to the unfortunate huntress since then.

Liselle found another chair and took a seat near the foot of the bed. From this angle, round-eyed, she studied the venatrix, then finally shuddered and pulled her gaze away, looking at Cerine instead. "She's rather pretty, don't you think? Not what one would expect in an Evanderian." She laughed uncomfortably. "One thinks of venatrices more along the lines of that gruesome Everild. I don't know that I'd trust a girl like this to protect me against shade-taken."

Memories of the fight she'd seen flashed through Cerine's mind. The young venatrix had not lasted long against Fayline.

But then again, who could truly fight powers like those possessing her sister?

"Is this the girl who saved you last night?" Liselle

persisted. "Is that why you're in here saying prayers for her?"

"Yes," Cerine nodded. "If not for her, I . . . well . . . It seemed the least I could do. And I couldn't sleep."

"Not at all?" Liselle tilted her head and *tsked* gently. "Cerine, dearest. Talk to me."

"I . . ." Cerine sighed and rubbed a hand down her face. One foot moved surreptitiously to touch the satchel beside her chair. She couldn't bear to leave it and its precious contents alone in her room. "What is there to say?"

Liselle pulled her chair closer, then reached across the space between them and gripped Cerine's hand. "They're doing the best they can for her," she said, meaning Fayline. "You know that, don't you? Those Evanderians must put an end to this."

"I know," Cerine whispered. And yet . . . did she? She had stared into her sister's face just last night, and she'd seen Fayline there. Furious, shade-mad, but . . . present.

And if Fayline's soul was yet intact, was it not theoretically possible to bring that soul back into ascendancy?

294

Liselle gave Cerine's hand another squeeze before sitting back in her chair. She fiddled with a pendant she wore around her neck, her gaze returning to the face of the sleeping venatrix. Her brows drew together, and her lips pursed. "She must be Venator Terryn's partner, don't you think? I wonder how long they've known each other. I wonder . . ."

She gave herself a little shake and looked away again, smiling across at Cerine. Then the smile morphed into a curious expression, and she tilted her head to one side. "What's that in your satchel, Cerine?"

"What? This?" Surprised, Cerine pushed the sack a little further behind her chair, hiding it with the fold of her robe. "Nothing. Just some books and papers."

"Oh?" Liselle frowned. "Something is . . . glowing."

"What?" Cerine looked down, brushing her robe aside. To her surprise, Liselle was right. Something in the satchel was indeed glowing a strange hue for which she had no name, but which blazed right through the thick leather. With a gasp of surprise, Cerine caught up the satchel and pushed open the flap, plunging her hand down inside.

Her fingers closed around a small, faceted orb.

She knew what it was even before she pulled it out, opened her hand, and saw a black diamond about the size of an eyeball. Even before she peered through its facets and saw whirling, living darkness deep in its center, pulsing with strange light that was more like anti-light.

The blood drained from her face. "It's an anchor," she breathed.

"What? Cerine, you're frightening me." Rising, Liselle leaned in for a closer look at the object on her friend's palm. "That looks like a gem. Why does it glow like that? Or *is* it glowing? I don't . . . I don't understand—"

Cerine jumped up so fast, her chair toppled over. "It's a curse anchor!" she cried. "Father told me about them. This is . . . this is what the Phantomwitch uses to . . . to . . . She must have planted it when she took my satchel!"

"Cerine." Liselle put out a hand. "You look sick. What is wrong? I don't know what you're talking about. What anchor? What—? Where are you going?"

Her words fell on deaf ears. Cerine was already out the door, calling back over her shoulder, "We've got to take this to the venators! Maybe they can still help! Maybe there's still time."

She scarcely heard Liselle's cries behind her as she raced from the sick venatrix's room and along the passage, her sandals slapping on the stone floor. Dominus du Glaive had left two of his lieutenants behind to guard Dunloch. Where were they? Outside, most likely, patrolling the perimeter. She must find them, must tell them.

In her haste, she almost fell down the grand front stairs. Servants moved in her peripheral vision, some of them calling out to her, offering assistance. She ignored them even as she ignored Liselle's voice at her heels. She threw herself at the huge front door, hauled it open, and stepped out into the blazing afternoon light, her breath nearly taken by a blast of cold wind.

For an instant, she stood sun-dazzled, unable to see or think. Then, her eyes slowly adjusting, she saw something. Off to her left, where the circular drive looped near the east wing of the keep.

A body.

"Noooo!" Her knees weak, Cerine slipped and

stumbled down the porch steps. By the time she reached the drive, she was running again. Within moments, she dropped to her knees beside the body. A man, lying flat on his stomach, his red hood covering his head. Her trembling fingers reached out, grasped the edge of the hood, and drew it back.

Cerine screamed and dropped the hood. The man's face was covered in spider-web patches of darkness, stretched beneath his pale skin.

"Goddess above!"

At the sound of Liselle's panting and footsteps behind her, Cerine pushed herself upright, her limbs shaking so hard, she feared she would collapse into herself with terror. She turned to face her friend, who had stopped several paces away, both hands pressed over her mouth.

"Is he dead?" Liselle gasped through her fingers.

Cerine nodded. She looked down at the stone clutched so tight in her hand that it cut into her skin. The darkness inside pulsed with energy.

The anchor was active.

"She's here," Cerine whispered. "She's already here."

CHAPTER 18

PUSHING UP ON HER ELBOWS AND TURNING HER EYES in the direction the soul tether pulled, Ayleth studied the pile of fallen stone further up the gorge. Through the film of clouds, she tried to catch a glimpse of Laranta, but the powerful *sòm* drug obscured her shade from view.

Still, Laranta's voice reverberated along the soul tether: *Shade! Shade! Mistress! Shade!*

There must be a shade-taken. Close. In the physical world. The physical world where her body lay unconscious. If Laranta could smell it even through the drug's suppression, it had to be powerful indeed.

In the waking world, where was her body? She couldn't remember. Thinking back as far as she could, she found some confused images of ruins . . . of a girl with shorn hair . . . of darkness, of *oblivis* . . . Beyond that, she wasn't sure.

It didn't matter. Laranta's voice grew more desperate with each yelped word. Whatever this shade-taken was and wherever Ayleth's body was, she and her shade were in danger.

She couldn't lie there on her face and do nothing.

"*I'll be back*," she growled, and scrambled to her feet, casting a regretful glance back at the memory spell. Goddess grant she would not forget it when she woke up! She threw herself at the pile of rubble and began to climb.

Rocks heaved and slipped, and the whole precarious mound shifted dangerously beneath her hands and feet. Her projected image was weak. Her limbs trembled, and her long, loose hair fell in her face. She pushed on, gnashing her teeth so hard, she could feel her physical jaw aching somewhere far away in the physical world.

At last she stood at the top of the pile, her bare feet planted on a broad stone that tilted if she shifted even slightly the wrong direction. Other stones beneath her groaned, strained. Any moment now, an avalanche would begin, and she'd be caught and crushed as it dragged her back down.

Hardly daring to breathe, she looked up at that distant gray sky. Up at the sheer gorge walls. Maybe five feet overhead, a little pine tree gripped the wall, growing at a strange angle, its roots exposed as they plunged into stone.

Five feet. If she had Laranta's strength in her, the leap would be nothing. But . . .

"*One shot.*" She drew a steadying breath, the words slipping out as she exhaled. "*You've got one shot at this.*"

She widened her stance, muscles tensing both in her projected form and far off where her body lay unconscious and helpless.

Mistress! Shade! Laranta howled.

"*I'm coming,*" Ayleth growled.

She leaped.

And the rubble pile gave way, crashing and grinding

beneath her.

Clutching Liselle's hand, Cerine ran up the porch steps, back into the keep. It didn't matter, she knew. No walls, no matter how tall or thick, could keep out the Phantomwitch.

But she couldn't just stand and wait for death to come.

"Where's the Red Hood?" she shouted at the first servant who caught her eye.

The wide-eyed boy in a courier's uniform stared at her, reading the horror in her face and mirroring it back at her. "Uh, he's . . . he's out the back way, round the embankment walk," he stammered, pointing through the keep itself.

"Take me," Cerine demanded. She realized she was still gripping Liselle and let her go, saying breathlessly, "Go to the sisters! Hide in the chapel and tell them to beg the Goddess's aid!"

"What? No." Liselle shook her head fiercely, golden curls flying. "I'm not leaving you, Cerine. I promised I'd look after you."

Innumerable protests mounded on Cerine's tongue. There was no time for any of them. She turned to the boy and ordered, "Take me to the Red Hood. Hurry!" and set off through the castle after him at a run, leaving Liselle to trail behind them in her rustling silk skirts. Familiar with all the byways of Dunloch, the boy led her swiftly through to a back door and flung it open.

Cerine stepped outside, blinking in the sudden glare. She saw the venator standing on the stone walkway above the steep embankment. Having forgotten his name, she cupped her hands around her mouth and shouted, "Red Hood!"

The man turned. He saw her. His head tipped questioningly to one side.

A burst of darkness exploded in the air behind him.

"*No!*" Cerine screamed.

The witch's arms wrapped around the Evanderian's neck and shoulders, her long fingernails gouging into his skin like knives. In a second flash they both vanished, leaving nothing but a coiling patch of rotten air and magic in their wake.

Liselle grabbed Cerine's arm, her fingers pinching to

the bone, and gasped, "Was that Fayline?"

Cerine didn't answer. She felt as though she would never move again, never draw another breath. Her gaze dropped to the stone still clutched in her hand. The diamond seemed to look back at her, a gleaming devil's eye.

With a wordless cry, Cerine dashed toward that stone walkway, toward that embankment. She drew back her arm to fling that stone over the walkway, out into the water. With all the force of her arm she threw it, sending the anchor in a high arc through the air.

Another black flash. A hand reached out of nowhere, caught the stone just as it began its downward descent, and Fayline—or that which possessed Fayline—tumbled to the ground and rolled up into a tight ball, clutching the anchor close to her emaciated chest. She unfolded herself and stood upright.

"That was foolish, sister mine," she said, rolling the stone in her long, slender fingers. "And it would have done you little good."

It was Fayline's voice, speaking with Fayline's mouth.

Cerine took a step back, her hands up in front of her.

Fayline stalked toward her, the rags of that once-glorious wedding gown fluttering about her long bare legs. Her hair streamed down her back, red as fire in the sunlight. But darkness pulsed under her skin, in the corners of her one good eye, and spilled out between her sharp teeth when she smiled.

"Did you really think I'd simply stand back and let you take my place?" she said. "Did you think I'd let you steal Gerard from me? I know you always fancied him, Cerine. But to stoop so low! And so soon after my . . . tragic demise."

Cerine fell to her knees, her quivering hands pressed together as though in prayer. She gaped, open-mouthed, at the monstrous thing wearing Fayline's body, speaking Fayline's pain, playing with Fayline's emotions.

"What?" The shade-taken loomed closer, her eye blazing with malignant magic. "No protests, no excuses? Surely you've got something you want to say to your own dear sister!"

"*You* are not my sister," Cerine breathed. She shook her head. "I won't speak to you . . . only to Fayline."

The witch's face twisted into a hideous snarl, and the

darkness crawling beneath her skin surged and deepened. Then she blinked. For an instant, the magic faded, the strange shadow-light dimmed, like clouds parting to reveal the blue sky of her one good eye. Fayline's lips moved soundlessly, then managed to quaver, "Cerine?"

A horrible shriek followed, and the shade-taken girl threw back her head, tearing at her own face and hair with vicious hands. When she looked down at Cerine again, the shadow-light was back and blazing. With lightning speed, her hand lashed out and struck. Cerine fell with a yelp of pain, clutching her cheek and momentarily stunned.

"Leave her alone!"

A flurry of silk and golden hair rushed past Cerine's spinning vision. "Liselle, no!" she cried even as her lady flung herself at the shade-taken, ferocious as a mother bear defending her cub. For a few breaths, the witch was so surprised she could not react.

Then, with a clap of darkness, the thing inside Fayline stepped out of this world, leaving Liselle clawing at empty space. Liselle choked on the air of some strange reality and backed away, her head swiveling wildly from side to side.

She'd not taken two steps in retreat when the witch reemerged, this time behind her. Fayline's arm wrapped around her neck and squeezed. Liselle gagged, clawed, and tried to pull away, but she was helpless to escape such a grip.

Remembering the Red Hood she'd just seen whipped out of this world, never to return, Cerine sprang up and caught Fayline's arm. "Don't take her! Don't hurt her!" she screamed, her voice half-mad with terror. "I'll do what you want, I'll go where you tell me. I won't fight you, Fayline. But don't hurt her. She's your friend. She's your friend!"

Liselle's eyes rolled back in her head. Her face turned ghastly purple as she gagged for want of air. She went limp in the witch's arms. Fayline let her fall in a heap on the ground. She turned and snatched Cerine's wrist instead.

"Very well, little sister. I've let her live. Now you will come with me, and we will see which of us Gerard loves best, won't we?"

For a hideous moment, Cerine believed she would be

dragged out of this world and forced onto one of those dark paths the witch walked so easily. But instead, the thing inside her sister turned and hauled her back to the still-open door of the castle. The messenger boy waited there, too afraid either to flee or fight, frozen in huddled terror just inside the door.

Fayline caught him by the hair on top of his head, yanking his face up. "You, boy," she said. "Take the fastest horse and find your prince. Tell him it's time he came home to me, his Fayline. He has until sunset, or else"—her teeth flashed in a blade-like smile—"I'll kill everyone in this castle, starting with my dearest sister."

CHAPTER 19

BLOOD. SHE SMELLED BLOOD.

Ayleth threw one arm up over the lip of the gorge and, fingers scrabbling against stone, pulled herself up and out. Her projected image collapsed and lay shuddering, cut and scraped all over by a hundred small wounds.

She breathed, and her nostrils filled with the stench of blood. It was strong enough, sharp enough, to drive away the stink of smoldering trees from her burned forest.

With an effort of sheer will, she propped up on her

elbows and gazed into her pine forest. The trunks were blackened, their limbs skeletal and bare as far as her eye could see. But already she saw signs of new growth. She wouldn't die of *oblivis* poisoning, at least.

But where did this stink of blood come from?

As she inhaled again, she realized the stench was not part of her mental world. It came from the physical world, and she breathed it in through her mortal body. Consciousness crept back along the edges of her mind.

Grinding out curses through her teeth, Ayleth pushed up onto her feet and took a step. Then another. Then a third, and then she was running, running through her burned forest. Darkness closed in, and the pine forest faded to black . . . the black of the world just behind her eyes . . .

She was back in her physical body.

At first the relief was so great, Ayleth didn't notice the pain. She was awake, or close to it, and that was victory in and of itself.

But how heavy her eyelids were! She tried to open

them, but gummy residue sealed them shut. Her torso burned from multiple cuts, and she felt the weird pressure of bandages across her breasts, around her stomach. Her fingers twitched, and she became aware of soft fibers. A blanket?

With an effort of will, Ayleth wrenched her eyes open, her gummed eyelashes parting unwillingly. An embroidered canopy arched over her head. For an instant, the creatures stitched in colored threads seemed to dance and spin before her vision. But they settled down into their proper shapes—an ugly depiction of a lion hunt, complete with bug-eyed huntsmen and a most scraggly lion. Hardly a welcome sight, but Ayleth focused on it as her other senses gradually came back under her control.

A scream echoed from somewhere far away. Ayleth drew a deep breath, every muscle in her body tensing. Another scream, and another followed the first. Far away, but not too far. Multiple voices. Terrified. Wailing.

She had to move. She had to act.

"*Laranta?*"

Her wolf shade shifted inside her head, but the *sòm* held her at bay. Laranta's powers were inaccessible.

Whatever was out there, Ayleth would have to deal with it alone.

Summoning what she could of her limited strength, Ayleth heaved herself upright. The world spun, but she refused to collapse back into her pillow. Her fingers clenched the blanket while more screams resounded through the thick walls and door. She tried to block them out, to concentrate on the needs of the moment.

Where was she? Dunloch. She was in Dunloch; she must be. The furnishings in this room were too rich to be anywhere else. Now, the more pertinent question: Where were her clothes? Currently she wore nothing except the bandages wrapped around her torso, and those were bloodstained, the source of the stench she'd followed up from her dream.

Across the room she spied a shift, but no trousers, no jerkin, no—

Another scream. She couldn't just sit here, clothes or no clothes.

Grinding her teeth, she flung back the blankets, somewhat startled by the sight of her own naked limbs. She climbed shakily to her feet, catching hold of a bedpost to steady herself. Tottering like an infant, she crossed the room and snatched up the shift, dragging it painfully over her head.

The screams faded then stopped. Was she too late? A distant murmur still reached her ears, and she had to hope that, whatever was taking place beyond her doors, she'd still be in time to help.

But she didn't have Laranta. And she had no weapons.

Pushing lank hair out of her face, Ayleth staggered to the door, cracked it open, and peered into the hall beyond. Slashes of afternoon light poured through windows, but the atmosphere was strangely gloomy. Even without Laranta's senses to guide her, Ayleth felt the oppression of shade presence near. A taste of poison lingered on her tongue.

There was no one in sight, and the only sounds she discerned came from a distance. Creeping on bare feet, Ayleth slipped into the passage and made her way silently along the corridor, keeping to the shadows. The murmur of voices increased as she went, whimpers and moans and prayers.

Ahead, at the end of the hall, she spied the open

guardrail overlooking the keep's front entrance. Using the wall for support, Ayleth slid carefully as far as she dared, and peered out through that railing, down into the huge hall below.

A cluster of Siveline nuns had gathered in a circle, kneeling in prayer. Outside their circle grouped the household: the chamberlain, the household guards, Chancellor Yves . . . everyone, even the scullery maids and the stable boys. All gathered together, crouched or kneeling, arms around each other.

One face stood out as familiar, though at first Ayleth couldn't place it. Dainty, pale, shorn-headed, and big-eyed. Oh, yes! The novice. The girl she'd met in the ruins of Cró Ular. Why were she and the Siveline Sisters here at Dunloch?

No sign of Gerard, Ayleth noted. Nor of Terryn. She recognized some of the guardsmen, but they were unarmed, all seated quietly with their hands behind their backs. Bound, Ayleth realized.

Who could have done this to them? Who could take the entire household of Dunloch captive?

A waft of darkness drew Ayleth's eye.

The witch strode through the center of the cringing throng, dragging shadows in her wake. Her long red hair flowed down her back, and her hands reached out to touch the heads and faces of those she passed, caressing them gently so that they whimpered and wept. She smiled, and her teeth flashed like fangs.

Ayleth drew back into the hall. Her heart hammered, and her already-weak limbs shook violently. Inren. She mouthed the name without sound.

Shoving her hand in her mouth, she bit down hard on the soft skin between forefinger and thumb, forcing a scream back down. Her mind clamored frantically: What could she do? What could she do? Think, think, *think*.

The witch could move impossibly fast, vanishing and reappearing in the blink of an eye. And if she caught hold of Ayleth again, she would drag her right back into that horror of darkness. Into the Haunts.

If she could find her weapons, perhaps she could take a shot with the Gentle Death? She carried no Evanescer poison, so paralysis was out of the question. But if she could shoot her with the Gentle Death, aim over the railing and take her down before the witch realized what was happening, she might be able to win this day. But where were her weapons?

Trembling violently, Ayleth slid back along the wall. With every breath, she sought to break through the haze of *sòm* keeping her from Laranta. The barrier remained firmly in place. She slipped back into her room, pushing the door closed but not shutting it all the way for fear the sound might catch the witch's ear. Her vision blurred with dizziness as she surveyed the room yet again, hoping for some sign of her weapons that she'd missed before.

Nothing.

"Think, Ayleth," she whispered, grabbing her hair above each ear and pulling, as though she could tug her drug-fogged brain into order. "You've got to arm yourself."

There was no way to take down a witch without weapons. She would have to escape, travel to Milisendis and come back. The idea was hateful to her. How could she leave these poor souls alone with that monster? But she couldn't help them without her poisons.

Blood pounding in her ears, she moved to the window, half-formed plans for escape racing through her brain. These all crashed to a halt the instant she looked out through the glass.

A dead man lay on the ground below. A dead man wearing a red hood.

"Terryn," she breathed.

The next instant, she'd thrown the window open. All caution forgotten, she swung her bare legs out over the casement, her toes finding crevices in the stone wall. Ivy grew thickly, and she used it for support, never fully trusting it to hold her weight. She half slid, half fell down the side of the castle, using window ledges and moldings where she could until she landed hard on the ground and collapsed to her knees. White pebbles cut into her skin, but she didn't care. At least the *sòm* dulled the pain of the injuries to her torso, even if it couldn't stop the wounds from opening and bleeding into her already-stained bandages.

Scrambling up, she ran and fell and ran again before collapsing beside the body of the dead man. With a heave, she rolled him over. The man's face was twisted almost beyond recognition, his skin blackened with curse-poison from the inside out, the whites of his eyes dark, and the blood trailing from the corner of his mouth foul with shadow blight.

But he wasn't Terryn.

Relief washed over Ayleth so profoundly, she sank back onto her heels, one hand still resting on the stranger's chest. Not Terryn. Not Terryn. *Breathe, breathe . . .*

Her fingers curled into fists. Relief passed, replaced by rage. This man, whoever he might be, was a member of her Order, and he'd been slaughtered by the witch inside. Ayleth knew what that death was like, the horror, the pain; she'd come so close to experiencing it herself. And worse still, the man's soul was lost. With no other venator on hand to separate his soul from that of his shade at the point of death, he must surely have been dragged with it into the Haunts. Doomed and damned.

The witch had to die.

All too aware that she was within sight of the front entrance, that if the witch chose to look through the front door, she would be seen, Ayleth yanked the quiver strap over the dead man's head and slung it across her shoulder. To her surprise, the man only carried two poisons with him—the Gentle Death, fletched in black feathers, and another fletched in white. None of the darts she carried had white fletching. What poison was this? Could this man have been armed with Evanescer to take down Inren di Karel?

Ayleth knew it was so. Grinning fiercely, she unstrapped the scorpiona from the venator's arm and hurriedly laced it to her own. It wasn't a perfect fit, but she could make it work. She also took his belt, hung with the Vocos and Detrudos pipes, and looped it around her waist, notching it as tight as it would go.

Feeling stronger now that she was armed, she staggered back to the wall beneath her open window with a plan forming in her mind. She would climb back up, then creep down the hall again to the railing overlooking the entrance. She would take the shot from above and kill the witch with a single dart.

Then she would use her Detrudos and drive whatever souls she found into the Haunts where they belonged.

CHAPTER 20

TERRYN AND GERARD LED THE WAY ACROSS WODECHRAN, taking the road to the southern fringe forests.

Fendrel watched them closely as he followed a few lengths behind. They rode beside one another, a matched set in their way. Terryn was taller and lankier than the prince, his hair and skin darker, his face sterner. Even as Fendrel himself had always been taller and sterner than his own brother.

It was the will of the Goddess that the older brother, a

tainted soul, should stand guard over the younger, should set him upon his throne. Were the sacred words not spoken in the *Seion-Ebathe,* the prophecy of old, translated by Saint Evander himself?

"Brother with brother, one shade-taken and one untaken, will stand together, establishing a new kingdom."

This holy text was the compass which had guided every aspect of Fendrel's life for as long as he could remember. Somehow, from the moment he'd first encountered those sacred words, he'd always known they were meant for him.

His was the tainted soul. And his brother, Guardin, was the pure and chosen king.

But prophecies didn't fulfill themselves. The will of the Goddess must be enacted by Her servants. Fendrel was willing to take action where necessary. It was he who had urged his brother into leading the revolt against the Witch Queen. It was he who had guided Guardin's every step of their long arduous journey to crown and kingdom and glory. It was he who had ensured that Guardin's sword cut Dread Odile's head from her body.

And it was he—Fendrel du Glaive, Venator Dominus,

Black Hood of the King—who saw to it that Dread Odile stayed dead.

But to have seen her face again . . .

Within the concealing folds of his hood, Fendrel shuddered. It was all a mistake. That girl lying on the bed back in Dunloch was not Dread Odile. She couldn't be. The resemblance was strange, uncanny even, but they were not exactly alike.

Not exactly . . . but too similar. Too similar for mere chance.

The small riding party left the main road at last, turning to follow the ruins of the old highway scarring the hilly landscape. Duke d'Aldreda rode on Fendrel's left, silent as stone. No doubt regretting the part he had played in this ongoing tragedy. Were it not for his foolish action, were it not for his decision to draw his sword and violently slaughter Inren di Karel when she knelt at his mercy, Fayline might even now be safe. If he could have suppressed his own need for vengeance, the Phantomwitch's soul would have spent the last twenty years and all of eternity in the torment of the Haunts where she belonged.

No good could come from chastising the duke for his error now. The four years since Fayline's possession had been punishment enough. One had only to look into Celestin d'Aldreda's single eye to see the ripples of regret running deep through his soul.

Cró Ular appeared below. Fendrel grimaced at the sight, drawing his horse up short. His shade-heightened awareness convulsed painfully at the assaulting sensations of old and sour curses. He'd never get used to it, no matter how many times he revisited this site.

But there was also deep satisfaction to be savored while gazing upon this vista. Here, they had won the first of their great victories. Here, he had led a host of two hundred powerful Evanderians to assault these blood-warded walls and overcome the defenses of Ylaire and Inren di Karel, slaughtering Dread Odile's servants and sending their damned souls on to oblivion. When the Evanderians' battle was complete, Guardin had marched in with his un-taken army, and they'd pulled Cró Ular apart.

Dread Odile had known then. Far away in her city, she'd trembled beneath that Eitr crown of hers. The prophecy would be fulfilled, and there was nothing she could do to prevent it.

Almost nothing . . .

"Dominus?" Terryn's voice broke through Fendrel's reverie, calling his attention back to the present. "Dominus, I recommend we leave our horses here and continue on foot."

Fendrel nodded and dismounted without a word. The others followed suit, and they made their way down the incline, creeping toward the broken walls. Fendrel cast his shade senses ahead, seeking traces of curse-anchor enchantment. To his surprise, he soon felt more than a trace; there was a definite throb of magic in the air, striking his mortal and immortal perceptions alike.

"The anchor," Terryn said, looking back at Fendrel, his eyes bright and cold. "I feel it."

Fendrel nodded. The Goddess's own luck was with them. The witch, for reasons he could not fathom, had left the anchor behind.

He signaled to Everild, who immediately veered off to the right, circling round the fallen stones of the wall. At a second signal, Terryn set off to the left, Gerard with him.

Fendrel motioned to d'Aldreda to stay at his side, and together they climbed over the broken gate and gazed into the courtyard.

D'Aldreda caught his breath. Fendrel glanced his way. It was here, at this battle, that the man who was now a duke had been liberated from his slavery. Most of the mortals serving under the witch sisters in Cró Ular had been slaughtered that day. Only a few had survived, favorite pets of Inren and Ylaire. Terryn had been one. D'Aldreda another.

The duke had not returned to Cró Ular in the twenty years since. Fendrel couldn't blame him.

"Celestin," he said, "do you need to retreat?"

The duke swallowed hard, then shook his head, his perfectly coifed hair falling slightly across his forehead. "No, Fendrel. I'm ready for this. Do we venture in?"

"Not yet." Fendrel slipped his Detrudos from its sheath. "First, we need to be certain that if the witch evanesces back to her anchor, she cannot escape."

He put the instrument to his lips and began to play the Song of Barriers, the same song he'd used to create the Great Barrier even now hemming in the Witchwood. This new barrier would be much less complicated, merely a circle with its circumference one mile from the anchor. Not a difficult task, especially with two trained venators to aid him.

As the spell song poured from his pipes and began forming its intricate enchantment in the air, Fendrel heard two other pipes begin to play as well, one on either side of him. Terryn and Everild understood his intention and wove their own spell songs to interlink with his. Soon Fendrel's shadow vision watched the shimmering fibers of his song binding with those other two variations, creating a powerful web of enchantment.

Inren di Karel could evanesce in. But she would never get out again.

Time seemed to stop as the Detrudos song played. When at last Fendrel finished, he couldn't tell if it had been moments or hours. D'Aldreda sat on a boulder, waiting with a warrior's patience, his stylish hunting coat oddly contrasting with his stern expression. "Are you done?" he asked shortly.

Fendrel didn't offer an answer, merely folded his Detrudos. Now he and his two fellow Evanderians must try to find a trace to follow.

While the duke and the prince waited, the three venators marched around the periphery of the spell-barrier for some while. Though they strained their shade senses, they caught no trace of a trail to follow. Only the anchor in the middle of the ruins, continuing to pulse with magic.

At last, they met again at the broken front gate, tired, hungry, and frustrated. The day was lengthening fast, the shadows cast by the fallen wall and tower deepening.

"I've been doing this for weeks," Terryn said, sinking down onto a fallen rock, resting his elbows on his knees. "Every time I get a trace or hear a rumor of the witch, she's long gone by the time I get there."

Fendrel nodded grimly. This was exactly how Inren had escaped him last time, directly after stealing Fayline's body. She'd planted anchors in clever places and swiftly evanesced from one to the next, leaving no trace behind. She was impossible to catch unless one knew for certain where an anchor was and set a trap. But even then, she must return to that anchor willingly, or the trap was useless.

"She'll not come back here anytime soon," Fendrel said, looking round at the looming ruins again. "She knows better."

"So, what?" Gerard demanded. "Are we just going to . . . give up?"

Everyone looked at the prince. No one spoke.

"We know she was here." Gerard shook his head, his face strangely dark and foreboding. "We're close. I know we are! We can't leave her; we can't abandon her!"

"Abandon her?" The duke snorted, though there was pain in his voice. "You're thinking about Fayline again. This is not Fayline we're talking about. This is Inren."

Gerard rounded on the duke, fists clenched, and for a moment Fendrel thought he might try to fight. Thankfully, he knew better. The prince turned away instead, cursing and staring into the ruins, as though he could somehow will the witch to manifest then and there.

"Sir?" Venatrix Everild said, addressing Fendrel. "What are your orders?"

Fendrel sighed and rubbed a hand down his face. His chest hurt from the cuts he'd made the night before, and the extreme use of his shade to work the purging spell had worn him out more than he liked to admit.

"We've established the Barrier," he said. "Without a trace to follow, there is nothing more we can do. It's time we return to Dunloch, see if d'Acelet and du Gy have any word for us."

Gerard cursed again and, without a word to the others, set off along the broken Queen's Highway, back toward the horses. Terryn cast Fendrel a quick look then hurried after the prince. Fendrel followed at a slower pace, flanked by Everild and d'Aldreda. He felt strangely heavyhearted. While he'd known all along that it was foolish to think they'd catch Inren, a small part of him had hoped. It would be good to cast this shade-taken out of this world once and for all. It would be good to rid himself of this one small shame.

Every one of Dread Odile's lieutenants who continued to exist in this world was a risk. They were loyal to their queen to the death. They would give everything to have her back again, to see her ruling over them as their adored goddess.

If they could, they would bring her out of her tomb.

The world around Fendrel darkened as clouds rolled

across the sun. It seemed to him as though his own thoughts drew the shadows in closer. Up ahead he saw Gerard and Terryn at the crest of the rise, already mounted, waiting for the other three to catch up.

The party rode in defeated silence back to the main road from Dunloch. It would be a long ride, ample time for each of them to consider all they had not done, all they could not do. Fendrel preferred not to let himself dwell on such things. Inren would show her hand again. Soon, most likely. She wouldn't get away this time as she had four years ago. He would see to—

"*Prince Gerard! Your Highness!*"

"Who the shades is that?" d'Aldreda muttered at Fendrel's side.

Fendrel shaded his eyes, peering ahead up the road to see a small, thin boy on horseback approaching.

"Billin?" Gerard called out and urged his own mount into a canter, hastening to meet the oncoming rider. "Billin, what's wrong? Have you word from Dunloch?"

Fendrel strained his ears and just heard the boy's words, choking through his sobs. "A witch! A witch is in the castle!"

A weight like the head of an ax fell on his heart.

CHAPTER 21

THE DOOR OF THE GREAT HALL STOOD WIDE OPEN and a cold wind blew through, winding round the pillars and brushing across the pale, frightened faces of the hostages. A particularly cold gust caught at Liselle's hair, blowing it away from her still features and freezing her skin.

Cerine tried to shield her friend as best she could. Crouched at the base of the stairs, she cradled Liselle's head in her lap. She showed no signs of waking since the witch's attempt to throttle her, but her chest rose and fell with each breath she took. She was alive at least.

All around them in the Great Hall huddled the people of Dunloch Castle. Servants, guardsmen, stable hands—everyone herded here like sheep waiting in the slaughter pen. The Siveline Sisters grouped together in the center of the floor, their blue hoods drawn up to shield their faces, as though they could somehow protect themselves from the witch's prowling gaze. Ducette was among them, on the outer edge of the group. Now and then she would flash a look Cerine's way, but she dared not speak. Cerine wished she could say something, offer some sort of encouragement.

This was her fault. All her fault.

If she'd stood her ground against her father, if she'd refused this ridiculous marriage . . .

The Phantomwitch stood in the open doorway, silhouetted in sunlight. For the better part of two hours, she had paced back and forth from the base of the stairs to that doorway. One hand unconsciously fidgeted with her curse anchor, but her gaze was intently fixed down the drive, toward the gate.

With a growl and a shake of her head, the witch turned away from the door and paced back across the room, pressing the anchor to her heart. With the light behind her, her face was cast in shadows, but her one eye flashed a horrible, otherworldly glow. She muttered as she walked, and the nearer she came to the stair, the clearer her words sounded in Cerine's straining ears: "He'll come. He'll come. He still loves me, and he will come. He'll set things right."

"You fool!" The voice that hissed in answer wasn't Fayline's, though it came from the same ravaged mouth. "He's already forgotten you. You saw that letter! He's replaced you with your own sister. Kill her. Kill her now. Take your vengeance, and let us be gone from here!"

Fayline's head twisted harshly to one side, straining her neck, her jaw. She whimpered, "No, no, no. He loves me. He'll come. He'll tell me; he'll explain."

Movement behind the witch drew Cerine's eye.

One of the household guards, taking advantage of the witch's turned back, cautiously edged toward the door. His gaze met Cerine's for an instant, and he raised his eyebrows, silently urging her not to look at him, not to speak, not to do anything to call the witch's attention his way.

Cerine immediately looked down at Liselle's face in her lap, stroking her hair and studying the shape of her ear. Her heart thundered painfully. She tried to will the man to not be stupid, to hold his ground. He couldn't possibly make it out that door, couldn't possibly escape the Phantomwitch.

But what then should they do? Wait for Gerard to be lured into this trap? Wait for the killing to begin?

Cerine's mind railed inside her, desperately trying to invent some plan, some plot, something she could try. Anything! But they were completely outmatched by this monster. No weapons they had could touch her, and even if one of them managed to land a killing blow, it would only drive the indwelling spirits into one of the many habitable host bodies on hand.

Perhaps the guardsman had a plan. Maybe he intended to intercept the prince, or to find other help. Cerine's fingers tightened into fists. She dared a last glance up.

The man stepped across the threshold. But the moment he did so, the Phantomwitch whirled. Her lips peeled back from her teeth in a demonic shriek. She flung down the curse anchor so hard that it cracked the marble floor. The next instant, she vanished, and a cloud of darkness surrounded the guard. Through that darkness, two skeletal hands reached and grasped him by the shoulders.

He was gone in an instant. Vanished.

Screams erupted all around. Men and women pressed their hands to their mouths, trying to stifle themselves, trying not to draw attention their way. From the cluster of Siveline Sisters, Ducette audibly sobbed. Cerine couldn't make a sound. All the breath seemed to have been stolen from her lungs.

The Phantomwitch reappeared in the hall. She paced over to where the anchor stone lay and picked it up again, twisting it between thumb and index finger. With a flick of her wrist she gestured at all those in the hall. "Don't any of you try that again!" she roared in Fayline's voice.

A chorus of voices choking on their own screams echoed in that open space. One voice continued to stand out from among the others as Ducette's sobs became more hysterical. Cerine wished she could reach her sister nun, wished she could hug her close, pinch her, whisper to her to control herself. Anything!

Instead, the Phantomwitch turned, her head twisting oddly on the end of Fayline's long neck. A growl in her throat, she stalked toward the cluster of nuns, grabbing them by their shoulders and heads, shoving them aside. They screamed and fell away, scrambling across the floor to get away from her, but her eye fixed on Ducette. Her hand whipping out with viper speed, she caught the girl by the back of her head, fingernails digging into her scalp so that blood welled and dripped, running through Ducette's shorn hair. The witch wrenched her head around, forcing her to look up.

Her free hand drew back, fingers curling like claws, ready to rip out the girl's throat.

"Wait!"

The witch froze. Her long nails clicked together with eager anticipation as she turned, eye blazing, and looked at Cerine.

Hardly believing she had just spoken, Cerine pulled awkwardly out from underneath Liselle and stood. "Don't hurt her," she said, drawing up tall. She blenched under the witch's gaze but would not let herself step back. "You're not cruel, Fayline. You don't want to do this."

"*I* don't want to do *any* of this!" the witch cried. Only it wasn't the witch now. It was Fayline—Fayline's voice in Fayline's mouth. She dropped Ducette, and the poor girl curled into a ball, stuffing the ends of her sleeves into her mouth to stifle her voice.

Fayline took no notice of her, staring instead at Cerine. She took a step, then another. "I don't want any of this, sister," she whimpered. "I want to be what I was born to be: with Gerard. His wife. His queen."

Her teeth bared, and she tucked her chin to her chest, twisting her jaw severely to one side. Her hands tore at the air as though she could shred reality around her. Then she looked up again, her mouth warped in a cruel smile. "But *I* want to be right where I am."

"Inren," Cerine whispered.

The Phantomwitch glided toward Cerine, no longer moving with the jerking, ungainly gait she'd been using. Now she was fluid, sensuous even, as though the silks she wore were new and not mud-stained tatters, as though her throat were adorned in jewels rather than pale growths. As though her swaying hips were full and the bones didn't protrude through skin and cloth alike. Her one good eye batted its shredded remnants of lashes.

"You don't look as much like your father as this host body I now wear," she said. "What a handsome thing he was! One of my favorite pets for many years. I named him Pretty, and he followed me around like a dog." Her mangled lips puckered as though responding to some lascivious memory. "I wanted a child by him. But alas, it wasn't to be!"

Sickness pooled in Cerine's gut. She'd always known that her father had been a witch's slave, but she'd not realized . . . this. The extent of his slavery, the degradation he suffered. Her mind whirled with this new, horrible revelation, with this sudden burst of understanding for the man she had always thought so distant, so driven. So uncaring.

"When he betrayed me," the witch continued, "I thought my heart should break. But that is how all you mortals are: traitorous, faithless, murderous." She was close now, within striking distance. Cerine could see every mottled tumor crawling up her neck with nightmarish clarity. "He told me he loved me."

Cerine spoke before she could stop herself. "You ensorcelled him. He didn't have command of his own will."

The witch's smile grew. "Oh, is that what he claims? Foolish child. My powers have nothing to do with ensorcellment. Whatever pretty lies he told, he told of his own free will." She shook her head, a thick burble of laughter in her throat. "Then what does he have the impudence to do? Go and make children with another. A *mortal* woman. When he could have sired *my* heirs."

With no warning, she hawked loudly and spat in Cerine's face.

Cerine closed her eyes, turning away. All in a flash, a memory filled her mind's eye. She saw her mother's body on the ballroom floor. Throat cut. Blood spilling over the bodice of her sapphire gown. And standing over her body—Fayline, eyes black with *oblivis*, bursting with the power of the witch who had just taken possession of her body.

"I promised my sweet pet that I would see him suffer for his betrayal," Inren purred through Fayline's lips. "I took his favorite daughter for my own soul's housing. And I killed that bitch he called his wife. Only you slipped through my fingers that night. The last little piece of my Pretty's heart." She stretched out a hand, fingers twitching as she reached for Cerine's throat.

But at the last instant, she turned and fell heavily to her knees. *"No!"* she cried. "No, no! You won't touch her. Not yet. Not until Gerard comes. Not until I know. Not until I know he loves me and not her. Not until . . . not until . . ."

Cerine's soul constricted in her gut, and her eyes burned. "Fayline," she whispered, almost daring to reach out to her sister but not quite able to summon the courage.

Fayline raised a silencing hand. The same hand which held the diamond anchor. Then, with a sudden growl, she turned and drove the stone into the floor, only inches from Liselle's unconscious face. The diamond's many black surfaces caught and refracted the sunlight spilling through the doorway.

Fayline slowly rose, still refusing to look at Cerine. She shook herself, straightened her shoulders, and began pacing once more. Staggering a little, breathing hard, she made her way to the open door and gazed down the drive.

Watching for her true love to come riding to her rescue.

The climb back up to her open window proved more difficult than Ayleth anticipated.

Haunts damn it! She'd grown so used to having Laranta's strength readily available at a moment's notice. Since coming to Wodechran, she'd stopped suppressing her shade as frequently or as deeply as had been her practice. To experience not only suppression but an actual block made her feel as though someone had cut off her right arm.

But one-armed or not, she was the only person who could deal with this witch.

Her limbs shuddered like dead tree branches in a storm by the time she pulled herself up along the moldings and vines and gained the window. Heaving her torso onto the ledge, she fell into the room and lay on the floor stunned for several breaths. Her heart raced, and she strained her ears for some sound of the witch's approach, half-convinced she heard footsteps in the hall. But that was ridiculous. The witch would simply appear in the room if she wanted to.

Forcing long, even breaths in and out from her lungs, Ayleth got up and adjusted the lacings of her scorpiona. She had to tie the ill-fitting bracer nearly tight enough to cut off circulation in order to keep the unbalanced weapon steady.

She pulled a switch; the arms sprang out into firing position. She slipped a Gentle Death dart from one of the two quivers she'd taken off the dead venator, but her fingers shook. When she tried to slot the dart into the scorpiona, it slipped and fell to the floor, landing point-down a mere hair from her bare foot.

Ayleth's heart stopped.

Then started again with a painful thud.

"Steady, Ayleth," she whispered. "Get to work."

If she stopped and thought about how close she'd come to inadvertently dealing her own death . . .

No. Now was not the time to think. She snatched up

the dart and, gritting her teeth, firmly slotted it into place.

She moved to the door and peered out into the hall. Nothing. Nothing but the distant murmurs and low moans of the captives. No sign or sound of the witch. She might as well take that as encouragement. She'd not been discovered, and while that remained the case, she stood a chance.

The shadows were deeper now as the sun shifted toward the horizon. Ayleth clung to those shadows as she slipped down the hall, her back to the wall, her firing arm up and finger on the trigger. Her bare feet made no sound on the polished wood floors. She slipped past the closed rooms to the end of the passage and the railing overlooking the front hall. There she paused, tilting her head only slightly to get another look down at the hostages.

No glimpse of the witch. She was probably pacing beneath Ayleth's current position. She'd come back into view soon enough.

Sinking into a crouch, Ayleth crept to the railing, peering through the lower curlicue of brass bars at the space down below. So many people! So many lives precariously in balance. If she misfired even by a fraction, she would send her deadly dart into an innocent person. Ordinarily, she wouldn't worry about missing a shot. She'd worked hard over the years to perfect her aim, after all. But her arm was trembling with the after-effects of the *sòm*. And the witch could move so fast . . .

Fear clawed viciously at her throat, trying to rise like a malevolent shade, to wreak havoc on her mind. She dared not give it an inch, not even for a second.

Shifting her weight, she rested her thumb on the triggering mechanism and breathed with careful precision to slow her heart rate, just as Hollis had taught her. She gazed out over the crouched bodies and bowed heads of the hostages, many of them hidden beneath the pale blue hoods of the Siveline Order. One of those hoods sat a little apart from the others, at the base of the stairs. Beside her lay a woman in rich garments, either unconscious or dead.

As Ayleth's gaze settled on that odd duo, the hooded head lifted. Huge round eyes blinked . . . and focused right on Ayleth's face between the rails.

They stared at one another, neither moving a muscle,

neither breathing.

Then the novice's eyes widened, and she screamed, "Watch out!"

Instinct took over.

Ayleth ducked, rolled, felt the catch and yank of fingers through her hair. She left behind a fistful of dark strands and came up into a firing crouch, her weapon trained on the witch, who stood where Ayleth had knelt a second before.

The witched hissed, black tendrils of poison seeping through her teeth. Dropping the fistful of hair, she lashed out at Ayleth's face.

Ayleth took the shot.

The dart struck the far wall, vibrating from impact. Empty black air swirled with the wind of its passing.

The witch would reappear anywhere, any moment. No time to reload; she had to *move.*

Ayleth lunged back down the passage, first in a crawl, then got to her feet and ran. A blast erupted in the air before her. Ayleth drew back, hands up as though to ward off the glare of fire, her stunned eyes blinking hard.

A sense of movement, and Ayleth felt a hand

snatching at her shoulder, trying to catch hold. She brought her left arm up, forgetting for the moment that she had no iron spike with which to ward off the attack. But she was quick enough to block the witch's grasp. With a twist of her arm, she slipped her own hand against the witch's elbow, grabbed hold, and pushed with all the strength she had against the natural bend of the joint.

A gasp of pain, and the witch fell onto her knee, twisted arm yanked up painfully behind her. For a breath, she was helpless, at Ayleth's mercy.

A clap of darkness and poisonous fumes. Ayleth released the witch's arm and sprang back, hitting the wall in her haste. She threw herself to the floor in the next instant, narrowly avoiding the reaching arms of her enemy as the witch reappeared in the space in front of her. Her fall and roll knocked the witch off her feet, sending her sprawling.

Ayleth was up in an instant, hurtling down the passage. The door to her sick room loomed into view, and Ayleth ducked inside, not bothering to slam the door behind her. The witch appeared on her left and caught Ayleth by the wrist. With a shriek of mingled rage and fear, Ayleth slammed the palm of her hand directly into the woman's nose. She felt it break, felt a gush of blood, and simultaneously felt the hold of those fingers loosen. The witch vanished again.

Ayleth withdrew, arms close to her sides, making herself as small a target as possible. In the back of her brain, reason clamored with her to load another dart into her scorpiona. But what good would that do her? She couldn't take the witch down with the Gentle Death, not now that they were actively engaged in battle. The shade inside would fight the poison, rendering the death violent. Violence would only empower the dark spirit. There were far too many vulnerable host bodies near at hand, ripe for an angered, liberated shade's plucking.

She had to strike it with the other poison, the Evanescer poison she'd taken off the dead venator.

Her hands were surprisingly steady now. Her blood was pounding, her spirit fully awake, even if cut off from Laranta still. A strange haze that might have been terror floated around the periphery of her awareness, but she didn't care about that. She pulled out the poisoned dart, gripped it in one hand like a dagger, and braced herself for the witch's return.

She took a breath. Held it.

For a split second, she thought she heard reality tearing.

Ayleth pivoted on her feet, slashing down with the dart into the dark cloud of poison through which the witch moved. Fingers like stone wrapped around her wrist, squeezing so tight she felt the bone crack. The witch's face appeared before her vision, alight with a manic smile that warped her ravaged features into something monstrous.

"You're not her," she snarled, gnashing the words through her teeth. "You look like her, but you're not her. I thought she'd killed both of you! How did you manage to escape her, pretty thing?"

"*Laranta!*" Ayleth screamed inside her head. The witch's host body was small, dainty, not a match physically for a venatrix. But Ayleth could not break that hold on her arm. "*Laranta, help me!*"

Behind the drug-barrier, her wolf shade howled, helpless.

"I suppose it's just as well," the witch said, tilting her

head to one side. She twisted Ayleth's arm, bringing her down to her knees. "Your blood is still needed."

A hand closed around Ayleth's windpipe, squeezing tighter and tighter. Darkness streamed through the witch's nostrils like smoke, forming a cloud around Ayleth's head.

"Close your eyes, little princess," the witch said. "We're taking a journey—"

She broke off with a gasp. Pieces of shattered pottery crashed and rained down around her head. Her grip loosened, and she fell to the floor in an unconscious pile of rags and red hair and tendrils of dark magic.

Behind her stood the novice, holding the remaining shards of a chamber pot.

Ayleth felt unconsciousness closing in as she struggled to draw breath. Fumbling with the quivers across her chest, she pulled out a black-fletched dart and tried to uncork its poisoned tip. It fell through her fingers as she collapsed on her side.

The novice sprang forward and caught up the dart. "Is this it? Is this the poison?" she demanded.

Ayleth nodded. Snarls of hair hung over her face, a

veil through which she watched the novice kneel beside the fallen witch. With trembling hands, the girl pulled the cork from the dart tip and held it over the unconscious shade-taken's exposed neck. She hesitated.

"Fayline," she whimpered. "I'm so sorry . . ."

With a gagging growl, Ayleth summoned the last of her strength and lunged at the girl. She snatched the dart out of her hand and slammed it into the witch's throat. The Gentle Death coursed through that tormented, shade-taken body. The witch's one good eye opened, flared, then faded as light and life departed.

Ayleth watched the souls rise from the witch's corpse. One shade fused so inextricably with the witch's soul that the two were essentially one. The Haunts opened to receive them, a crack of chaos drawing those loosened souls toward its depths. A last glimmer, and Ayleth thought she saw another soul, a human soul, writhing as it was pulled up and out of the host body.

"Fayline." Ayleth's mouth tried to form the word. Her hand fumbled for the Detrudos pipe slung from the belt around her waist. She had to catch that soul! She must prevent its being dragged away with the others, damned . . .

But it was too late. She was too weak. She couldn't get the pipes free of their sheath. She slumped to her elbows, then collapsed facedown.

The Haunts swallowed all three souls and closed like snapping jaws.

CHAPTER 22

THE SUN WAS SETTING AS TERRYN AND GERARD galloped their horses up to Dunloch's gate. Finding it open and unguarded, they hastened through and across the bridge. No torches were lit in their posts, and the circle drive before the keep was dark with deepening twilight.

The keep was dark as well save for a light flickering in one window. Terryn's gaze shot to that window, instantly recognizing it as the window to Ayleth's sick chamber.

Someone was present in that room, or had been recently enough to light a candle.

Gerard was ahead of him, his black stallion outpacing even swift Fleeta. At the steps he skidded the exhausted beast to a halt and sprang from the saddle. "Gerard, wait!" Terryn called out, pulling up Fleeta beside the stallion. The doors at the top of the stairs stood open, but only darkness waited inside. Who could say what horrors they would find within Dunloch's walls?

And the witch . . . Inren. She must be aware of their coming.

Heedless of any warnings, Gerard raced up the porch steps. Terryn followed, checking the firing mechanism of his scorpiona. Perhaps, if the Goddess was with him, Inren would be distracted by the prince long enough for Terryn to get a clean shot. He could hope . . . He could pray . . .

He collided with Gerard as he passed under the doorway arch. The prince had come to a stop just inside the door, staring into the front hall. For a terrible moment, Terryn looked over Gerard's shoulder and believed the hall was strewn with dead bodies.

But no. No, these were living souls. With shadow vision bright in his eyes, he saw the shine of all those spirits still indwelling their mortal hosts. They huddled together, holding each other close, staring with round-eyed terror as though expecting demons to attack from the shadows at any moment. But they were alive.

"Cerine?" Gerard called, taking a tentative step forward. Without shadow vision to light his way, he must be nearly blind. "Cerine, are you there?"

"Your Highness!" The reedy voice of Chancellor Yves quavered with utter terror. There was movement among the bodies, then the chancellor stood, his hands clasped and shaking. "Your Highness! The witch is here! She put a binding on us all, and we must not leave this room, or we will perish, dragged into the Haunts. Don't come a step nearer, or you might also be snared—"

The prince was in motion before Yves could finish. Terryn made a grab for him but wasn't quick enough. Gerard ran for the stairs, stumbling and staggering through the crowd of hostages, his vision not yet fully adjusted to the twilit gloom. With a growl, Terryn went after him, using shadow vision to guide his steps. A quick scan of the hall's periphery revealed no sign of the curse Yves had described. Could it be the witch had lied to her captives? Or that the enchantment had faded since she cast it?

Or was Inren already gone?

He was near the base of the stairs when his foot caught on something. An outstretched hand. A dainty woman's hand.

"Liselle?" Terryn crouched beside the lady's still body, his heart plunging painfully. Though he knew he should hurry after the prince, he reached under Liselle's long golden hair to feel her neck for a pulse. A breath whooshed from his lungs, and he closed his eyes briefly. She lived. She was unconscious, her heart beat a fast and furious rhythm, and her eyes moved back and forth behind her delicate eyelids as though she experienced some terrible dream. But she lived. And, as far as his shadow vision could discern, she was not cursed.

Gerard was already up the stairs and disappearing into the hall. Terryn gritted his teeth, but there was nothing he could do for Liselle now. Leaving the lady where she lay, he charged up the stairs, pivoted hard at the landing, and caught Gerard before he'd taken many paces down the dark hall of the east wing.

"What are you doing?" he snarled, yanking on the prince's arm. "You can't fight Inren!"

"Cerine isn't with the others." The whites of Gerard's eyes gleamed. It was too dark in this unlit hall for him to see much of anything, and his gaze couldn't quite focus on Terryn's. "Neither is Ayleth. And there was a light in Ayleth's room. I know you saw it. They might be there."

Any attempt to make Gerard retreat down the stairs and stay quiet among the others would be futile. Terryn lifted his scorpiona arm high and shouldered his way in front of the prince. "Watch my back," he said in a tight whisper. "And stay close."

The two progressed along the passage, nerves jumping with tension and terror. Every door was shut except the one at the end of the hall. A crack of light gleamed in the darkness. Straining his ears, Terryn thought he heard something moving inside.

Had Inren found Ayleth and decided to complete the murder she had nearly accomplished in the ruins?

His jaw clenched tight, but Terryn refused to hasten

his careful approach. If the Phantomwitch was in there, he would kill her. He would take her down before she knew she was hunted.

A murmuring voice touched his ear. He could not yet discern what it said, but another few steps, and he recognized a familiar cadence:

"GoddessHeart have mercy. GoddessSoul have mercy. Goddess-Head have mercy."

"Cerine?" Gerard tried to push past Terryn.

Terryn thrust out his left arm, blocking the prince's way. On silent feet he moved to the door and carefully peered through the crack. He saw it all in a flash: Fayline's corpse lying dead on the floor, her grotesquely mutated face lit by a single candle; Cerine kneeling beside her sister, hands cupped in prayer, eyes closed and tears streaming.

And beyond her, Ayleth.

Adrenaline surged through his limbs, urging him to burst into that room. Only the strength of many years' training kept him standing in place like stone. What else might be in that room? He reached out with shadow senses, searching for the slightest trace of shade presence.

Nothing. Not even a shiver of Ayleth's shade. Which meant . . .

Which meant Ayleth might be dead.

He shoved the door open and dropped into a defensive crouch, his scorpiona aimed ahead. Cerine screamed and fell away from Fayline, then shouted, "Don't shoot! Don't shoot! She's gone! She's dead!"

"Cerine?" Gerard pressed in behind Terryn. His gaze landed on the body beside Cerine. "Fayline . . ."

Terryn let him pass. The prince collapsed to his knees across from Cerine, staring at that growth-covered, mutated face. His body spasmed as though he would vomit, and his arms shook so hard, he almost couldn't lift the dead girl. But Cerine helped him, and he soon cradled her head against his heart, rocking her gently. His eyes sought Cerine's, full of questions, full of entreaty.

"She's gone," Cerine whispered again, tears pouring steadily down her face. "She's gone, Gerard."

Gerard shook his head. Then he lowered his face to the top of Fayline's head. As he wept, Cerine caught hold of her dead sister's hands and resumed singing the prayer song: *"May the Mother receive you, who hath called you, and may the heavenly spirits conduct you to the Gates of Life.*"

Terryn wrenched his eyes from the three of them. Ayleth lay close by, and he was suddenly, agonizingly afraid. Afraid to move closer, to kneel beside her. Afraid to check for a pulse . . .

He swallowed his fear and snapped his scorpiona out of firing mode. Dropping to his knees, he caught hold of Ayleth's shoulders and rolled her onto her side. She wore nothing but a shift over the bandages on her torso, and the flimsy cloth was dark with blood. But he saw no fresh wound. An ill-fitting scorpiona was strapped to her right arm, and loose belts and quivers draped over her shoulders and around her hips. Not her own equipment. Where she'd come by these weapons, he didn't like to guess.

With a trembling hand, he pushed limp dark locks of hair back from her forehead. The moment he saw her face he knew: She was still alive. Her skin was puffy with the after-effects of *sòm*, swollen until she was almost unrecognizable. But the black stain of *oblivis* poison was gone. And she breathed. Goddess above be praised, she breathed!

Then his gaze landed on her right hand, still grasping the end of a Detrudos pipe. A pipe only partially drawn from its sheath.

Terryn's heart went cold.

CHAPTER 23

THEY WERE, EVERY LAST ONE OF THEM, TOO AFRAID to help.

Sisters of the Order of Saint Sivella believed all shade-taken to be impure. Physical contact with one required purification rituals that took a full month to complete. Therefore, none of them, not even Ducette, would go anywhere near Fayline's dead body.

Cerine, however, was not a Siveline Sister anymore.

In the end, Venatrix Everild helped her carry Fayline's

corpse to a quiet chamber, where Cerine worked alone to prepare the body. After peeling away the soiled, ragged wedding gown and undergarments, she stood a moment, viewing what was left of her sister. Nothing could be done about the hideous growths covering her body like fungus on a tree. Nothing could remove the mottled patches of darkness under her skin. The horrible thing lying on the bed scarcely resembled Fayline anymore.

Yet Cerine set to work. She washed her sister's corpse with great care, even taking the time to trim and polish her claw-like nails. She washed and combed out the lank, patchy, tattered strands of hair, still burnished red under the grime. Among the garments her father had brought to the castle, intended for his younger daughter's use, she found a gown of forest green. With Everild's help, she slid Fayline's emaciated form into the folds of soft velvet; and when they were finished, she looked almost human again by soft candlelight.

Then Venator Fendrel and Venator Terryn entered the room and assisted Venatrix Everild in carrying the duke's dead daughter down to the chapel, where the altar had been prepared for her body. Cerine took a few moments to change her own garments, to wash her face and hands. She found a gauzy veil and covered her head and face.

Pausing to view herself in the tall glass on the wall, she scarcely recognized the pale waif meeting her gaze through the veil with glassy, purple-smudged eyes. Part of her wished to retreat to the safety of her Siveline robes and hood. However, considering the day's events, she felt it more respectful to her sister's memory to finally accept the situation. The facts could not be changed. Fayline was dead. She would not be saved. She would not return to marry Gerard as she was intended to do.

Cerine would fulfill that duty in her sister's stead.

Steeling herself, Cerine left her room and made her way through the stricken halls of Dunloch to the castle chapel. She caught fleeting glimpses of people around her, but her gaze focused only on the floor beneath her feet. No one spoke to her. She spoke to no one. She entered the chapel alone.

Singing voices echoed from the high stone arches. Cerine spotted her sisterhood in the shadows to the left of the altar, their hoods pulled low over their faces, their hands upraised in supplication to the goddess. Ducette led them in the funeral-prayer hymns, her chantress voice ringing clear and sweet. A pleasant surprise: Cerine had not expected Grand Mother Didienne to allow her girls to sing the solemn prayers over the body of a shade-taken.

Above the altar at the far end of the chapel hall, three glorious stained-glass windows depicted the spreading branches of a rowan tree, sacred to the Goddess. Celine deliberately approached, thinking how strange it was to see Fayline's body, illuminated by the light of numerous candles, lying still and cold beneath this holy image. Fayline, who was so full of life. Fayline, who was so madcap and witty. Fayline, who could dance an entire night away and never tire, who could outride any man in the kingdom, who could outshine any woman of the king's court.

Fayline . . . broken, lost Fayline.

Tears choking her throat, Cerine collapsed to her knees before the altar, clasping her hands in prayer. But no words came. She could only kneel in silence while the voices of the Siveline Sisters washed over her in sacred laments.

She didn't know how long she'd been kneeling there

before a rustle of skirts told her she wasn't alone. The next moment, Liselle knelt beside her and took hold of her hand. Cerine peered through her veil at her friend, noting the ugly bruises around her neck where Fayline . . . no, where *Inren* had tried to strangle her. Her golden curls hung limp and unbound around her shoulders. Her eyes were too bright; her mouth was too stern.

Her throat tensed as though she fought back tears as she gazed upon the dead form on the altar stone. Swiftly turning to Cerine, she gasped, "I'm so sorry!" Tears spilled over, and she was too distraught for several moments to continue. At last she managed, "Oh, Cerine! I'm so sorry I could not protect you . . . or her!"

Cerine squeezed her hand back. Leaning her head against Liselle's, she said firmly, "This isn't your fault."

Liselle sat with her for at least an hour. Eventually, however, she leaned over, kissed Cerine on the top of her head, and left. Cerine continued her vigil alone, accompanied only by the sisters in their alcove.

After a time, her father joined her. He was the most disheveled Cerine had ever seen him. Not even on the night of Fayline's possession and his wife's death had d'Aldreda revealed any trace of weakness. Now, he sagged down onto his knees beside Cerine, his jacket unfastened, his hair falling over his forehead. Stubble darkened his jaw.

They didn't speak to each other for some while. The terrible secrets Inren had revealed that afternoon returned to Cerine now. She shuddered, wishing she'd never learned the truth of her father's enslavement. She hoped he never found out what she knew.

The Siveline Sisters finally ended their chants, their voices tired. As they slowly filed out of the chapel, the candlelight cast their shadows like dark phantoms behind them. When they had gone, the silence between Cerine and her father felt heavier than before.

"The Venator Dominus and his people are hunting down any anchors left behind," d'Aldreda said at last. "The witch is dead and banished, but Fendrel has assured me he will take no chances. They'll see that Dunloch is secure for the wedding."

Cerine gaped at her father, unable to believe her ears. "You . . . you cannot seriously intend to proceed with wedding plans," she said, struggling to restrain her anger.

"Not *now*."

Her father glanced her way, one eyebrow quirked. "Of course we will. We must. If we let it be postponed, Inren wins. Again." He shook his head, swallowing hard as he faced forward. His gaze, Cerine noted, did not rest upon Fayline's body, but lifted instead to the air above her. "I shall see you the queen of all Perrinion, my daughter. The blood of d'Aldreda will rule throughout the Golden Age. We will live on as joint heirs to the prophecy of the Chosen King. This is the path we will walk, come what may."

Bitterness rose like bile in the back of her mouth, burning as she swallowed it hard. Her gaze rested on Fayline's face, on those distorted contours beneath the softening veils. At sunrise, the venators would carry her body down to the shore of the Holy Lake. There it would be burned along with many sacred spices, and her ashes would be gathered to be returned to her father's house for burial. Just as though she had died a natural death. Just as though her soul wasn't damned.

The duke left at last. Exhausted, Cerine sank down heavily onto the stone floor, leaning her head against the altar stone. One hand crept up to find Fayline's. Her fingers felt cold and unnatural, but Cerine held on anyway.

She couldn't have said how long she sat in this way before she heard Gerard's footsteps approaching. She had known he would come eventually, and she had wondered if she ought to leave before he did. But this was her last night with Fayline.

Besides, she really ought to share this moment of mourning with the one other person who truly understood all that had been lost.

"How is the venatrix?" she asked without looking around.

The footsteps paused. He didn't answer at first. "Sleeping," he said at last, his voice muted in this solemn setting of candlelight and sorrow. "They bound her wounds and put her in bed. She's not in any danger. Terryn is watching over her."

Cerine nodded. "She saved us," she whispered. "Fayline . . . Inren . . . would have killed us all."

Without responding, Gerard knelt beside her. He assumed an attitude of prayer, murmuring sacred words.

Cerine did not interrupt him. She listened to his voice, heard how many times it caught in his throat. But he made it through the whole prayer without stopping.

When he was done, he turned around and sat with his back against the altar, drawing one knee up to his chest. She dared to glance his way through her veil. How pale and tired he was tonight!

"Were you with her?" he whispered, turning and catching her eye. "At the end?"

Cerine nodded. She didn't trust herself to speak.

"I'm glad." His voice cracked, and he looked down quickly, though not quickly enough to hide the sheen in his eyes. He unexpectedly turned and placed his hand atop hers, which still grasped Fayline's cold fingers. "Cerine," he said, her name soft on his lips. He looked at her, his heart in his eyes, full of sorrow. "Cerine, I must be honest with you. Our lives are all so fragile, our futures so uncertain. I don't want to miss whatever brief chance I may have—"

Cerine released her hold on Fayline to slip her hand out of his grasp, then folded both hands in her lap, staring carefully down at them. "I know," she said. "I understand, Gerard."

She understood that he needed to take back what he'd said in that foolish letter of his. She understood that he wished to apologize for attempting to pretend that he felt for her what he felt for Fayline. They must marry; the law decreed as much. And Gerard, noble soul that he was, felt he must make a show of love, to try to justify this whole horrible masquerade.

She understood. And she could not bear it.

She felt his eyes on the side of her face. "Cerine, I don't think . . . I don't think you believe me."

Cerine met his gaze and, with a tremendous effort of will, held it steadily. "My sister just died," she said. "My sister, who loved you and whom you loved."

"Cerine—"

"We both of us know our duty." She abruptly rose to her feet, pulling back the long folds of her skirt. "A duty we will fulfill for the sake of our people. But there can be no good in pretending. I ask only that you always be honest with me."

Gerard rose as well. The candlelight glowed gently on the contours of his face. He took a step, moving closer to her than she liked. His hand stretched out toward hers, and she felt the warmth of his fingers less than an inch from her own.

"And you, Cerine?" he said, his voice thick. "Will you be honest with me?"

She turned away and left him standing beside Fayline's dead body. Her heavy skirts dragging behind her on the stone floor, she fled into the dark shadows at the far end of the chapel. She found the door and pushed it open, gasping a little as the cold wind blew her veil flat against her skin. The sky was just blushing with dawn, and across the courtyard, she saw the Red Hoods approaching. Coming to carry her sister's body down to the shore.

It was over. It was all over.

CHAPTER 24

AYLETH WALKED ALONE IN HER PINE FOREST. THICK fog clogged the air, undulating sluggishly between tree trunks and along the ground. She knew what it meant: *sòm*. They must have dosed her with more of the *sòm* to make her sleep, to make her stay quiet and calm in her bed. She staggered, unsteady in her mind, and leaned one shoulder heavily against a tall dark tree. Bits of ash shook down from the limbs above.

With desperate effort she tried to organize her

thoughts, to pull them into shape. What happened? She had faint memories of battle, a bizarre image of climbing out a window. But the fog was too thick; she couldn't see through it.

"*Laranta?*" she called.

Her shade was near. She felt her along their soul tether, somewhere in the fog. But she couldn't see her, couldn't hear her. The *sòm* was much too dense.

"*Haunts damn it,*" she growled, pressing her hands against her chest. The drug blocked whatever pain her physical body experienced, but if she concentrated, if she focused her strength, she could make herself feel the cuts on her torso.

The projection of her body shuddered, and she gasped as skin parted as though sliced by an invisible knife and blood welled up between her fingers. She could make it go away by shifting her focus again, by letting the obscuring *sòm* take her. But she couldn't bear it.

Grinding her teeth, she leaned into the pain, and soon she smelled it. Once the sense of smell returned, it was only a matter of time before—

She opened her eyes. Her real, physical eyes. For a terrible moment, she believed she had gone blind. Utter darkness filled her vision. The drug addled her brain but no longer blocked the pain, and she was lost, disoriented, terrified.

With a gasp, she tried to sit up but lacked the strength. She only managed to roll. She felt the heart-stopping instant when she reached an edge, that instant where her balance still held. Then she fell, and a strangled cry clogged in her throat.

She landed hard on one shoulder, and blankets fell on top of her. Slowly her mortal vision adjusted to the darkness, taking in what little light glowed from the dying fire on the stone hearth. She took stock of her surroundings. A bedchamber. A bed, from which she'd just fallen. A fireplace, a looming wardrobe. An empty chair.

Cold. Dark. Alone.

Ayleth rolled over and tried to gather her limbs beneath her, but they wouldn't obey. She only managed to knock the blankets aside, leaving her body exposed to the frigid air. Shivering, exhausted, she lowered her cheek to the stone floor, half ready to let herself return to the drugged stupor.

The door opened. She heard it but lacked the strength to lift her head and see who entered. Heavy footsteps reverberated against the ear pressed to the floor. Blearily, she thought she saw a flash of perfectly polished silver spurs, then a pair of knees.

Strong hands gripped her shoulders, rolling her over and pulling her up until she lay cradled, her head lolling back across an arm. Her hair caught and pulled, but she couldn't shift into a more comfortable position, could only lie there, pressed up against a solid, warm body. Her bare legs, stretched out across the floor, prickled with cold. She tried vainly to move them.

"What does it take to keep you in bed?" a deep, dark voice rumbled from beneath the shadows of a hood.

"Terryn." His name came out all wrong when she tried to speak it. Her tongue couldn't quite sound out any vowels. "The . . . the witch. I must kill . . . the witch . . ."

He adjusted his arm under her, shifting her up so that her cheek lay against his shoulder. "Come on. Come on, di Ferosa," he said, as though speaking encouragingly to a child, and caught her around the waist, pulling her up to her feet. She couldn't quite find her balance, so he scooped her behind the knees and awkwardly bundled her onto the bed. As her head hit the pillow, she groaned and nearly flopped onto the floor again. He stopped her fall, adjusting her until she lay on her back.

Then he snatched up the blankets from the floor and began to spread them over her. As he laid them across her chest, he paused, leaning closer to inspect the bandages. With a shake of his head, he let the folds of fabric drape down over her torso. How warm and close he was. His jerkin was unbuckled, his quivers and sheaths gone, and dark hair fell across his forehead.

With a sudden flash of will, Ayleth reached up and clutched him by the front of his shirt, twining her hand into the fabric. He caught his breath, surprised, as she pulled his face closer to hers. His eyes flicked to her mouth, to her lips as they pulled back in a pained grimace.

"The . . . witch . . ." she panted.

A rough chuckle rasped in his throat. "You killed the witch," he said, his forehead puckering as he gave his head a little shake. "You killed her. Wounded, drugged, unarmed, you took down Inren di Karel." Another chuckle, which turned into a rueful, disbelieving laugh. "You are truly mad. I've never met a woman your equal for pure insanity."

She gazed up at him, unable to comprehend what he said. Something was wrong. Something . . . she couldn't remember . . . Her gaze fixed on the ugly scar marring his cheek.

A word swam through the haze of her mind: *Liar.*

He had lied to her. About what?

Witches. In the borough . . .

She breathed hard, still holding tight to his shirt. He turned his face to one side, as though trying to hide the scar, and started to pull away. Ayleth tightened her grip, using all that remained of her strength. "Don't!" she whimpered, her voice very small in the darkness. "You . . . don't . . ."

She couldn't find the words. She knew only that she couldn't let him go. She had to stop him, somehow.

He gazed down at her for a long, silent moment. Then, placing his hand over hers, he gently pried her hold away from his shirt. "All right," he whispered, lacing his fingers with hers. "I'll stay. I promise."

Cold blue eyes glittered beneath the shadow of his hood. Ice blue, like a winter sky. They shone as two bright beacons even as the rest of the dark world blurred out around him.

Ayleth sank back on her pillow, still holding his hand as she fell asleep.

She woke with a start, her eyes flying open and her fingers tightening around . . . a handful of blanket. Not fully aware of what she did, her hand fumbled across the bed, searching for a hand that wasn't there.

"*Laranta?*" she asked inside her head. To her relief, she immediately felt her shade's presence moving to the forefront of her mind.

Here, Mistress, Laranta said. *Here, here.*

Ayleth let out a long, long breath, closed her eyes, and pressed her hand to her face. Her temples throbbed, but her mind felt clearer than it had been for a long while. Clamorous memories pressed in upon her awareness, memories of too-recent terrors, which she could not face just then. She pushed them away, concentrating instead on her breathing, on the sensation of Laranta in her head.

But her hand felt strangely empty, and she couldn't say why.

Opening her eyes again, she realized someone sat beside her bed. Her heart gave a little lurch, and she turned, her mouth opening to say a name. That name froze on her tongue, however, and her eyes widened.

"Your . . .Your Highness," she breathed.

Gerard wore no jerkin, and his linen undershirt billowed loose as though he'd unconsciously pulled the front lacings. He sat in a chair drawn up close to her bed, leaning forward with his elbows on his knees. Bright afternoon sunlight spilled through the nearby window and turned his tawny hair to gold. His eyes were red and raw, his cheeks hollow.

"Hullo there, Ayleth," he said. His smile was still beautiful. "You're looking much better this afternoon."

Ayleth tried to sit up, but regretted it at once and pressed a hand to her bandaged torso. Now that the *sòm* had worn off, there was nothing to block the pain from those cuts. How had she come by them anyway? Looking down, she realized that she still wore next to nothing, and while the bandages served well enough for modesty, she blushed and pulled her blanket up higher.

"Don't trouble yourself, please," Gerard said kindly, lifting a reassuring hand. "I don't wish to distress you. I asked if I might sit with you a while. In case you woke up."

"You . . . you're very kind, Your Highness," Ayleth croaked. Her voice was dry in her throat. Gerard got up at once and moved across the room to where a pitcher of water stood waiting on a small table. He poured a cup and brought it to her bedside.

She stared as he offered her the drink, unable to fathom that she, of all people, should be served by the Golden Prince. It was too much. She couldn't make herself take the cup.

Gerard, misinterpreting her lack of action, held the water to her lips instead. She couldn't very well refuse and let him pour water down her front, so she gulped and spluttered. "Steady," he said, and when she'd drunk her fill, he set the cup on the floor to one side. Then he bowed his head and drew a long breath.

"I have to thank you," he said.

Ayleth winced.

"For saving Lady Cerine"—he rushed on—"and all of Dunloch." When he paused again, Ayleth thought she saw a flash of tears in his eyes. But he mastered himself and continued: "Venator du Gy and Venator d'Acelet were both found dead. They had remained on hand to guard my household and inhabitants from the Phantomwitch, but she killed them. They never even had a chance. But you . . ." His lips twisted in a mirthless smile. "You took down Dread Odile's lieutenant. It's quite remarkable. I believe commendation has been sent to the Grand Vanderian, and you will be honored for your service."

The words flowed over her, dragging with them a full tide of woe. Ayleth bowed her head, unable to continue meeting the prince's eyes. She didn't want to hear him say these things. She didn't want his praise. She'd only done her duty; she'd performed to the best of her limited abilities.

"Ayleth," Gerard said, his voice a low, tight whisper. "Ayleth, I must ask . . . I must know if . . . if *Fayline* was present for your final battle. Present within her body, I mean."

She wanted to lie. But she knew he would never forgive her for it. Unable to say the words aloud, she slowly nodded.

Gerard drew a painful breath. "Very well. Did you . . . did you manage to . . . Were you able to save her soul?"

"No." The word slipped out without sound, scarcely more than a breath.

She heard him choke. From the tail of her eye she saw how his body shuddered in his chair. She couldn't bear to look at him. For some moments they simply sat there, not looking at each other. Not speaking.

Finally, the prince rose to his feet. "You did well, Venatrix di Ferosa. You did what you had to do." With those words, he turned and left the room, shutting the door behind him, leaving Ayleth alone with her memories. Alone with the vision of those three twining souls rising out of Fayline's corpse.

Swallowed into the horror of the Haunts.

She crumpled back into her pillows and smothered her sobs in blankets.

EPILOGUE

YLAIRE TOSSED ASIDE THE SPADE AND RUBBED SWEAT from her forehead with the back of her hand, leaving a smear of dirt across her pale features. It was done. To the best of her ability.

Digging a grave in cold winter soil was hard labor, but . . . She stomped on the mound a few times to pack the earth harder. It wasn't as though anyone would miss the old hermit. He'd been isolated out here in the country. No one would notice his absence for several weeks at least.

By then she would be long gone.

Wiping her hands on her skirts, she turned to face the little leaning hovel that had been the old man's home. It was dark inside, but her shadow sight saw a glow of magic through the sagging doorway. Nilly's shade was ascendant.

Good. She had need of its powers.

With quick strides, Ylaire crossed the distance between grave and hut and ducked her head to enter. The girl waited for her, sitting quietly in the center of that single room, her hands folded in her lap. Ylaire hoped she had not witnessed the moment when she broke the hermit's neck. She tried to take care of such ugly business privately, away from the child's sensitive gaze. The Seer's powers were more effective when its little host was calm.

"Rasanala," Ylaire said. "It is time."

Nilly's eyes raised. But it was her shade that peered out from inside. Her mouth moved, and that strange multitudinous voice spoke: *"My Nilly is hungry."*

"And she will eat." Ylaire crouched in front of the girl and gently touched her cheek with one long, dirt-crusted nail. "As soon as you have done what I ask, she will eat."

The shade spirit flashed rebelliously, and for a moment, Ylaire feared it would refuse. Then it nodded its host body's head and held out a hand. "*I will need blood to channel my path,*" it said.

Ylaire swallowed hard. But what choice did she have? She reached into the front of her gown and withdrew the little vial of blood. So little and so precious! She hated to give up any more of it.

She pulled out the stopper and, holding her breath, tilted out a single drop into Nilly's open palm. Nilly closed her fist and lowered her hand back to her lap. She bowed her head, falling at once into a trance, concentrating on that blood and all the secrets it could reveal. Pulses of power rippled out from her core.

Ylaire stepped back. The glow of magic was so bright, she couldn't bear to look at it, so she switched from shadow sight to mortal vision and silently watched the child. Nilly held perfectly still, her legs crossed beneath her, her shoulders back, her chin dropped. Her breathing slowed until it almost ceased entirely.

Then her lips began to move.

Ylaire narrowed her eyes. Though she strained every sense, she could not discern any words. She took a step closer. "Rasanala?" she whispered.

The strange shadow voice breathed from Nilly's soft lips. "*Blood to blood. Bone to bone. Blood to blood. Bone to bone. Blood to blood, bone to bone, blood to blood . . .*"

"Rasanala?" Ylaire cried, taking another step. Her whole body vibrated with tension, with hope, with fear. "What do you see? Show me!"

Without warning, the child's eyes lifted, blinding bright with magic power. Ylaire tried to throw up her hands to shield her eyes, but Nilly's hand darted out, the hand holding the smear of blood, and caught hold of the witch's hand.

A burst of magic exploded in Ylaire's head.

The next moment, she landed on her back. The hovel groaned, and the entire structure shifted perilously before settling back on its foundations. Ylaire stared up at the old thatched ceiling, at the cracks of moonlight shining through. Her hand smarted as though burned, and she pressed it, quivering, to her breast. For several moments she couldn't breathe.

At last her lungs shuddered, and she drew in a great gulp of air. As she let it out slowly, her mouth curled into a smile.

"I see," she whispered. "I see."

Nilly huddled in a corner of the hut. Ylaire saw her cowering in the darkness, her small arms wrapped over her head. Shadow sight revealed the magical aura of her Seer shade surrounding her like a shield.

Ylaire's smile grew. "You've done it, child. You've done it at last! I know where she is. I know what I must do."

After struggling to her feet, she staggered to the door of the hovel and leaned heavily on the frame to stare out into the night, across the shallow hermit's grave, over the rolling hills. On to that distant place where moonlight shimmered on a lake and made white turrets glow in the darkness.

"I know what I must do." The witch licked her eager lips, and her hands clenched, nails drawing blood from her palms. "I must return to Cró Ular. I must find Inren."

ABOUT THE AUTHOR

Sylvia Mercedes makes her home in the idyllic North Carolina countryside with her handsome husband, sweet baby-lady, and Gummy Bear, the Toothless Wonder Cat. When she's not writing she's . . . okay, let's be honest. When she's not writing, she's running around after her little girl, cleaning up glitter, trying to plan healthy-ish meals, and wondering where she left her phone. In between, she reads a steady diet of fantasy novels. But mostly she's writing.

After a short career in Traditional Publishing (under a different name), Sylvia decided to take the plunge into the Indie Publishing World and is enjoying every minute of it. The Venatrix Chronicles is her first series as an independent author, but she's got many more planned!

Don't miss the continuation of Ayleth's adventures in
Book 4 of The Venatrix Chronicles!

*Venatrix Ayleth made a vow of loyalty
to her Holy Order.
But is the Order loyal to Ayleth?*

DANCE OF SOULS

Meanwhile don't miss Song of Shadows:

Visit www.SylviaMercedesBooks.com
to get your free copy.